"You think me and Rose would be happy here. I think you're crazy, cowboy."

"Crazy about you, Shannon, that's for sure, even if you are way out of my league."

"I wish you'd quit saying that." Shannon rose to her feet. "I have to tuck Rose into bed."

"You could come back afterward," Billy said. "Watch the stars shine down."

She smiled, a sweet curve of her lips in the gathering twilight. "You really need to get some rest."

"What I really need to do is kiss you."

For a moment he thought she was going to leave. Just turn and walk away and leave him sitting there, like a rejected fool. Just as she had ten years earlier. But she didn't. She bent over him, her fingertips touching his shoulders, her lips barely touching his. The gentlest of kisses, and far too brief.

Dear Reader,

This was a tough story to write. I left my home in western Maine seven years ago when the mountain where my father's ashes were scattered was leveled to make way for twelve industrial-scale wind turbines. Several years later I went back to visit my old mountain haunts, but nothing was the same, and I didn't stay long. John Muir said, "Going to the mountains is going home," but I've since learned that mountains are not renewable, and going home can be a painful thing.

The characters in this story share many of the same experiences I did, viewed from opposite sides of the fence. Shannon McTavish believes wind power is green and good for the planet. Billy Mac sees it as an environmental disaster. To complicate matters, Billy works for Shannon's father, who's the only holdout among the major landowners who stand to make big bucks leasing their land to the wind power company. Battle lines are drawn, but there's a whole lot more at stake than the outcome of a wind project. Hearts are on the line, as well as the future of Shannon's little girl. Shannon has to decide whether to walk away, or try harder to protect what turns out to be the two most important things to all of them: home and family.

I love to hear from my readers. Contact me at nadianichols@aol.com and check out my author's page on Amazon.com.

Nadia Nichols

HEARTWARMING

A Family for Rose

———

Nadia Nichols

Recycling programs
for this product may
not exist in your area.

ISBN-13: 978-1-335-63379-8

A Family for Rose

Copyright © 2018 by Penny R. Gray

Printed in U.S.A.

™ www.Harlequin.com

Nadia Nichols went to the dogs at the age of twenty-nine and currently operates a kennel of twenty-eight Alaskan huskies. She has raced her sled dogs in northern New England and Canada, works at the family-owned Harraseeket Inn in Freeport, Maine, and is also a registered Master Maine Guide.

She began her writing career at the age of five, when she made her first sale, a short story called "The Bear" to her mother for twenty-five cents. This story was such a blockbuster that her mother bought every other story she wrote and kept her in ice-cream money throughout much of her childhood.

Now all her royalties go toward buying dog food. She lives on a remote solar-powered northern Maine homestead with her sled dogs, a Belgian draft horse named Dan, several cats, two goats and a flock of chickens. She can be reached at nadianichols@aol.com.

Books by Nadia Nichols

Harlequin Superromance

Across a Thousand Miles
Montana Dreaming
Buffalo Summer
A Full House
Montana Standoff
Sharing Spaces
Everything to Prove
From Out of the Blue
A Soldier's Pledge
Montana Unbranded

Visit the Author Profile page at Harlequin.com for more titles.

For my father, who once told me that one of the hardest decisions we ever face in life is choosing whether to walk away or try harder.

CHAPTER ONE

WYOMING WAS A far stretch from Nashville, but Shannon McTavish hadn't forgotten the way home. Ten years had passed since she last drove down this long, lonesome stretch of road, but she remembered every curve, every hill and every gully. She knew the names of the mountains she was driving toward—Whiskey and Wolverine, Wolf Butte and Wind River. She knew the names of the creeks she crossed and how sweet the wind would taste when she rolled her window down to fill her lungs. She remembered the sound of the soul-deep thunder that the wind made when it blew across the wild wide open.

This was a big, empty land that looked as if nothing had changed, yet everything had. When Shannon left, her future had seemed so bright and she'd been so in love. Ten years ago she'd vowed never to return to the lonesome place on the edge of nowhere, yet now she couldn't wait to get there.

Each mile brought her closer, but there were two more obstacles to overcome—and they had nothing to do with the miles or the mountains in between. Her father didn't know she was coming home, and he was unlikely to welcome her.

Shannon glanced in the rearview mirror. "How're you doing back there, Rose?"

"Good, Momma. I'm counting cows, like you told me to."

"How many so far?"

"So many I can't go that high," Rose said, all blue eyes, fair skin and sweetness.

"We must be in Wyoming, then," Shannon said.

"Are we almost there?"

"Almost, sweetheart. I'm going to stop for gas at this little store up ahead, and then it'll be just a few more miles and we'll be home."

"Will there be horses there?"

"I don't know, Rose. There used to be lots of them, and I hope there still are."

Hope. The word mocked her. She'd done nothing but hope this whole long drive. Hope her father would be glad to see them. Hope he'd sell her that little piece of land she coveted, so she could build a house and haven for herself and Rose on that little pine-clad knoll above the creek near the ranch gate. Hope she could make a new life for herself and her daughter, and mend fences with her father.

Hope and pray Travis wouldn't follow them here.

Shannon pulled alongside the gas pumps out in front of Willard's General Store. The sign was a little more faded after ten years, but the store's facade looked the same. The weathered bench in front of the store was empty, but it would be at four o'clock on a summer afternoon during haying time. She unbuckled her seat belt and got out, stretching cramped muscles. The air was warm and clean and smelled of sweetgrass and sage. She drew it into her lungs, remembering past summers, other times. The screen door opened with the familiar tinkling of the brass shop bell and Willard Jackson emerged, pulling on a pair of leather work gloves. Same old Willard. Gray hair and beard, wiry and spry, eyes bright behind gold-rimmed glasses. He started down the steps as the screen door banged shut behind him and then came to an abrupt stop when he spotted her.

"Shannon?" he said. "Shannon McTavish! Well I'll be hanged. How are you, girl? It's been a dog's age since you went and got famous on us. Good to see you!"

Shannon had to restrain herself from hugging him, her reaction was that acute. She shook the hand he offered with a glad smile. "It's good to see you, too, Willard. It's been a while, for sure. I've come back to visit Daddy and my gas tank's about empty. I'd appreciate if you'd fill it with regular. How are things with you? How's Wilma?"

Willard began pumping the gas. "Oh, things around the store are the same as ever. Wilma's fine. Not much has changed since you left." He canted his head as if reconsidering what he'd just said. "Your daddy know you're coming?"

Shannon shook her head. "I wanted to surprise him. Why? Is everything all right?"

"Well..." Willard began reluctantly, then stopped. His jaw dropped as he looked through the open car window at Rose. "By the sweet ever lovin'. Is that little'un yours?"

"She sure is. Rose turned six last month. Say hi to Mr. Jackson, Rose."

"Hi, Mr. Jackson," Rose said.

"Hello, Rose. You're as pretty as your mother, you know that? You planning on staying awhile?"

"Momma says we're gonna live here, and I'm going to ride horses every day," Rose said.

Willard nodded. "Glad to hear it. Your momma sure could ride, before she got herself famous in Nashville." He topped off the tank and replaced the gas cap. "You planning on moving back here for real?" he asked, that same cautious look in his eyes.

Shannon reached inside the car for her purse. "Willard, to tell the truth, right now I can't say whether I'm coming or going. It's been a long journey and I'm really tired."

He nodded his understanding. "The ranch road's gotten pretty rough since you been gone. There're some washouts that fancy car of yours might not like. Things at your daddy's ranch might look a little different now from what you remember."

Shannon wondered what he was trying to tell her, then shrugged off her fears. "Everything changes, Willard. I'm just glad to be home."

"We're glad to have you. If you need any supplies out there, anything at all, just give me a holler. I'll drive 'em out myself after closing time."

"That's kind of you, but I'm sure we'll be okay." Shannon counted off the bills for the gas and gave them to Willard. "Give Wilma my love."

The ranch turnoff was less than a mile from the store, and the entrance to the ranch road looked pretty much the same. Same massive cedar poles set on either side, two feet in diameter and twelve feet tall, with the ranch sign up high, spanning the distance between them.

The sign was painted steel, rusting gracefully, with a cutout of a running horse. *McTavish Ranch* was lettered in gold against the dark red painted steel. Her mother had made the sign, using an arc welder to cut out the big silhouette of the running horse. When it first went up, folks had come from miles around to admire it, and after all these years it was still a handsome sign, welcoming her home and making her feel as though everything was going to be all right.

That feeling lasted until she saw the new house that was being built not a stone's throw from the ranch turnoff, on the banks of the Bear Paw, smack-dab on the spot where she used to wait for the school bus.

She braked abruptly, her fingers tightening around the wheel, and for a moment she couldn't believe her eyes. It was as if someone had found her childhood diary with the drawing of her little dream house in it, the house she'd planned to build in this very same spot one day. Only nobody knew what her dream house looked like. She hadn't told a soul she was coming back. Nobody would've built that house for her on the little knoll overlooking the creek.

"I don't believe it," she said aloud.

The building was a small, story-and-a-half ranch with a wide porch across the side facing the creek. Simple and pleasing to the eye. The structure was framed up and closed in, sheathed in house wrap, but the roof was only half shingled and the siding wasn't on yet. No windows had been installed in the framed-out openings. No doors. She could see a generator under a lean-to near the house. Stacks of roof shingles and lumber were neatly arranged in the yard.

"Are we there, Momma?" Rose asked from the back seat, perking up.

"No, honey, not yet."

"Why're we stopped?"

"I'm looking at a house."

Rose hitched up in her seat to see out the side window. "Who lives here?"

"Nobody...yet. It isn't finished." Shannon was still trying to process it all. Was it possible that her father was building this place for her and Rose? Was it possible that, all along, he'd been waiting for her to come home? Hoping that she would? Awaiting the day? Had she been wrong about him, thinking that all these years he was still angry with her, that he never wanted to see her again? Could this little house be proof that he really loved her and hoped she'd come back?

"No," Shannon concluded with a shake of her head. "Never in a million years would Daddy be building that house for me."

The final stretch of road to the ranch was worse than rough. One of the first things she'd have to do would be to trade her Mercedes for a pickup truck. If her father let her stay, that was.

But she might have destroyed all chances of that ten years ago. Daddy'd warned her about quitting school and running off with Travis Roy. The day she'd left home they'd had a terrible fight, said terrible things to each other, things they could never take back. Shannon figured he'd get over his big mad, but he hadn't, not even after ten years. Hadn't answered any of her letters, hadn't asked her to come visit or expressed any interest at all in his granddaughter. Worst of all, every single thing he'd warned her about had come to pass. He might not have spoken to her in forever, but for sure he'd say these four words to her when she came crawling home. He'd say, "I told you so," and he'd be right.

"Momma, I have to pee," Rose said from the back seat.

"Hold on, sweetheart, we're almost there."

Shannon crested the height of the land where she could see the ranch spread out in the valley below, surrounded by mountains that looked close enough to touch and were crowned with sailing-ship clouds scudding across the wide-open July sky. She stopped the Mercedes. "See, Rose? Down below us in that valley? That's the McTavish Ranch. That ranch has been in our family for a long, long time."

Rose's face scrunched up in pain. "Momma, I *really* have to pee."

Shannon got out, freed Rose from her seatbelt and helped her from the back seat.

"Go behind those bushes. I'll wait right here."

Rose obediently walked to the side of the road and looked behind the bushes. "Momma, there's no bathroom here."

"If you want fancy indoor plumbing, you'll have to hold it till we reach the ranch."

"I'll wait," Rose said with a pained look and turned toward the car.

Shannon leaned against the car door. It seemed as if the wind was clearing away the weary fog that muddled her thoughts and sapped her energy. Wyoming wind was a yondering wind. She'd always loved its wild, far-flung power, and right at this moment, standing in the shadow of those rugged mountains, she felt young again, as if her dreams were still within reach and life was just beginning.

"Momma?"

Rose's plaintive voice interrupted her reverie, reminding her that ten years had passed and she was now the mother of a six-year-old girl who really had to pee.

The rutted dirt road serpentined a slow descent into the valley and their car kicked up a plume of dust that would announce their arrival minutes before they pulled in to the yard, assuming anyone was looking.

Shannon noted the sad condition of the fences and gates on the ranch road. Willard had warned her, but it looked like Daddy hadn't done any maintenance since she'd left. It was ominous that the gates were ajar, all three of them, including the main gate just off the black road. The cattle and horses could wander clear to the Missouri River if they had a mind—unless there weren't any left to wander. Maybe Daddy had sold all the livestock. Maybe he planned to sell the land off in ten-acre parcels. Mini ranchettes. Maybe that little house being built on the Bear Paw River was the first of many.

She closed the gates, one after the other, two sagging on broken hinges, the last hanging from a rotting fence post. Her parents had taught her always to close the gates and keep them closed, so she did. It would've felt wrong to leave them open.

She parked in front of the house beside the faded blue pickup that was her father's, the same pickup he'd had when she left. Ford half ton. It had been starting to rust then and it was a whole lot rustier now.

The house looked weather-beaten. Shabby. The roof needed shingling, the windows needed a good cleaning. There were a couple of soda cans under the wall bench on the porch, an oily rag on the bench itself next to a greasy jug of winter-weight chain saw oil.

She did a quick assessment of the rest. Porch could use a good sweeping. House needed a fresh coat of paint. Gardens were gone. Her mother's beautiful roses and peonies had long since succumbed to years of neglect in a harsh land. Barns and outbuildings were desolate. Corrals were empty. It looked as if nobody had ever cared about the place and nothing good had ever happened here.

But Shannon knew better. The ghosts of the past weren't all dead. She and her parents had had good times here. Until her mother died.

She cut the ignition. "You wait right here, Rose."

The wind lifted a dust devil as she climbed the porch steps. "Daddy?" She rapped her knuckles on the doorjamb and peered through the screen door into the kitchen. "Daddy, you home?"

She heard the slow click of approaching paws and she peered through the screening. An ancient border collie crossed the kitchen linoleum toward her in a stiff arthritic gait. For the second time that day, Shannon felt a jolt of shock down to the soles of her feet.

"Tess?" She stared in disbelief, then opened the screen door as the dog approached, blue eyes milky with cataracts. The border collie sniffed her outstretched hand and after a moment her tail wagged and her blind eyes lifted, searching. Shannon dropped to her knees and enclosed the frail dog in her arms, overcome with emotion.

"Tess," she choked out as her throat cramped up.

"She waited a long time for you to come back," a man's voice said.

Shannon knew that gruff voice as well as she knew the old dog she held in her arms.

She looked up, blinking through her tears. Her father stood in the doorway, folded-up newspaper in one hand. She rose to her feet and swiped her palms across her cheeks to blot her tears.

"Hello, Daddy."

His expression was chiseled in stone. For the longest moment Shannon thought he wasn't going to respond, but then he gave a curt nod. "Fool dog still looks for you every afternoon, about the time the school bus used to drop you at the end of the road. She never stopped waiting for you to come home."

His words were like a knife twisting in her guts, but of course, that had been his intention. To hurt her. Shannon would've dropped down beside the old dog and bawled her heart out if he hadn't been standing there.

He was thinner, older, but still tough. A couple days' worth of stubble on his lean jaw. His hair had gone completely gray and was cut short, like he'd always kept it. Neatly trimmed mustache. Sharp blue eyes that could still make Shannon feel guilty about things she hadn't done and never would. Blue jeans, worn boots and a reasonably clean white undershirt. Handsome in a steely-eyed, weathered way.

"You might've let me know you were coming. Phone still works," he said.

Shannon shoved her hands into her pockets and lifted her shoulders in an apologetic shrug. "I'm sorry. It was a spur-of-the-moment trip. I brought Rose with me, Daddy. I thought you might like to meet her." She raised her voice and turned toward the car before her father could send them both packing. "Rose, come on and meet your grampy." The car door opened. Rose stepped out and stood in the dust of the yard, staring up at them. To her father, Shannon said, "She's a little shy with strangers, but it doesn't last long. C'mon up here, honey. It's all right."

Rose just stood there, watching them.

"Where's Travis?" her father asked in that same flat, hard voice, eyeing the car.

"I left him, Daddy. I should've done it a long time ago. We're divorced. It's over. I guess that's why I'm here. I didn't know where else to go. Come on, Rose. It's okay."

Rose climbed the porch steps one at a time, holding on to the railing. She stared gravely at her grandfather with her dark blue eyes.

Peaches-and-cream face. Tawny curls. How could he not fall in love with her? Shannon thought. How could this sweet little girl, his own flesh and blood, not melt his heart?

"Hello, Grampy, I'm Rose," she said, and, like they'd rehearsed, she held out her small hand to him.

He took it in his strong, calloused one after a startled pause. "Hello, Rose," he said, and released her hand awkwardly. Shannon was relieved to see his expression had softened.

"Is this your dog?" Rose asked him.

"That used to be your momma's dog. Her name's Tess."

"Her eyes look funny."

"She's blind," her father said bluntly. "That happens sometimes with old animals."

"Do you have horses?"

"A few."

"Are they blind, too?"

"No, but they oughta be. They're old enough."

Rose's expression became pained. She looked at her mother. "Momma, I *really* have to go pee."

"The bathroom's inside, up the stairs and

on your right. Go on. And don't forget to wash your hands after."

The screen door banged behind her and light footsteps raced up the stairs.

"Been a long time since there were any kids in this place," her father said.

"I passed a house being built on the way in," Shannon said, figuring it was best to get it out of the way. "In that pretty spot where I used to wait for the school bus."

Her father nodded, rubbed the bristle of gray stubble on his chin and carefully studied the distant mountains. "I sold ten acres out by the black road to someone you used to know. Billy Mac, from the rez," he said. "He paid some cash up front and he's paying cash for half of each month's mortgage payment, giving me the balance in work. I charged him interest just like a bank would. Seemed fair."

For a few moments Shannon struggled to process what he'd just said. *Billy Mac!* Then the blood rushed to her head and her Scots/Irish spirit took over.

"You sold ten acres of land along the Bear Paw to Billy Mac? A guy you wouldn't even let me date in high school?"

"Property taxes were due and the town…"

"Billy Mac?"

"I needed the money to pay back taxes, and you left, Shannon. I didn't drive you off, you left of your own free will."

Shannon pressed her fingertips to her temples. "You're taking half the mortgage payment in labor?" Shannon glanced around at the neglected slump of the place. "Doesn't look like he's in any danger of drowning in his own sweat from all the work he's doing around here. How much did you sell him the land for? Two hundred an acre?"

Her father never flinched. "He's working hard and doing all right by me. I got no complaints," he said. He shoved his hands deep in his pockets and rounded his shoulders. He refused to look at her, just gazed across the valley. The silence between them stretched out, long and awkward.

"I'd have bought that piece of land from you, Daddy," Shannon said quietly. The anger drained out of her and, with it, the hopes and dreams of her fairy-tale homecoming. "You know how much I loved that spot."

"Too late for that, isn't it?"

"Too late for a lot of things, I guess." Shannon felt empty inside. She'd been a fool to think that coming home would make life better. If it weren't for Rose, she'd get back into her car and leave this place for good.

"How long were the two of you planning to stay?" he said, still not looking at her.

"I was hoping you might let us stay for a night or two," Shannon said. "If it wouldn't be too much trouble."

They heard Rose's footsteps descending the stairs at a gallop. "You can stay as long as you need to," he said. Curt, clipped, brusque. He wasn't going to bend. Wasn't going to soften. Wasn't going to cut her any slack. Never had, never would.

"Thanks, Daddy," Shannon said, biting back the angry words that burned on her tongue. "We won't be much bother. We might even be of some help. I still remember how to do chores, how to drive the mowing machine and how to pitch bales of hay. I noticed the fields hadn't been hayed yet. It's getting late for the first cut and there can never be too many hands at haying time."

Rose pushed the screen door open and rejoined them on the porch. She dropped to her knees beside the old border collie. "Hello, Tess. I'm sorry you're blind."

"Be gentle with her. She's very old," Shannon said. "Fifteen years, anyway."

"I'll be gentle, Momma. Do you think she's hungry?"

"Maybe."

"I'm hungry, too. We haven't eaten since forever."

"That's not true, we ate lunch. You didn't finish yours, remember? I said, 'If you don't finish your sandwich, Rose Chesney Roy, you're gonna get hungry real quick.' And now you're hungry and we don't even know if your grampy can feed us."

Her father bristled at her words. "You like beans and franks?" he asked Rose, gruff as a bear.

Rose nodded up at him, wide-eyed. "And I like burgers and french fries."

"You'll have to settle for cowboy fare tonight."

"Okay," she said eagerly, scrambling to her feet. "Can you teach me to ride tomorrow, Grampy?"

He matched Rose's intense blue gaze with one of his own and fingered his mustache. "This is a real busy time of year. I doubt I'll have a chance." They heard a vehicle approaching and Shannon turned to see a dark pickup truck bouncing down the last rutted stretch of ranch road, kicking up dust. "That'll be Billy Mac. He's been staying here while he builds his house."

The anger that had drained from Shannon returned with a vengeance and heat rushed back into her face. "Billy Mac's living *here*? With *you*?"

Her father nodded. "Bunks in the old cook's cabin. Likes his privacy."

The truck pulled up next to Shannon's car and the engine cut out. Door opened. Driver emerged. Stood. Looked up at them. Shannon stared back. It had been ten years and people changed, but the changes in Billy Mac were the result of more than just the years. He stood just as tall, with those same broad shoulders and the lean cowboy build that had made him a star quarterback and rodeo rider. But he wasn't a kid anymore. Whatever he'd been through in the past ten years had turned him into a man. He reached his fingers to the brim of his hat and gave her a formal nod.

"Hello, Shannon," he said. "This is quite a surprise."

"Hello, Billy. You sure got that part right,"

Shannon replied. Her face burned as she remembered like it was yesterday his passionate and unexpected kiss, and how she'd slapped him afterward. "This is my daughter, Rose."

Billy nodded again. "Nice to meet you, Rose."

Rose skipped down the porch steps and stuck her hand out. "Momma told me it's polite to shake hands when you meet people," she said.

Billy took her little hand in his own for a brief shake. "Your momma's teaching you good manners."

"Supper's about ready," her father said. "Come on in."

Billy hesitated. "The two of you have some catching up to do. I don't want to intrude."

"You're not intruding," her father said, then turned before Billy could respond. The screen door banged shut behind him.

"Nobody argues with Ben McTavish," Shannon said. "You should know that by now. You're working for him, aren't you? Come on in." As much as Shannon dreaded sharing supper with Billy Mac, she dreaded sharing it alone with her father even more.

Billy'd gained a limp—probably from getting thrown off some snuffy bronc or bull. The injury made climbing the steps slow.

"Are you a real cowboy?" Rose asked when he reached the top step.

"Not anymore, Rose, but I used to be a fair hand at rodeo."

"What's rodeo?"

Billy glanced at Shannon. "Your momma hasn't told you what rodeo is?"

Shannon smiled and tousled Rose's curls. "I've been remiss."

Billy gave Rose a solemn look. "Better ask her to bring you to the next rodeo, so you can experience it firsthand."

"Can we go, Momma?" Rose asked, excited.

"We'll see. Come on, supper's ready and we need to get washed up."

Billy opened the screen door and held it while Shannon, Rose and Tess went inside. Shannon had envisioned dirty dishes stacked in the sink, counters crowded with empty cans of food and trash everywhere, but the kitchen looked much the same as it had when she'd left. More tired and worn after ten years, but surprisingly neat. Her father was adding another can of generic pork and beans to the pot on the old propane cookstove.

"Won't take long to heat," he said.

"I thought Rose and I could share my old room," Shannon said. When he didn't respond except to nod, she took her daughter's hand and led her up the stairs, remembering the feel of each worn tread, the creak of the floorboards, the way the late afternoon sunlight beamed through the west-facing hall window and splintered through the railings at the top of the stairs.

"Is this where we'll be living, Momma?" Rose asked as they stood in the open doorway of the small room at the top of the kitchen stairs. The room was just as Shannon remembered. Just as she'd left it. Bed neatly made. Braided rug on the floor beside it. Posters of country-and-western singers pinned to the walls. High school text books stacked on the battered pine desk, as if waiting for her to return and finish up her senior year, as if she could step back in time and magically erase that unforgivable mistake she'd made, running off to Nashville with the slick-talking Travis Roy.

"I don't know, Rose," Shannon said, because in all honesty, she didn't. "We'll be staying here for a few days, anyway." She felt a little dizzy, standing in this musty-smelling time capsule. A little sick at heart and a little uncertain. Coming back home hadn't been such a good idea, after all, but she was here. The only thing she could do was try to make the best of it. She had to get beyond the little house Billy Mac was building on the very spot she'd coveted—and the fact that Billy Mac was downstairs in her father's kitchen.

Billy'd had a tough-guy reputation in high school, maybe because being born on the rez had left him with a chip on his shoulder the size of Texas. But he'd been a wonderful athlete, and handsome enough to make all the girls swoon. He'd had his pick of them, too.

He'd asked Shannon out a couple of times, but even her father had heard that Billy was a player and warned her away from him. Though she'd heeded his warning, that hadn't stopped her from being attracted to him, and it hadn't stopped Billy from trying.

Though she'd been a year younger, Billy'd been her lab partner, and they'd shared an edgy class fraught with a different kind of chemistry that could have taken her down a completely different path and very nearly did. But along about then, Travis Roy moved to town, asked her to sing with his country-and-western band and then dazzled her with promises of a life of fame and fortune in Nashville.

Billy had asked her to his senior prom, but she'd gone with Travis, instead, and not just because of Billy's reputation with the girls. Travis's band was playing at the prom, and she'd written a song for him to sing. He was going to dedicate it to the graduating class as well as the song they'd recently recorded for an agent from Nashville. The song that was about to pave their way to fame and fortune. But Billy'd been at the high school dance, and he and Travis had gotten into it out in the parking lot. Billy'd flattened Travis in a fit of jealousy, busted his nose, then had the audacity to tell her he loved her.

As if that wasn't enough, he'd showed up at the ranch a few weeks later under the guise of apologizing and found her crying on the porch after yet another argument with her father about her wanting to head to Nashville with Travis. He attempted to comfort her and one thing lead to another, culminating in The Kiss.

It was a kiss she'd never forgotten, a kiss that ignited enough passion to make her momentarily forget she was with Travis, but she'd come to her senses, slapped Billy and stuck with Travis, believing her life would be far more rewarding in Nashville with a country music star than with a guy whose sole aspirations were to win a rodeo belt buckle and to have his own ranch someday.

Shannon already knew about ranch life. She'd lived it for seventeen years and wanted something a whole lot more glamorous for the next seventy.

Shannon didn't dwell on the fact that, had things turned out a little differently, if Travis hadn't come to town, she might have ended up being a rancher's wife. She'd never tell Rose about any of this, because there were some things a mother didn't talk to her daughter about, but she still remembered that kiss and how it had made her feel. Ten years hadn't dimmed the memory.

Rose fidgeted. "I'm hungry, Momma."

"Me, too," Shannon said. "I'll let the room air out while we eat supper. We can share the bed tonight, so long as you promise not to thrash around too much. You kick like a little mule."

"I won't kick tonight, Momma. I promise."

Shannon raised the window and leaned out on the sill, looking across the valley toward the craggy bluffs lining Wolf Butte, hazy and grayish blue in the afternoon sunlight. She drew a deep breath of the clear, cool air and let the wind draw it from her lungs.

She felt like weeping, but couldn't. Not with Rose watching. She was still an outcast, unwanted and unloved. Daddy'd been happier to see Billy Mac than he had been to see his own daughter after ten long years. He'd let them stay as long as they needed, but they weren't welcome here. He'd made that plain enough.

"Momma?" Rose's hand slipped into hers. "Can we go eat now?"

"Yes," Shannon murmured past the painful cramp in her throat and turned away from the window to accompany her daughter downstairs.

CHAPTER TWO

BILLY WAS SETTING the food on the kitchen table, cowboy style: pot of beans next to the pot of franks next to the plate of sliced white bread. Stack of mismatched plates, a coffee can full of silverware. Plastic tub of generic margarine. Plastic salt and pepper shakers. Roll of paper towels. Jug of milk. Four chipped cups that would do double duty for milk or coffee. Shannon smelled the sharp aroma of coffee as it started to perk.

Her dad was nowhere in sight.

"Your father went to the tractor shed," Billy said, reading her questioning expression. "Said not to wait on him. He didn't know how long he'd be."

Shannon felt another bitter stab. He'd gone to find one of his bottles of whiskey. He used to have them stashed all over the place, hiding bottles the way squirrels hide their nuts. He was sitting out there somewhere, drinking cheap hooch to avoid his daughter and granddaughter.

"Come wash your hands in the sink first, Rose," she said as her daughter started to sit at the table. They shared the soap, warm water and towel. Billy removed his hat before sitting, revealing a short haircut that didn't quite hide a nasty six-inch scar on the left side of his head above his ear.

Rose stared at it as she climbed into her chair. "Does that hurt?"

Billy shook his head. "Looks worse than it is. The doctors had to put a metal plate in my skull. Here, Rose, have some beans." He dished some out for her, adding a hotdog and a slice of bread.

"Thank you," she said. "Why did they put metal in your head?"

"Rose, it's not polite to ask questions like that," Shannon said as she took her own seat. She tried unsuccessfully to catch her daughter's eye, but Rose was still staring unabashedly at Billy.

"It's all right," Billy said. "I got hurt when the vehicle I was riding in hit a roadside bomb when I was in Iraq. The doctors had to put me back together again the best way they could."

Shannon wondered how many more ugly surprises the day could throw at her. "You joined the military? I always thought you were going to be a big rodeo star or the highest paid quarterback ever for the Dallas Cowboys."

"That might be a first for an Indian off the rez." Billy's grin was sardonic. "Signing up with the Marines seemed like a good idea at the time. The recruiter made it sound like an opportunity I'd be crazy to pass up. I'm glad things worked out better for you in Nashville, Shannon. A lot of talented musicians go there hoping to make a name for themselves, but not many do. You did real good."

Shannon served herself up some beans and franks, avoiding his eyes. "Thanks."

"Bet your next song tops the charts, same as all the others."

"There aren't going to be any more songs. For ten years I lived mostly on a bus and never knew when I woke up what state or town I was in." Shannon concentrated on cutting up her hotdog into precise segments. "I'm done with that life."

Billy had the good sense not to pursue the subject. He helped himself to the beans and took two slices of bread, laying them carefully on the edge of his plate, then hesitated, his fork poised. "Your father probably told you I bought that piece of land by the creek."

Shannon studied her hotdog segments. "Yes, he did."

"He put a for-sale sign out on the road about the same time I came back home. I didn't have much money saved—the military doesn't make a man rich—but I didn't want anyone else buying a piece of the McTavish ranch, so I went to talk to him about a job. He ended up selling me the land and hiring me on at the same time."

"Lucky for you," Shannon said drily, poking at a piece of hotdog.

"I work at Willard's part-time, too. Your father can't pay me, but he's letting me work off my mortgage."

There was an awkward silence. Shannon forked her beans and hotdog segments together in a pile in the center of her plate and stared at them. She'd never faced a more unappetizing meal.

"I guess my father isn't gentling mustangs

anymore," she said. "I don't see any horses down in the corrals."

"We shipped five out to auction last week. The Bureau of Land Management's due to bring another batch in any day now, but McTavish doesn't make much money taming wild horses for their adoption program. Barely enough to buy groceries, really."

"What about horse training for the film studios?"

"He had some sort of falling-out with a studio over a dog being killed on location maybe five, six years back. He blamed them for it and quit. I don't know the details."

Shannon prodded her beans with the fork. The bread was stale and the swelled-up franks were downright suspicious. Who knew what they were made of? She pushed her plate away and reached for her glass of milk, taking a tentative sniff to make sure it hadn't soured.

She gazed across the room to another time. "My mother was the mover and shaker around here. She trained the horses and the dogs. Daddy learned from her after he got busted up in that horse wreck and couldn't work as a stuntman anymore. He did all right with it, but my mother was the best of the best."

"She was a legend around these parts," Billy said.

Shannon was surprised he remembered the strong-willed, independent-minded woman who had been her mother. She caught his eye and felt herself flush. "Finish your beans, Rose."

"But, Momma…"

"Clean your plate and I'll take you out to the barn to see the horses."

Rose dutifully lifted her fork while Billy scraped his chair back and pushed to his feet.

"Coffee's done," Billy said. "I'll pour."

Shannon downed her milk in four big swallows and held her stained Bear Paw Bank and Trust cup out. He filled it with hot strong coffee. "Thanks," she said. "How many hours are you putting in a week to work off your mortgage? What're you doing, exactly?"

Billy set the coffeepot back onto the stove and returned to his seat with his own mug. "I work at Willard's store, stocking shelves, mostly at night. For your father, I help with the mustangs and other odd jobs. Right now I'm working on the fence line down along the black road. It's slow going. Most of the posts are rotted off and need replacing."

"I don't doubt that, but what difference does a good fence make if the gates are left wide open for the livestock to wander through?" Shannon was aware her voice was sharp but the question needed to be asked.

He pulled his chipped John Deere Dealership mug close to his chest. "There's no livestock on the place. We're planning on picking up some young stuff together at the fall auction, but the fences have to be repaired before we can do that."

We? Shannon thought. "Daddy told me there were horses."

"The only two horses he kept were Sparky and Old Joe. He gives them the run of the place, and they never roam too far from the barn."

Shannon took a quick swallow of coffee, which burned her mouth. The pain helped her gain control of her emotions. Sparky and Old Joe had to be twenty-five years old if they were a day. She'd practically grown up astride Sparky, and Old Joe had been her mother's favorite horse. She set down her mug, deeply shaken yet again. As gruff as her father acted, he still had a heart. For the animals, at least.

"I won't beat around the bush, Billy. This place is falling down. It's a shambles. My father may be broke but I'm not. Not completely, anyhow. I can pay whatever it takes to hire you on full-time. That is, if you think you can do the work, and I understand if you can't, with your injuries. It's a big job, a lot harder than stocking shelves at the store, but you'll pay your mortgage off all the sooner."

Billy's eyes locked with hers and the heat in his gaze hit her like a forceful blow. He pushed out of his chair so abruptly that he lost his balance and had to grab for the edge of the table. He straightened, carried his plate and cup to the sink, then limped to the door, took his hat from the wall peg, pushed through the screen door with a squeak and a bang, and was gone.

"Is he mad, Momma?" Rose said in the silence that filled the room.

"I think so, honey." Shannon sighed. "Finish your supper, Rose, and we'll go find Sparky and Old Joe down in one of the barns."

BILLY WAS ON his way to the cook's cabin when he spotted McTavish down by the machinery shed, working on the tractor. Billy pulled his truck up beside the old red Moline tractor and cut the ignition. He and McTavish had been working on the tractor for a week now, every evening after supper. Robbing parts from three other tractors in various stages of decay to build one that could take on the job of haying. Robbing Peter to pay Paul, McTavish called it. The first mowing was already three weeks late. The grass was tall and going to seed. The neighboring ranchers already had their first cutting stored away in their barns.

McTavish wiped his hands on a greasy shop rag. "Thought I might try to fire her up tonight, see how she goes."

Billy adjusted his hat, glanced toward the ranch house then back at the tractor. "Those plug wires look bad. I should've picked up another set today."

"She's got new plugs, new oil filter, new oil, fresh gas, good hydraulic lines. Tires are old but they'll do. She might go, cracked plug wires and all."

"If so, we could start haying first thing to-morrow," Billy said.

McTavish nodded. "Be good to make an early start. We're a little late this year." McTavish hauled himself up onto the metal seat, pulled the primer knob and kicked her over. The Moline sounded as tired as the both of them put together. The tractor's engine turned over but wouldn't fire. McTavish's shoulders slumped. "If just one damn thing would go right around here," he muttered.

"I'll go to town first thing and pick up a new set of plug wires at Schuyler's," Billy offered. "He opens early. We could still be haying by seven. Get the top field done, anyhow, maybe half of the lower."

McTavish nodded again. "Save the slip. I'll deduct it from your monthly payment."

A killdeer flew across the front of the tractor and landed near the corral. Billy watched it hunt for insects in the weeds along the fence line. He plucked a stem of tall grass and nibbled on it. "Been thinkin'. Maybe I could cut my hours at Willard's so's I can work more hours here, when it's busy times, like haying. And the fencing needs to be done before we buy the stock."

"I can't pay you, Billy. We talked about that before."

"I don't need much to get by."

McTavish looked at him. "You're building a house. That takes cash."

"I got what I need to close it in for the winter," Billy said softly. "There's lots that needs doing around here if we're bound to get this ranch back on its feet. Part-time won't cut it. I'll stock shelves at the store if I need spending money. Working full-time for you, I'll pay off my mortgage all the quicker."

He paused. Hearing the words aloud, he realized they made sense, and the humiliation and anger Shannon's words had triggered started to bleed away. She hadn't been attacking him personally, merely telling him she could afford to hire full-time help, and if he couldn't do it, she'd hire someone who could. It was his job to prove to her he was up to the task, in spite of his injuries. "Must feel good, having your daughter back."

"She shouldn't have left." McTavish climbed down from the tractor, his movements stiff. "But she's come to her senses. She finally divorced Travis Roy."

Billy tossed the grass stem away to hide his surprise. "She plan on staying?"

McTavish shook his head. "Doubt it. Willard showed me a picture of her house in one of those entertainment magazines. Looks like the White House, pillars and all, ten times as big as all the buildings on this ranch put together. After living that fancy life for ten years she'll never be able to live here again."

"I can't think of any better place to raise that daughter of hers."

McTavish gave him a jaded look. "I dunno about that. Shannon couldn't wait to get out of here."

"She came back, didn't she?" Billy plucked another blade of grass. "With all her money she could have gone anywhere, but she came home. That says a lot. She still cares about you and she cares about this place, that's as plain as a summer day is long. Speaking of which, it's getting late. I'll see you in the morning, bright and early. We got some hay to cut."

SHANNON TOOK ROSE to the horse barn after cleaning up the kitchen. They walked down in the golden light of early evening. She tried to focus on the beauty of the setting, the rugged mountains and the fertile McTavish Valley, but all she could see were the broken fences, the missing shingles, the sagging roofline of the barn. A land empty of horses and cattle and young dogs. A land devoid of hope.

She pulled open one half of the big barn door and stepped into the dimness, holding Rose's hand in hers. "This barn used to be full of horses and sweet-smelling hay, barn cats and cow dogs. I always loved coming in here."

"Where are the horses, Momma?"

She gazed down the row of stalls. "Looks like nobody's home at the moment." She raised her eyes to the empty hay mow. Dropped them to the wide aisle, littered with dried manure and straw, not neatly swept and raked, the way she'd kept it. She sighed. "Sparky and Old Joe must be outside somewhere, maybe down by the creek."

"Can we go find them?"

"Sure. It's a nice evening for a walk."

They were walking past the tractor shed when Shannon saw her father sitting on an upended bucket, working on the guts of an old red tractor. She changed direction and headed toward him, leading Rose along.

"We missed you at supper. I set aside a plate," she said when he finally paused to acknowledge their approach. Shannon let her eyes flicker over the old machine and shook her head. "Can't believe this old relic still runs."

"It don't. That's why we haven't hayed yet."

Rose spotted Tess lying beside the old shed. "Can I pet her?"

Shannon nodded. "Just be gentle and remember she's old and frail." When Rose was out of earshot, Shannon shoved her hands in her pockets and rounded her shoulders. "Daddy, can we talk?"

He fitted a socket wrench onto a nut and torqued on it hard. It didn't budge. He glanced up at her for a few moments, then said, "I'm listening."

"Rose has been through an awful lot. The past two years, things got pretty bad between me and Travis, and toward the end she was old enough to understand what was going on."

Her father's expression hardened. "She see Travis hit you?"

The carefully applied makeup clearly hadn't hidden the evidence of Travis's last fit of drunken rage. "Yes," Shannon said. "Travis got mean when he was drunk, and these past few years he was mean and drunk most of the time."

Her father laid the socket wrench down at his feet and pulled a rag out of his hip pocket. Wiped his brow and his neck, shoved it back in his pocket, picked up the socket wrench, and tackled the job again, all without ever looking at her. "You don't have to worry about me. I haven't touched a drop since you left, and I sure as heck ain't going to hit either of you."

Shannon flinched inwardly. Her father clearly remembered the last heated words they'd hurled at each other, ten years ago when she was about to leave home. "You walk out of here right now and I no longer have a daughter!" he'd hollered.

She'd whirled around and shot back, just as mad, "You haven't been a father to me since Momma died. You're nothing but a useless drunk!" Then she'd walked out to Travis's truck, climbed in and driven away, bound for Nashville, fame and fortune. That was the last time they'd seen each other, and those were the words that had festered between them for the past ten years.

Her father had stopped working to look directly at her. "You left one useless drunk behind and ran off with another," he said. "I'm sorry about that."

"I'm sorry I said what I did, Daddy," she said. "We both said things we shouldn't have. I'm hoping you'll forgive me and I'm hoping we can make a fresh start. Rose needs to get to know her grandfather."

He dropped his eyes and didn't say anything for a long time, long enough for Shannon to draw a deep breath and square her shoulders. "It's okay if you don't want us. I have friends in California, and I've always wanted to see the big redwoods."

Her father stared at the wrench in his hand and shook his head, still not meeting her gaze. He looked old and beaten. "I couldn't make anything work after your mother died. Losing her wrecked me."

Shannon was surprised by his admission. She felt her eyes sting at the defeat in his voice. She wanted to reach out to him but didn't know how. "I guess maybe when she died, the heart just went out of both of us. I'm going to walk down to the creek with Rose and look for Sparky and Old Joe."

"They'll be by the swimming hole," he said, still staring at the wrench as if it was the sorriest thing he'd ever seen. "They come up to the barn near dark, looking for their grain."

"I'm glad you didn't sell them, Daddy."

He sat back down on the bucket and started working on the tractor. "Nobody'd want 'em," he said gruffly. "They're so old they're no good for anything, not even dog food."

Shannon knew that's not why he'd kept them, but he'd never admit he loved a horse, not in a million years. Crusty old bastard. "C'mon, Rose," she said, reaching for her daughter's hand. "Let's go find us a couple of useless old hay burners."

CHAPTER THREE

DAWN CAME AND Billy was halfway to town before the first slanting rays spangled through the big cottonwoods along the far side of the creek. The parts store wasn't open yet, so he had to roust Schuyler out of bed. The older man cussed and coughed up thirty years of a bad habit as he came to the door, pulling on a pair of greasy old jeans.

"What the hell you doin' here this time of night, Billy?" he said, blinking red-rimmed eyes and scratching his whiskers.

"Need a set of plug wires for McTavish's Moline. We're making hay today. And it's morning, Schuyler, in case you haven't noticed."

"Do tell. Been a while since McTavish did much of anything out to his place. This have something to do with that rich and famous daughter of his coming back home?" He already had a pack of cigarettes in his hand and was tapping one out. "I heard she might be plannin' on stickin' around for a while. That right? Seems kind of funny, a famous singer wanting to stick around a place like this."

"I need those plug wires, Schuyler. The day's half wasted."

After he'd gotten what he came to town for, Billy stopped by Willard's and asked for the day off, told him about his new work schedule and drove back to the ranch through the three open gates. He thought about how they really should be closed, how the horses never should've gone from this place, or the beef cows...or Shannon. McTavish said she wouldn't stick around for long, and he was probably right, but she'd come back here looking for something, and he hoped she found it. He hoped she'd make up her mind to stay and raise her little girl here. It was a good place to raise a kid, and Rose seemed like a good kid.

McTavish was up and waiting, and the coffee was hot and strong.

"Been thinkin'," Billy said after he'd poured himself a steaming mugful. He stood at the kitchen door and looked out across the valley, watching as long fingers of golden sunlight stretched across the land. "Maybe we could fix up that old windmill, the one that used to pump water to your upper pasture. Might make the grass grow better. We'll need a lot of hay to winter the stock we buy this fall." McTavish said nothing in reply, just pulled on his jacket. Billy took a swallow of coffee. "I got the plug wires installed and the tractor's ready to go whenever you are."

"Don't know what difference any of it'll make in the long run," McTavish said.

Billy set his mug in the sink.

"We'll find out," he said. "Let's make us some hay."

SHANNON SLEPT SOUNDLY and awoke with a start, surprised that the day was already in full swing. She glanced at her watch but didn't need to. She could still measure the morning hours of ranch life by the sounds and smells and the sunlight. It was 8:00 a.m., the day half gone.

"Rose, honey, it's time to get up." She nudged the small bundle curled beside her in the bed, smoothed her palm over the warm curve of her daughter's cheek. Rose made a soft mewling and burrowed deeper beneath the quilt, never quite awakening.

Shannon tucked the quilt around Rose and left the warmth of the bed, moving to the window. The air still held the cool of the night but was rapidly warming. She could hear the distant guttural growl of a tractor.

Her bedroom window overlooked the barns, the molten shine of the creek, the roof of the cook's cabin and the old bunkhouse. The lower fields were out of sight, on the other side of the creek, but she suspected the sound came from there. If Billy was helping her father, there really wasn't much she could do in the fields until the hay was baled tomorrow. Today she'd go to Willard's, buy some decent groceries and cook them a decent meal.

She could wash the windows and cut down the weeds growing around the sides of the house. She could sweep off the porch and pick up the trash. Brush the burrs out of Sparky's and Old Joe's manes and tails. Take Rose for a ride. There was no end of chores to keep her busy, and certainly no excuse for her to be lying abed when so much needed doing.

She showered in the small, drab bathroom

with the peeling wallpaper and wiped the steam from the mirror afterward, staring at the thin face with the blackened left eye.

The swelling was almost gone and the colors around her eye had morphed, gradually, from dark purple to a mottled greenish yellow. Makeup helped to hide the bruises, but there was no forgetting, especially when she looked in the mirror, how awful the last few years of her life had been. Travis's last visit had come after the divorce was finalized, and he'd left her lying on the foyer floor. The very next day she'd filed for a restraining order, packed her things and left with Rose.

Shannon dried and brushed her hair, dressed swiftly in jeans, a T-shirt and a fleece sweatshirt, and carried her shoes down the kitchen stairs. The coffeepot on the gas stove was still warm. She poured herself a cup and carried it out onto the porch. Tess was sleeping at the top of the porch steps, letting the morning sun warm her old bones.

Shannon sat beside Tess, drinking her coffee and letting the sun warm her bones, too, while she gently stroked the old dog. Yesterday she'd wondered if it had been a mistake to come back. Today she felt a little better about things. She had no idea how long she and Rose would stay, but right now she wasn't going to worry about the future. She was going to fix breakfast for her little girl and then go to town and get some groceries.

There was hay to make…and she had her own fences to mend.

THEY QUIT AT NOON, not because they wanted to, but because the cutter bar broke. The field was almost finished when the bolt sheared off. McTavish had gone back to the barn to get more gas when it happened. Billy heard the sudden disjointed clatter and disengaged the cutter bar. Diagnosing the problem was easy. The fix would be, too, as soon as he picked up a new bolt, but that meant another trip to town if he couldn't find a replacement in the tractor shed.

By the time he'd removed the sheared-off bolt, McTavish had returned with the gas. He climbed out of the cab, slammed the door of the truck, lifted the gas can from the back and turned to face Billy.

"Shannon's gone," he said bluntly. "Took Rose and left. No note, nothing. I knew she wouldn't be able to settle for this place."

Billy shook his head. "She'd have told you if she was leaving."

McTavish took his hat off and whipped it against his pant leg. His eyes narrowed as he looked across the vast expanse of newly cut grass. "Didn't make a damn bit of difference, this morning's work."

Billy didn't know what to say. The wind had picked up and the sweet smell of fresh-cut hay filled the air. It had been a good start to a good day, but suddenly the sky didn't look quite so blue. "We need a new bolt for the cutter bar," he said, holding up the shorn piece.

McTavish was still gazing across the big hay field. "I never could talk to her." He shook his head. "Never could."

"There might be a spare bolt up in the trac-tor shed," Billy said.

McTavish didn't respond. Just stood there, holding the gas can and staring off into the distance. Billy started walking back toward the ranch. He was about to duck inside the tractor shed when he heard a vehicle com-ing down the road. A rooster tail of dust plumed behind the dark-colored Mercedes as it emerged at the bottom of the steep grade and headed toward the ranch, pulling to a stop up by the house.

Shannon was in the process of unloading boxes from the car when Billy reached her. She stopped at the bottom of the porch steps with a box in her arms and gave him a wide open smile. It was so beautiful and unexpected that he stopped and struggled to catch his breath while his heart did backflips.

"Morning," he said.

"Good morning," she said. "Rose and I went to town and picked up some real food, or as real as food gets at Willard's. I'll fix some sandwiches, so's you and Daddy can eat quick and get at it again. Rose, honey, Tess'll live without you for a few more minutes. Can you come here and give your momma a hand with these groceries?"

The little girl jumped up from where she'd been crouched beside Tess on the shaded porch and raced to her mother's side even as Billy closed the distance between them.

"Here," he said. "Better let me take that one, that looks heavy." He lifted the big cardboard box from Shannon's arms.

"Thanks. I picked up enough to get us through the haying. No more canned beans and franks with stale bread, thank you very much. My mother was a good cook and she taught me a few things."

"Your father came back to get some gas for the tractor, saw your car was gone and figured you'd left for good."

Shannon was gathering another box of groceries into her arms. She glanced up with an exasperated expression. "I pinned a note beside the screen door. The wind must've blown it off. If he'd checked my room he'd have seen my things. He was probably happy to think I'd left so soon."

Billy climbed the steps one at a time, slowly, but he climbed them, carrying the heavy box of groceries. He set the box on the table and she set hers right beside it. Rose added the five-pound bag of russets she'd lugged up.

"He's hoping you stick around."

"Be nice if he showed it." Shannon turned away to unpack the box she'd carried up from the car. "Thank you, Rose," she said. "Why don't you bring that bowl of water out for Tess, in case she's thirsty."

When Rose had left the kitchen, carefully balancing the water bowl, Shannon continued unpacking. "I'll get the last box," Billy said, and descended the porch steps, wondering how Shannon and her father had ever drifted so far apart. Shannon was organizing the groceries as he reentered. Her expression had become introverted. Thoughtful.

"Tuna sandwiches okay?" she asked.

Billy nodded. "Sounds great. I came back to find another bolt for the cutter bar. I'll go look for one in the shed, then get your father. He's still out with the tractor."

The wall phone rang as he was heading for the kitchen door and Shannon set the cans of tuna on the counter and reached for it. "Mc-Tavish Ranch, Shannon speaking," she said, and then Billy watched as her expression changed and her entire body went rigid. She listened in silence for a few moments before interrupting.

"Don't you dare come here, you hear me?" Her voice was low, taut with emotion. "I'll have you arrested if you violate that restraining order. I mean it. You stay away from me, and you stay away from Rose." She hung up without waiting for a reply. Her face was pale, and when she raised a hand to smooth the hair off her forehead, the tremble was

noticeable. She cast a quick glance out the kitchen door to where Rose crouched beside the old dog, coaxing her to drink, then drew a shaky breath and crossed her arms around herself. "I'll have lunch ready by the time you get back."

Billy paused with one hand on the doorknob. "Your father told me about your divorce."

"I bet he did," she said bitterly.

"You're safe here, Shannon," he said, ignoring her reaction. "If Travis Roy is stupid enough to show up, there won't be much left for the sheriff to arrest."

AFTER THE PHONE call from Travis, Shannon could barely focus on the simple task of making a stack of sandwiches and heating a pot of soup. She told herself that Travis wouldn't come here, he wouldn't dare, but he still had family in Lander. Lander was a ways from their valley, but it was still too close as far as Shannon was concerned. He'd said he just wanted to talk to her, to see Rose. Said he had something for her and swore he'd quit the drinking and the drugs, but he'd made every promise in the book these past few years and broken them all, over and over again. She was through believing his lies and living in fear. The divorce was final. She was done with him. The only thing left for the courts to decide was the custody of Rose, and she was confident she'd win that battle.

She stirred the soup as it came to a simmer, cut the sandwiches and put them on a platter. Poured some tortilla chips into a bowl and put that on the table along with a pitcher of milk and four glasses. Finding four soup bowls proved a challenge, but she came up with three mismatched bowls and washed out the bowl she'd mixed the tuna in, filled an old mixing bowl with the fruit she'd bought, and put that on the table as well, dead center.

The screen door squeaked open, banged shut and Rose burst into the kitchen. "Momma, can we go riding now?"

"No, honey, it's lunchtime. Go get washed up."

"Can we go riding after?"

"Maybe."

Rose studied her for a moment, her expression becoming fearful. "Did Daddy find us?"

Shannon felt her heart wrench. She was still too emotionally raw to hide the effects of Travis's phone call from her daughter. "Go wash up, Rose. It's all right, we're safe here."

"Are we going to stay with Grampy forever?"

"For now. I don't know about forever. Nobody does. Go wash up."

After Rose had gone upstairs she heard boots climbing the porch steps and moved to the door. Billy had returned, alone.

"Your father's truck was gone when I got back to the tractor," Billy explained as he came into the kitchen. "I went ahead and fixed the cutter bar on the mower. I'll finish that field after lunch and start on the second. Ought to be able to turn the hay once before dark." He hung his hat on a peg by the door and eyed the table. "That looks mighty good."

"It's just a stack of sandwiches," Shannon said.

"You haven't seen the chow we normally eat around here."

"Oh, I got a pretty good taste of it last night," Shannon said, ladling out the soup while Billy washed at the sink. She filled three bowls and set the remainder on the stove for when her father got home.

"You probably got used to eating pretty

fancy while you were living in Nashville," Billy commented, dropping into the same chair he'd used at supper the night before. Rose thundered down the stairs and claimed her own seat, eying the food expectantly.

"We were pretty spoiled," Shannon admitted as she joined them at the table, passing the platter of sandwiches. "Rose especially loved our cook, didn't you, Rose?"

Rose shook her head vehemently and made a face. "She made me eat yucky things."

Shannon laughed. "Rose doesn't like fancy food."

"Neither do I," Billy confided to Rose. "Give me plain and simple any day."

"Plain and simple's all they shell out at Willard's, so the both of you should be very happy," Shannon said. "Napkin in your lap, Rose."

"It's not a napkin, it's a paper towel, Momma."

"Pretend it's fine linen and remember your manners, young lady."

Rose heaved an exaggerated sigh as she put the paper towel in her lap. "Are you always going to have a plate in your head?" she asked Billy.

"Rose!" Shannon chastised her.

"Yup," Billy said. "The docs told me the plate was permanent. I asked if they could throw in a fork, knife and spoon but they couldn't fit 'em in there."

Rose giggled until Shannon caught her eye. "How long were you in the military, Billy?"

"Eight years. After four tours of duty I thought my life was pretty much over when I was wounded. That little piece of land and the house I'm building beside the Bear Paw is the best thing that's ever happened to me. I owe a lot to your father for making that possible."

Shannon felt a twinge of resentment. It was noble of Billy to have served his country, and terrible that he'd been so horribly wounded in action, but he'd stolen her dream. That was *her* little house he was building in *her* special spot. Billy and her father had stolen her dream and it was hard not to resent them both for slamming the door on the future she'd planned for herself and Rose here at the ranch.

Billy wolfed down two sandwiches and dispatched his soup with equal enthusiasm. Rose matched him, mouthful for mouthful. For a six-year-old, she ate like a horse. Shannon took a bite of her sandwich and played with her soup. The phone call from Travis had effectively destroyed any appetite she might have had, and she was brooding about her future. Where was she going to raise her daughter if there was no place for her here?

"Not hungry?" Billy said, already finished.

"I ate a big breakfast," Shannon lied. "Wonder where my father's at."

Billy shook his head. "We talked about fixing the windmill. Maybe he decided to make a start on it. He lost all interest in haying when he thought you'd left."

Shannon shook her head with a frustrated sigh. "Soon as I get all the groceries put away, I'll pack him a lunch and walk up there."

"But you said we could go riding," Rose protested.

"We will, after we make sure your grampy's fed."

Billy pushed away from the table and reached for his hat. "I'll get back to haying. Thanks for lunch." He paused with his hand on the door. "Cell phones don't work all the time out here, Shannon. If anyone unwelcome should show up, call the police on the landline right away, then call my cell. The number's written on the wall beside the phone."

Shannon felt an unexpected twinge of gratitude. "Thanks, Billy, but we'll be okay."

He held her gaze a moment longer, then turned and went out the screen door with a squeak and a bang. She watched him walk down toward the bridge over the creek. Watched him until he walked out of sight, grudgingly admiring the strong set of his shoulders and the quiet, solid competence of him.

Eight years of soldiering had given him the kind of masculinity that only came from encountering and surviving adversity and hardship day after day, year after year. The years since high school had changed them both in ways they'd never anticipated.

She'd come back home bruised and battered from a failed relationship, spooked as a deer and afraid of her own shadow. Billy'd been through different fires and was scorched around the edges by his years in the military, but those fires had given him a depth and substance that many men would never achieve.

True, she resented him for buying the piece

of land she'd dreamed of building her little house on, but after Travis's phone call, she was glad Billy was here. Keeping Rose safe from harm was her top priority, and Billy had as much as promised that no harm would come to them here.

"Do you think Billy could teach me to ride?" Rose asked, coming to stand beside her.

"If anyone could, it'd be Billy. He was a rodeo champ before he was eighteen. Just a kid, but he beat 'em all, even the best of the best."

"Momma, what's rodeo?"

Shannon looked down at her daughter and gave a rueful laugh as she reached to tousle Rose's tawny curls. "Rodeo's a crazy part of the wild spirit of the West, Rose, and I promise I'll take you to see one, first chance we get. Now let's pack up a lunch for your grampy and find him, if we can."

BILLY FINISHED CUTTING and turning both fields by sundown. He wanted to make good on the day because of Shannon. Not only because she doubted he could physically handle the full-time work, but also because of how vulnerable she was right now. She was nursing wounds from a failed marriage, she'd given up her singing career, returned home with Rose and was looking for a safe place to rebuild her life. Billy was hoping she'd realize her father's ranch was the place. He was hoping she'd want to stay.

Shannon had always been different from the other girls, even back in high school. Strong willed, with a self-confidence that went way beyond her years. She was smart as a whip, prettier than an October sunset and she could sing. Man, could she sing.

Billy had been used to having his pick of pretty girls. That territory came with the rodeo championships and being a winning quarterback. But Shannon was the kind of girl who intimidated most guys.

It was alphabetical luck that paired them as lab partners in chemistry class, and he got to know Shannon pretty well. She had a quick, wry sense of humor and an opinion about everything that left nobody wondering where she stood. There was a reason she was president of the debate club. Shy she was not. He looked forward to every moment of their lab time together and tested the waters very carefully before asking her if she wanted to go along with him to his next rodeo.

But still, when he asked her out, she'd very politely and coolly told him, "No, thank you," without so much as a pause, adding, "My father says I should stay away from guys with only one thing on their minds, and I agree."

"Have I made a move once during chem class? Come on, give me a chance."

"Billy Mac, you've dated every pretty girl in this high school and then some. I'm reasonably sure you'll find half a dozen fans to go with you to your next rodeo and they'll jump up and down and wave pom-poms when you win that fancy belt buckle."

Billy hadn't given up. He'd done his best to win Shannon over, figuring that she must surely feel the chemistry simmering between them, chemistry that had nothing to do with the lab work they shared. After all, every time their hands touched, Shannon blushed. Their conversations ran the gamut from world affairs to the gossip heard at Willard's General Store, and Billy began to hope that, in spite of the differences between them, in spite of the fact that he was just a half-breed off the rez and she was on track to be a country-

and-western star, she might realize that she was falling in love with him.

But it was not meant to be, because that was the year Travis Roy's family arrived in Bear Paw. Travis was a city boy and a slick talker. He could sing and play guitar. He started a country-and-western band and Shannon was his first recruit.

Before long, they were playing gigs at all the local watering holes. Then they were playing gigs in the big towns. Cities. The band entered a regional contest and won. Went to Nashville to enter a bigger contest and won there, too, handily. They were televised on a national star-search TV show just a few months later, which they also won.

They were young and on fire, and in retrospect, Billy couldn't believe he'd had the nerve to ask her out that second time, to his senior prom, no less, knowing full well she'd turn him down once again and cut him off at the knees. But he asked her anyway, figuring he had nothing to lose, and she'd politely thanked him and said she already had a date.

Travis, of course.

So Billy took the head of the cheerleading squad to the prom and had to watch Shannon and Travis having too good a time together on the dance floor. That was the same night he blew any chance he might have had with Shannon by breaking Travis's nose in the parking lot.

As soon as he could screw up the nerve he'd gone over to her ranch to apologize and he'd found her crying on the porch, her arms clutched around Tess. She'd had a fight with her dad about wanting to leave for Nashville, one of an endless string back then. Billy understood wanting something different than what you had. He'd gone to Shannon and held her for a long while…and then he'd kissed her.

He hadn't meant to, hadn't planned it, but Shannon's body instantly melted against his, and she'd kissed him back with all the passion he knew lived within her. For a few brief, glorious seconds, Billy thought he'd finally won her heart…until she froze in his embrace as she realized what she was doing, wrenched herself out of his arms and slapped him, accusation in her eyes. "What happened to not making a move, Billy?" she'd said. "My father was right about you!"

Hurt and ashamed, he'd lashed out: "What's

the matter? A half-breed off the rez isn't good enough for a McTavish?"

"I don't care about that, Billy. Never have. I wish you could say the same." Then she'd disappeared into the house, slamming the door on Billy's hopes and dreams.

Shortly thereafter, with the promise of a recording contract with a big producer, Shannon and Travis left Wyoming and headed for Tennessee to cut their first single.

It was a smash hit.

Billy had wondered about her often in the years that followed. He kept up with her life through the songs on the radio, the tabloids at the grocery store and through letters from friends back home.

So he knew she'd married Travis. Had a baby girl. Gotten famous. But in spite of all that fame and fortune, her marriage had failed. As far as Billy was concerned, her coming back home was good. She needed to mend fences with her father, and McTavish needed Shannon and his granddaughter in his life more than he'd ever admit.

And her being home gave Billy a chance to prove two things to Shannon: that this was the perfect place to raise her daughter, and that Billy, in spite of his injuries, wasn't just some half-breed Indian off the rez riding a dead-end horse.

What wasn't good was that Travis Roy knew where she was. Travis had hurt her, and Billy could think of few forms of life lower than a man who would abuse his woman. If Travis showed up here, there'd be hell to pay.

Billy felt uneasy leaving Shannon alone at the house while he hayed, but he could watch the road from some of the fields, and even where he couldn't, he'd be able to see the cloud of dust a vehicle kicked up when it approached the ranch.

He kept his eyes peeled all afternoon, sitting on the old Moline, driving back and forth, back and forth, across the fields, making hay.

SHANNON WALKED UP to the old windmill after lunch. She carried a hamper containing sandwiches and a thermos of hot coffee in one hand and held Rose's hand in the other. The windmill wasn't too far from the ranch, but after they'd hiked half an hour Rose began to complain.

"Momma, I'm tired."

"Almost there, sweetie, just a little farther. Maybe we'll see some horses up there, or a cow that might have escaped the roundup."

The trail followed the creek, and Shannon scanned for tracks. There were some old hoofprints left by horses and cattle, and she thought she saw the impression of a bear paw in a soft patch of mud alongside its namesake creek, but nothing really fresh and no boot tracks. This didn't surprise her. Her father would've driven the truck to the site using one of the old ranch roads. The windmill hadn't worked in many years. After her mother died, everything had started to slide downhill.

"My legs are tired," Rose said. "Can you carry me?"

"No, honey. You're big enough to walk."

"Why couldn't we ride?"

"Because you don't know how to ride yet."

"But you said you'd teach me."

"I will, but first we have to find your grampy." Shannon was worried, though she tried to keep that from Rose. Her father thought she'd left the ranch and taken Rose. Billy said he'd been upset. Would he be angry to see them or pleased? Or would he be just his old stoic self and show no emotion at all? If only she could have left Rose back at the ranch. But with no one to watch Rose, she'd had no choice but to bring her along.

Should she tell her father about Travis's phone call or would that just make things worse?

They crested the last stretch of steep climb and stopped for a breather. "There's the windmill," Shannon said, "and there's your grampy's truck." She was relieved to see it, and Rose tugged at her hand, forgetting how tired she was.

"Come on, Momma. Let's bring Grampy his food."

Her father was sitting inside the cab of the truck. The windows were rolled down. The truck was facing the windmill, so he didn't see them until he noticed movement in his side-view mirror. He turned his head and Shannon could tell instantly from his red-rimmed eyes that he'd been drinking. She pulled Rose to a stop beside her, her stomach churning. She wished she hadn't come, but it was too late.

"I went to town after breakfast to get some

groceries," she said. She held up the hamper. "We brought you some lunch."

"Do you like tuna sandwiches, Grampy?" Rose asked.

He dragged his forearm across his face and cleared his throat. "I do, yes," he said roughly.

"We brought you some," Rose said. "And Momma made you some coffee."

"Thank you." He nodded, not meeting Shannon's eyes. "I'll get back to work right after I've et."

"Then I guess we'll see you at supper." Shannon set the hamper on the hood of the truck and tightened her grip on Rose's hand. "C'mon, Rose. You can help me get Old Joe and Sparky into the barn. We should give them a good brushing."

"But, Momma…" Rose protested as Shannon tugged her down the path away from the windmill.

"You said you wanted to go riding, didn't you?"

"But, Momma…!" Rose was struggling to keep up with Shannon's brisk pace.

"We can't go riding until the horses have been groomed, and we need to check the saddles and bridles, too, and clean them so they're nice and shiny."

"But...!"

"It'll be easier going back down the trail than it was hiking up. Come on, we've got a lot to do before suppertime."

Rose dug her heels in and brought her mother to a halt. *"Why was Grampy crying?"*

Crying? Shannon had just assumed, when she saw his red-rimmed eyes, that he'd been drinking. Had she been wrong? Was Rose right? Was that why he'd wiped his face? Filled with self-doubt, Shannon turned, knelt down and met her daughter's somber gaze.

"Maybe because he thought we'd left him, and he was feeling sad. But he'll be okay now that he knows we're still here. He'll eat his lunch and work on the windmill and we'll see him at suppertime. Don't worry, your grampy'll be fine." She gave her daughter an encouraging smile. "Let's go get Old Joe and Sparky all dolled up so we can show Grampy how good they look when he comes home."

Rose's face brightened. "Okay," she said. "Maybe then Grampy'll teach me to ride."

Shannon glanced over Rose's shoulder toward the old pickup truck. She'd seen her father cry only once, the day her mother died. Maybe Billy had been right. Maybe he really was glad she'd come back home. Maybe he'd even missed her a little bit all these years and just couldn't show it.

Or maybe he just had.

"Maybe," she said softly, hoping with all her heart it was so.

CHAPTER FOUR

THEY BROUGHT THE horses up to the barn and Shannon showed Rose how to hold the brush and currycomb, how to use a firm, gentle pressure and make the geldings' eyes half close with the glorious pleasure of being groomed. Then she worked on getting the old burrs out of their manes and tails. Lord knows how long it'd been since they'd last had a good grooming, but the two old geldings clearly enjoyed every moment of it.

Sparky remembered her. She'd half thought he wouldn't, but the way he lipped her jacket pocket, figuring she'd have a treat secreted there for him, was a dead giveaway. She gave him a piece of carrot, showing Rose how to present it on the flat of her palm so her fingers wouldn't get mistaken for the treat.

"Hey, old Spark, I bet you still like to run, don't you?" she said, rubbing his withers as he crunched on the carrot.

"Does he run fast?" Rose asked.

"He used to, and he could jump a four-foot fence. He's too old for that now, but when he was young we competed in the barrel racing, and he'd always win for me. Always. He might not be pretty, but he sure could move."

"I think he's pretty," Rose said, stepping up beside Shannon to stroke the gelding's shoulder.

"I'm with you. I think he's handsome and smart and talented. Now, let's give Old Joe a treat. He's a retired movie star. Your grandmother trained him, and he's starred in more horse movies than any other. He's a thoroughbred. See how much taller he is than Sparky? Sparky's a quarter horse. Quarter horses can run really fast for a quarter of a mile, but thoroughbreds can run really fast for a lot farther."

"Was Old Joe a racehorse?"

"He was a racehorse in most of his movies but not in real life," Shannon began, then stopped when she heard the distant rumble of a vehicle approaching. Her heart rate trebled and she snatched Rose's hand and pulled her out of the barn to find out who it was. Travis wouldn't dare come here. He wouldn't dare!

She craned to see up the valley, then felt the tension rush out of her when she noticed a big truck hauling a gooseneck stock trailer. "I bet it's that new shipment of government mustangs for your grampy to train," she said, light-headed with relief. "Let's open up the corral gate for them."

Ten minutes later the driver of the truck thanked her and departed, leaving behind six wild-eyed, scruffy-looking mustangs. Shannon kept Rose pulled tight beside her as they watched the horses circling the corral, the whites of their eyes flashing with fear. They were caked with dust and mud and sweat, and their manes and tails were tangled, yet they were wild and beautiful. "You stay away from these horses, Rose," Shannon warned. "They're wild and they could easily kill you if you went into the corral."

"I won't hurt them, Momma," Rose said.

"I realize that, honey, but they don't. All they know about humans is that we took them away from their band and brought them to a strange place. We robbed them of their freedom. They have no reason to trust us or like us."

"Do you think they ever will, Momma?"

Rose asked, watching them stampede around the corral, her eyes as wide as theirs.

"That's Grampy's job, to make sure they do, and he's good at it. Come on, let's turn Sparky and Old Joe loose and carry the saddles up to the house. We can work on them out on the porch and keep Tess company."

Shannon carried the saddles and Rose held the bridles. Had saddles always been this heavy? Her arms were aching by the time she set them down on the porch. Tess lifted her head and gazed up at her for a long moment, thumped her tail twice, then returned to her nap. Shannon was just settling down to the job of cleaning the saddles when she heard the approaching growl of the old farm tractor. It was Billy, and he was making for the house at full throttle, still hauling the tedder behind him. He braked below the porch and cut the tractor's engine.

"I saw the dust coming down the road," he explained in the sudden silence. He followed Shannon's gesture, spotted the horses in the corral and relaxed. Shannon realized he'd half expected to find Travis here. Maybe he'd been hoping Travis was dumb enough to come, so Billy could flatten him again like he had on prom night. The thought of Billy protecting her brought a flush of warmth to her cheeks.

"They're a good-looking bunch," she said. "A little spooked right now, but they'll settle down."

"They'd settle down a whole lot faster if it was the dead of winter and they were cold and hungry." He paused.

"You find your father?"

Shannon nodded. "He was up at the windmill. How's the haying coming along?"

"Fields are all mowed and turned once. With any luck we'll be done by nightfall tomorrow. They're predicting rain tomorrow night. Heard the forecast on my way back from town this morning."

"That's cutting it real close."

"If the tractor doesn't break down again we'll make it."

"Maybe." Billy was looking a mite whipped, but Shannon wasn't about to say so. "I can help you out, but we'll need another hand or two to get it into the barn before it rains."

"Thought I'd head into town after supper, see if I can scare up some more eager volunteers," Billy said.

"Good help's usually pretty scarce when it comes to pitching hay bales."

Billy grinned. "True enough. But once I mention they'll be working alongside a famous country-and-western singer, the whole town of Bear Paw'll turn out."

"Fine by me," Shannon said. "The more the merrier when it comes to haying. I'll start a big batch of spaghetti sauce tonight and plan for a big feed tomorrow."

"Sounds like a plan. I'd best get to work." Billy started the tractor, gave her a nod and pulled away from the porch. Shannon watched him, pondering what strange twists of fate had drawn both her and Billy Mac back to Bear Paw.

"Momma, can I help tomorrow?"

"Sure, Rose. You can ride in the hay truck and count the bales as we load them on."

"How many bales will there be?"

"Lots and lots. Enough to feed a bunch of horses all winter long, and maybe some cows, too."

"What if I can't count that high?" Rose asked, frowning.

"I'll give you a piece of paper, and when you count ten bales being loaded, you make a mark on the page. Then start counting to ten again and make another mark. Each mark will count for ten bales, and that way you'll keep track for us. Now let's get to cleaning these saddles. It's almost time for me to start supper."

They settled on the porch together, side by side, feet swinging over the edge, sponges in hand, saddles sprawled beside them. Rose made lots of suds with her sponge. Tess slept and twitched her way through the active dreams of a younger dog. Shannon breathed in the good smells of saddle soap and leather, and paused from time to time to look out across the broad sweep of McTavish Valley toward Wolf Butte. For the first time in years, she felt like she was truly home.

She wondered how long the feeling would last.

BILLY WAS DOG TIRED. His leg hurt. His side hurt. His shoulder hurt. The pain was acute, and the more he tried to ignore it, the worse it got. He tried to focus on the machinery. On loading the baling twine into the baler. On the anticipation of a home-cooked supper prepared by Shannon McTavish.

He'd overdone it today, that's all. The pain would pass, along with the scare he'd gotten, seeing that big rooster tail of dust moving toward the ranch house, toward Shannon, and thinking it was Travis Roy.

He'd seen a lot of ugliness over the years. A lot of death. He should be immune to violence by now, but he wasn't. Just the opposite. He'd been numb for a long time, but it was as if the pain in his body had become a conduit to all the pain and suffering he'd witnessed.

Seeing Shannon's bruised face and how she'd tried to hide the bruises with makeup twisted him up inside. She insisted Travis wouldn't come here. He hoped she was right, because he wasn't sure what he'd do if he ever got his hands on that bastard. Or maybe he was sure, and that's what scared him. Shannon was out of his league and always had been, but that didn't keep him from caring about her, and it never would.

Billy gave up on the baler. He needed to walk the pain out. He'd go up to the windmill, check on McTavish. The wind was dying and the air was sweet with the smell of fresh-mown hay. It was going to be a pretty evening. A pretty sunset.

There was no one to see him, no one watching. He could limp. He could crawl on his hands and knees and it wouldn't matter. That was the wonderful thing about living on the edge of nowhere. A man could find himself, re-create himself or lose himself, all without anybody watching.

McTavish was crouched at the base of the windmill, tools scattered around him, covered with grease. "I think I've about got 'er," he said, wiping his hands on a rag.

Billy leaned against the front of the truck. He was sweating. He took off his hat and let the wind cool him. "I finished cutting the fields and turned them all once. Figured we could bale in the morning. I'll head into town after supper and find us some help. With a good crew we might get all the hay in by dark, if we go at it hard."

He let himself slide down the truck's bumper, keeping his leg out straight, until he was sitting on the ground. "Shannon's fixing supper, and you just got a new delivery of six mustangs from the government. Good-looking horses. Wild and wooly. I would've had 'em all broke by now except I'm plumb wore out."

McTavish rubbed the stubble on his chin.

He shook his head, wearing the faintest of smiles. "By God, but we're a pair."

Billy would've laughed if he'd had the strength.

TEN YEARS OF having a chef had spoiled Shannon. She'd forgotten all the basic cooking skills she'd picked up from her mother, who could shoulder a full day's work on the ranch and still manage to produce savory home-cooked meals. As Shannon rummaged through the lower cupboards for the proper cookware, she tried to recall what she'd bought for groceries. She had two hungry men and a hungry daughter to feed in short order.

What to cook? How to keep them all happy?

"Momma, I'm hungry," Rose said, pushing through the screen door with Tess at her heels.

She'd promised the men a good feed. They'd both be hungry. She had hamburger. Lots of hamburger. She'd fix the spaghetti sauce tonight and they'd just have to eat it two nights in a row.

"Eat a piece of fruit, Rose. It'll tide you over until supper's ready," Shannon said, reaching for a skillet. "I'm making spaghetti. You like spaghetti, don't you?"

"With meatballs?"

"With meat sauce. Sorry, no time to make meatballs. We spent too long cleaning the saddles."

"They look nice and shiny, Momma."

"They sure do, and they'll look even nicer on Sparky and Old Joe."

Shannon lit the gas burner and plunked the deep cast-iron skillet down atop it. She opened two cans of spaghetti sauce and poured them over the hamburger as it cooked. With a little doctoring, she could make the sauce look and taste like homemade.

Shannon paused, frowning. She'd forgotten about Sparky and Old Joe. They were probably down at the barn by now, wondering where their grain was. What about the mustangs in the corral? They had water, but they'd need to be fed. And what of her father? Had he been crying or drinking? If he'd been drinking, had he put the cork back in the bottle?

"Rose, I have to toss some hay to the mustangs in the corral. I won't be two minutes. Stay here with Tess and I'll be right back."

She paused at the door, scanning the small kitchen, the spaghetti sauce starting to bubble in the skillet, the old dog finishing her meal over in the corner, and the young child waiting and hungry. She wondered if she'd ever be able to juggle feeding horses and a haying crew while effortlessly mothering her own child.

She couldn't leave Rose alone in the kitchen. What had she been thinking? "Grab an apple and come with me, honey. You can watch, okay?"

Rose took an apple from the bowl on the table, crossed the kitchen and took Shannon's outstretched hand. "It'll be okay, Momma," Rose reassured her with all the trusting innocence of a child. And for one blindingly beautiful moment, as that small, perfect hand slipped into hers, Shannon believed that it truly would.

SUPPER WASN'T SERVED until 8:00 p.m., which was early for Shannon but very late for her father and Billy, who were both so tired they spoke in monosyllables as they methodically cleaned their plates and then made short work of seconds. The spaghetti was good, and she served it with garlic bread and a big salad. Her fears that her father might have been drinking up at the windmill had been laid to rest. He was stone-cold sober and dog tired.

"I'm afraid it's the same menu for tomorrow, but I'll bake an apple pie, too," she promised as she cleared the table.

"Been a dog's age since I've had apple pie," her father said, leaning back in his chair. "Your mother could make the best pie crust. Light as a feather."

"Well, Daddy, I hope you'll settle for a store-bought crust."

Billy was sitting quietly, finishing off his cup of coffee. "It'll be great."

"What's that?" Shannon asked, her hands full of plates.

"Your apple pie."

"Better save your praise till you've tried it," she said as she piled the dishes in the sink. "Rose, it's time for you to get washed up and ready for bed."

"But I don't want to go to bed."

"Tomorrow's going to be a big day. You'll be counting the bales for us, remember? That requires a good night's sleep."

Billy's chair scraped away from the table

and he pushed to his feet. "That was a good supper, Shannon," he said. "Thank you."

"You're welcome." She dropped her eyes from his and turned back to the sink to hide her blush.

"Guess I'll head into town and see if I can rustle us up some recruits for tomorrow," he said, reaching for his hat. He paused for a moment, fiddling with the hat brim in his hands. "It's Friday night. Thought maybe I'd get a beer at the Dog and Bull. You're welcome to come along if you like, Shannon. I'll buy you a beer."

Shannon froze at the sink, her hands dripping with soapy water.

"I'll watch Rose," her father volunteered in the awkward silence, "and I know how to clean up a kitchen. The two of you go out and have some fun."

"Grampy and I can watch TV together, Momma," Rose said, excited by this sudden turn of events. "Just one show won't hurt."

Shannon didn't know which surprised her more, Billy's invitation or her father's offer to babysit. "All right," she relented. "Just one little program on that little TV, and you're off to bed. Daddy?"

"Just one," he said. "And maybe some popcorn."

"I love popcorn!" Rose said.

Shannon turned her attention back to the dishes, feeling Billy's eyes on her. "Might be fun to see the old hangout again. Give me ten minutes."

Billy pushed past the screen door and Shannon blew out her breath. Dove back into the hot sudsy water and finished the supper dishes. It felt good to do domestic things, to wipe the counters down, clean off the table. Her father and Rose were already in the living room, trying to choose a program. Rose picked a Western. *Gunsmoke*, from the sound of it. Shannon had just finished the dishes when she heard Billy's truck pull up to the porch. He leaned out of the driver's-side window when she stepped out. "Ready?"

"Almost. I need to change."

"You look fine just the way you are."

Shannon hesitated, wiping her hands on the kitchen towel. "Maybe this isn't such a good idea."

Billy tugged his hat brim lower. "These are the same folks you used to rub shoulders with back when you had cow manure on your boots and horse slobber on your shirt. They don't care if you aren't dressed fancy."

Blunt and to the point. Shannon blew out another breath and nodded. "I'll be right down."

She raced upstairs to the bathroom, where she washed up in furious haste, brushed out her hair, feathered more foundation over the greening bruise, glossed her lips and called it good.

Billy'd said she looked fine. He was being polite, she knew, but right now she needed to hear it. She needed to feel pretty. Like she still had talent. Still mattered. And he was right. The sooner she went into Bear Paw and resumed life on a Wyoming scale, the sooner she could plan her future, whatever that was and wherever it might take her. After a tiny spritz of perfume to fend off odors of leather, hay and horses, she snatched up her denim jacket and purse, and headed back down the stairs feeling like a young girl on a first date.

She smelled popcorn before she reached the kitchen. Her father was standing at the stove, shaking the pot over a high flame. It struck her suddenly how old he looked, and she stopped dead at the foot of the stairs, caught in a painful time warp, wondering how this had happened to them both.

"Thanks for watching Rose, Daddy," she said. "You be good." She bent down to plant a swift kiss on Rose's soft cheek. "One TV show, that's all, then off to bed."

"One show and *popcorn*," Rose corrected her.

And then Shannon was climbing into Billy's truck. As he swung out of the yard, she caught a brief glimpse of the familiar outline of Wolf Butte, glowing in the sunset. Then her eyes rested on Billy's profile. Lean and chiseled, as strong and rugged as the mountains. She wondered how her life might have turned out if she'd said yes when Billy first asked her out to cheer him on at the rodeo.

"Do you ever miss rodeo?" she asked. His sidelong glance was brief and it took him a few moments to reply.

"I figured out a while ago there's more to life than riding snuffy broncs, Shannon. I couldn't ride like that anymore even if I wanted to, but you can still sing. You don't have to give it up if you don't want to. You could stay right here and raise your daughter, and sing, too."

BILLY WASN'T SURE if it was the right thing to say, but the words were spoken. Shannon turned her gaze away and folded her hands in her lap, her fingers twining around that little glimmer of a purse.

"You can't live way out here on the edge of nowhere and be a country-and-western star," she said quietly. "But that doesn't matter anymore. My singing days are over."

After that she was as quiet as a church mouse until they reached his house. Billy pulled in to the driveway and sat with the engine idling. He'd been planning this house for years. Drawing floor plans and elevations on scrap paper while sniper fire pinned him down. Revising them on paper towels in the mess tent. Using up an entire pad of graph paper during those endless months at the hospital stateside.

"Your father told me what you said about wanting this piece of land to build your house on," he said. "He wouldn't have sold it to me if he knew you were coming back."

"It doesn't matter," Shannon said quietly. "I shouldn't have said anything to him. It's just a piece of land."

"It isn't just a piece of land. You used to

wait for the school bus right here," he said. "For two years I rode that bus with you, and I never forgot how you used to look, standing there by the side of the road with your books and your guitar. You had greatness in you then, Shannon, and you still have it. You don't need Travis Roy or anyone else to prove how good you are. Everything you'll ever need, you already have inside of you."

Shannon shook her head. "That was another lifetime ago. Whatever I had back then is gone now."

"You've been through a lot. Give yourself time to heal. It took me a while to get beyond what happened to me in Iraq. Don't make any big career decisions until you've had a chance to think things through."

Shannon gave him a wry smile. "Oh, I've been thinking things through for the past two years. I'm not a dreamer anymore. I won't lie to you, Billy. When I found out my father had sold this piece of land to you, at first I was mad as a wet hen, but now I realize how selfish I was being. He needed the money, you needed a place to call home and the truth is, I don't even know if I'll be sticking around.

My dream about that piece of land was a foolish one."

Billy looked down toward the Bear Paw. He considered what she'd just said and wondered how he could make it right. "This valley's a good place for you to raise your daughter. I can't think of a better one. Your dream was a fine one. Just say the word and this land is yours."

Shannon shook her head. "It's your dream now, Billy. Now, how about that beer you promised me?"

CHAPTER FIVE

THE DOG AND BULL was a busy place for a town the size of Bear Paw. Pickup trucks filled the parking lot. Even as Shannon and Billy approached the front door of the town's only saloon, two more vehicles arrived, parking side by side. The occupants discharged and started for the saloon as a foursome, spotting Shannon en route and coming to an abrupt stop.

"Well, I'll be hanged if it isn't Shannon Mc-Tavish! I heard you were back in town," the heavyset guy with the dark-rimmed glasses and short beard said. "Remember me? Ralph, Ralph Sayres, we were in algebra and college writing class and history together. This is my wife, Kitty." He slung his beefy arm around the shoulders of a petite smiling brunette who looked about ten months pregnant. "She was Kitty Clark then. You might remember her, too. She was a year behind us but she finally caught me up. The short, ugly dude on my right is Steve Little. He's the mayor of this one-horse town. And the gal with him is Holly Duncan, she's a lawyer with Patriot. You planning on singing tonight, Shannon?"

After Ralph's onslaught, Shannon appreciated the firm placement of Billy's hand on the small of her back as he guided her inside the Dog and Bull.

And they left her alone, all of them. There was no stampede. The patrons nodded, smiled, raised their glasses in typical Western salute, but there was no paparazzi-like invasion of her privacy. Shannon and Billy sat at a table to the rear of the room, farthest from the band and the bar. Billy ordered two beers, and when they came in frosty mugs she took a sip and looked around the crowded room at all the people drinking and dancing. She glanced back at Billy and smiled. Lifted her glass to him. "Thanks."

He raised his own mug and smiled.

"What's Patriot? Ralph seemed to assume I'd know."

Billy set his beer mug down and leaned toward her. The band was loud and not all that good.

"There's a company called Patriot Energy that wants to build a wind farm in the valley. They've bought up leases on thousands of acres around town, but the key piece of land they need is owned by your father, and he won't talk to them. Won't sign their leases. Wants nothing to do with the project."

Shannon pressed closer, not sure she'd heard him right. "Seriously? But he needs the money. The ranch is falling down. Why won't he sign?"

Billy removed his hat and set it on the table. "He thinks wind power's the biggest taxpayer subsidized consumer fraud going, as well as being an environmental disaster, and he wants nothing to do with it."

Shannon sat back in her seat, confounded. She drew her mug of beer close and watched the band for a few minutes. "Can't you talk some sense into him?"

Billy shook his head. "I happen to agree with him."

She frowned. "Then you're both crazy. Seems like a no-brainer to me."

"You haven't done your homework."

Stung, she changed the topic. "If we're going to recruit helpers for tomorrow's haying, we'd better start before everyone gets too drunk," she advised him.

"Wait a few sets. They'll have to be drunk before they volunteer to help hay," Billy said.

Shannon laughed. "That wasn't what you told me back at the ranch. You said all you had to do was mention my name and the whole town would show up to pitch in."

"True enough, but a lot of 'em are real mad at McTavish for holding out against the wind company. Bunch of folks stand to make a lot of money from leasing their land for the turbines. They'd be building the project by now if McTavish wasn't holding things up."

"What's so special about our land? If my father's being that pigheaded, can't they just go around him?"

"That ridge you drive over to get to the ranch house? That's the section they need to join the project to the transfer station down on the black road. They want to put twenty turbines, each of them nearly five hundred feet tall, along the ridge that runs down your valley, paralleling the Bear Paw, along with transmission lines to the substation, also on your father's land. That would connect the two other proposed groups of turbines, including a bunch on Wolf Butte. One hundred seventy-five turbines in all. Going around your father's land would add four miles or better to the transmission corridor. That's a huge expense."

"I passed lots of those things driving across the Midwest. They're all over the farmlands, but they didn't seem that tall." She took a sip of beer. "How much would my father get if he leased the land?"

"Rumor has it the going rate for each turbine lease is five grand a year—so possibly one hundred thousand dollars a year, plus maybe more for the transmission right-of-way. What the developers don't tell anyone is that there are real health risks associated with these big machines. Noise, shadow flicker and ice thrown from the blades, habitat fragmentation and water quality issues. But probably the low frequency sound waves are the worst health threat. Oh, and they kill birds and bats, lots of 'em. But lots of ranchers and farmers around here need the money. So you can understand why it could get ugly."

"Mind if we join you for a bit?"

Shannon glanced up to see Steve Little and Holly Duncan. Steve was in his early fifties, feeling the tug of time and trying to fight it. Shannon could read the struggle all over him, especially in the way he looked at Holly, who was young and pretty, and overdressed for the Dog and Bull in a conservative skirt suit.

"It's great to see you, Shannon," Steve said, pulling his chair close to the table, leaning forward on his elbows and giving her a wide smile. "Hope you plan to stick around for a while."

"Thank you. I haven't made any long-term plans yet, but it's nice to be back."

"Bear Paw's a great place to live, you know that, but it could be a lot greater." He rocked forward, his eyes boring into hers. "I'd much rather have this discussion out at your ranch but your father won't let me step foot on it. There are important things happening around here, Shannon. *Big* things. Patriot Energy wants to erect wind turbines all over this county."

"Billy told me a little bit about it."

"Their project would put this little town on the map and create a lot of jobs. The increased tax base would lower everyone's property taxes, and because wind is free, our electricity rates would drop to practically nothing. Besides all that, it's the right thing to do for the planet. Wind power is clean and green and it'll wean us off foreign oil. Almost everyone in town is all for this project."

"Actually, half the residents of Bear Paw are against it," Billy corrected. "The ones who don't stand to make money from the leases but have to live with forty-story-tall towers standing over their houses, reducing their property values and destroying their health. And it's already been proven that wind energy increases electricity rates."

"None of them understand how important this is for Bear Paw and for the climate," Steve Little said, flushing at Billy's words. "McTavish just stirred up a lot of trouble."

Shannon turned her beer mug between her palms. "And you're hoping I can talk some sense into him? Obviously you don't know my father."

"This project can't go through without your father's cooperation, Shannon. You should try to convince him. These past years have been tough for him. Real tough. And this could make him a lot of money."

"That may be true, Steve, but my father's as tough as the times, and he has a mind of his own. A pretty good one, as a matter of fact." Shannon felt a big headache coming on. "Right now, all I'm concerned about is getting our hay in tomorrow. How would you and Holly like to come out to the ranch and pitch bales? We'll be starting around six a.m. The work's hard but there'll be a big spaghetti feed, all you can eat, and coolers of cold beer when the day's work is done."

The mayor of Bear Paw laughed. "It's good to have you back in town, Shannon," he repeated, pushing out of his seat and helping Holly do the same. "We hope to be talking to you again soon." He gave a curt nod to Billy, then escorted the attorney, who hadn't spoken a single word, over to their table.

"Well, that doesn't bode well," Shannon said, catching Billy's eye. "I'm beginning to think we might not have much help tomorrow."

"Steve Little wouldn't have been of much help, no matter which way you pointed him, and I doubt that attorney ever pumped her own gas, let alone heaved a bale of hay into a hay wagon. Besides, they've both been putting the screws to your father."

Shannon was about to ask him what he meant but another person interrupted.

"Shannon McTavish?" She looked up to see the lead singer of the band that had been up onstage. She hadn't even realized they'd stopped playing. "I just want you to know how honored we are to have you here tonight."

"Thank you. I'm having a great time. You really got the crowd dancing."

He took his hat off and crushed it nervously in his hands. "We were wondering, the boys and me, if you might want to sing just one song. Just one, for old times' sake. I know it's not right, me even asking it of you, but you're the best of the best, and to be here in the same place with you, well, that's just special. If you don't want to sing, that's okay. We're just glad you're here. We're really honored."

Shannon wanted to tell him sorry, no can do, she'd given it up when she and Travis split, but she just couldn't. She remembered what it was like to be in his shoes. So she nodded and smiled. "What's your name?"

"Spencer, ma'am. Spencer Wallace. Our band's called Badlands."

"Badlands. I like that. I'll need a guitar."

"I'd be honored if you borrowed mine. Anything else?"

"Nope." Shannon caught Billy's eye. "I'll be right back," she said as she rose to her feet. When she stepped onto the stage all the talk stopped and the room grew still. Shannon felt a bit of the old magic stir in her blood and wondered, as she adjusted the mic, if she'd ever find anything else in her life that made her feel quite like this.

"Hello, Bear Paw," she said with a smile. "It's great to see you're all having such a good time tonight. My name's Shannon McTavish, and I thought I'd sing a brand-new song I wrote a few months ago, if it's okay with you."

The crowd let loose with hollers, cheers and whistles as she set the mic back in the stand and took the guitar Wallace offered. She tried a few chords. Spencer Wallace might not be able to sing a lick, but he had an ear for tuning a guitar and for that she was grateful.

"I wrote this song for my little girl," she said, as her fingers softly and deftly picked the strings. "Her birthday fell on a Sunday and it rained. It rained so hard the caterer couldn't make it, the magician cancelled, the roads flooded and only four kids out of thirty showed up, but none of that mattered to Rose," she said as her fingers continued to strum soft chords. "My little girl doesn't care about any of that stuff. She taught me that what's really important are the people you love. This song is called 'Rainy Day Girl,' and I hope you like it."

Stage fright had never plagued Shannon. As long as she had a guitar in her hands, she was centered. Everything else faded into the background: the crowd, the lights, everything. As soon as she began to sing, she slipped into a trance. Another dimension.

Sometimes, after a concert, she'd be in a daze for hours, trying to reconnect with reality. She'd tried to explain it to Travis once, but he'd just laughed. Said she was just coming down from what he called "entertainer's high."

Maybe that was it. Maybe singing was her opiate. Her religion. And it had blinded her to the realities of life. To thinking life on the road with an abusive and unpredictable drunk was a good one, and that as long as the concert hall was packed and the applause was deafening, nothing else mattered. Not even Rose.

Wasn't that why she'd given it up? Walked away from her abusive marriage and her career? Wasn't that why she was in Bear Paw tonight, looking for a bunch of people to help get the hay into her father's barn before it rained? Hadn't she made the decision to give up her singing career and focus on getting her life in order so she could be a good mother to her little girl?

But there was no denying how good it felt to be standing up on the stage in this little backwater saloon in Bear Paw, singing Rose's song. No denying how good it felt when the crowd poured out enthusiastic approval and demanded more. So she sang some of the ones that had taken Travis and her all the way to the top, and when Wallace and his boys jumped in to back her up, she flashed them an encouraging smile. The dance floor filled. Energy levels climbed, but after the sixth song she bowed gracefully away.

"Thank you all, it's been great fun tonight." She hesitated a moment, then held up her hands to stop the applause. "We're making hay out at the McTavish ranch tomorrow, and as a matter of fact we're a mite shorthanded. If any of you feel like working hard and playing hard, there'll be plenty of food and drink and maybe another dance, if anyone's still standing after the hay's in the barn. Good night and thank you all again. Bear Paw's the best, always was and always will be!"

She handed the guitar back to Wallace, who leaned close so she'd hear him over the applause. "Me and the boys'd be proud to help you out with the hayin', if you'd have us."

She gave him a wide smile. "We start at daybreak. The coffee'll be hot and there'll be plenty of food. Thank you so much for offering, and for letting me sing with you tonight."

Billy had ordered a pitcher of ice water in her absence and he poured her a glass as she took her seat. "You were great," he said.

"Thanks." She drank the water and he refilled her glass. "We have four recruits already," she told him. "Spencer and his band said they'd be coming to help out."

"That's good to hear. Four's plenty."

"It's four more than we've ever had before," Shannon said with a rueful laugh.

Shannon realized, in that moment, that she'd been looking forward to the work. Growing up, she'd always dreaded haying time, but now she wanted to be a part of it. She wanted to pitch the bales onto the hay wagon until her arm muscles burned with exhaustion. Get covered with chaff, scorched by the sun, feel the thirst after hours of sweaty labor and the mindlessness of absolute exhaustion.

She wanted to stand under a hot shower afterward and think that nothing in the whole wide world felt any better than that. She wanted to fall into bed and be asleep in the next breath, untroubled by thoughts of the future. What she wanted most of all was to go back in time so she could do a few things differently. But in lieu of that, she'd help with the haying.

But did she also have a responsibility to help her father fend off the wind company? Even if she believed it was in his best interests?

"So, tell me a little more about Steve Little and this lady attorney who've been putting the screws to my father."

"Your father was behind in his property

taxes when I got back this spring," he said. "Five years behind. Patriot Energy made it plain they needed his ridgeline. They visited him in person, told him all the neighboring landowners had already signed on, and how much he'd make every year from each turbine lease and the transmission right-of-way. Then your father kicked them off the ranch. Told them he didn't care about the money. He didn't want the towers and transmission lines on his land, and that was that.

"Steve and Ms. Duncan came out to the ranch the same day I bought that piece of property from him. They didn't know about the land he'd just sold me or the money I'd just paid him toward it. Steve told your father if he didn't sign the lease, the town was going to take the ranch for back taxes. Ms. Duncan had the lease agreement in her hand.

"So your father went inside, wrote a check for the total amount of the back taxes, put it in Little's hand and told him to haul his ass off his property and never return. Those were his exact words. Told him it'd be a cold day in hell before a single one of those towers went up on his land."

Shannon took another sip of water as Wallace and the boys got into gear again onstage. "Will the wind project go through if my father doesn't sign that lease?"

Billy thought awhile before answering. "I don't know. This is a pretty big deal, Shannon. Patriot Energy is an LLC owned by an energy company in Spain with ties to big oil in Qatar. The company stands to make a lot of money. And they've promised the townsfolk lower property taxes, cheap energy, better roads, good-paying jobs. They make it sound like wind energy's the pot of gold at the end of the rainbow."

"So my father's against it. What about you?"

He refilled her water glass a third time, then looked her directly in the eyes. "Like I said before, I'm with your father, and not just because I work for him or he sold me that land. I happen to believe it's the most environmentally destructive consumer fraud being peddled on Wall Street." He pushed his chair away from the table. "We have a big day ahead of us tomorrow. We should get back."

Shannon was dog tired, but didn't want the night to end. Not just yet. She pulled her water glass close and studied him. "What brought you back here, really?" she asked after the band finished their song. "You wanted to get out of Bear Paw just as bad as I did, or you wouldn't have joined the military."

Billy didn't answer for a few moments, just sat watching the band start to break down their equipment, then he shook his head. "I joined the military to get my education and see a little of the world, but the day I got my discharge papers, I headed for home. I never forgot where I came from. I know where I belong, even if I'm not wanted by some folks, and I'm staying put." He rose abruptly to his feet and picked his hat up off the table. "If you're ready, we'd best be going. Morning comes early."

He left money on the table to cover the beers and the tip, and guided her out the door. It was a relief to gain the darkness of the parking lot, see the bright stars spangling the night sky, feel the cool air coming down from high mountain places. Billy's truck loomed in the darkness. He opened the door for her and she climbed in.

"Thanks for coming tonight," he said.

"Thanks for asking me," she replied. "And no matter what anyone's said to you, Billy

Mac, you have a future here, and I'm sure it's a bright one."

He closed her door, climbed into the truck and they headed for home.

THEY TALKED ON the drive back. About little things. Safe things. Shannon was lulled by the sound of his voice. The deep masculine calm of it. She felt safe with Billy. Secure. Which was odd given that her objections to dating him in high school were based on his reputation. But the military had changed him, and when he turned off the black road and began the last two miles of their journey, she felt a pang of disappointment that soon this magical night would be over.

The first thing she noticed when Billy's truck crested the ridge were the lights. The ranch buildings were all awash with light. Lights blazed from the ranch house, from both barns, from the tractor shed and from the spots that illuminated the corrals. Shannon sat up straight and braced her hand against the dashboard.

"Billy," she said. "Something's wrong."

"Maybe one of the mustangs got loose..."

"Drive faster!"

"We're almost there, Shannon."

"Oh, God. Damn my selfish soul to hell, I should never have left Rose!" Shannon wrenched the truck's door open and her feet hit the ground before the truck came to a stop in front of the ranch house. "Rose! Daddy! *Rose!*" Her daughter's name was a shriek in the night. She flew up the porch steps, burst through the kitchen door and ran straight into her father.

"Whoa!" he said, steadying her. "Everything's all right. Travis came by but he's gone. Rose is fine. She's upstairs asleep. Never even knew he was here. I put all the lights on just to show him he couldn't hide in the shadows, that's all. He left over an hour ago. He's long gone."

Shannon felt her muscles turn to water as her worst fears were confirmed. "Travis was here? He was *here*?"

"I told him not to come back," her father said. "It's all right. Rose is safe."

Shannon dodged past him, taking the stairs two at a time with her heart in her throat. She came to a stop in the doorway, breathless with fear. The hall light spilled softly across her childhood bed, the same bed where Rose now slept in blissful innocence. Safe. Secure. Just as her father had said.

Shannon approached the bed slowly and knelt to kiss that warm, smooth forehead. "Momma's home, Rose," she murmured. She arranged the blanket against the cool night air. She sat for a while, long enough to regain her breath, long enough for her heartbeat to steady and the sick surge of adrenaline to ebb. Then she kissed her daughter again and rose to her feet. She paused in the doorway, looking back to make sure Rose was safe and sound. Still trembling, Shannon descended the stairs into the kitchen, where her father and Billy waited.

"She's asleep." Her voice sounded taut, strange. "Rose is fine." *But I'm not!* her whole being silently screamed. *I've never been so afraid!*

Her father nodded. "I checked on her after he left. Like I said, she never woke up."

Shannon brushed the damp wet of fear from her forehead. "I can't believe he came here. At night. After dark. I can't believe it. I warned him not to come, Daddy. There's a restraining order on him. I'm going to call the sheriff in the morning to report this."

"He said he needed to talk to you," her father said. "Said he'd changed his ways. Said he was sorry about everything and he had something for you. He left when I told him to go. Didn't kick up any fuss, just nodded and left. I turned the lights on as a precaution and got my rifle."

Shannon was deeply shaken by the realization of how close she'd come to losing Rose. Travis hadn't come here to tell her he'd changed his ways. He'd come to snatch his daughter, and her father had stopped him in his tracks. Her father still had that power passed down through four generations of Wyoming McTavishes. He was as tough and hard as the land and nobody dared cross him, not even Travis.

"He won't be back," Billy said. "Not tonight, anyway, and not ever, if he knows what's good for him." He met Shannon's eyes. "It's late. We got us a haying crew coming tomorrow, first thing. Get some sleep. I'll see you both in the morning."

He pulled his hat back on and without another word turned to go. The night closed in around Shannon and her father, and the quiet.

Shannon released a pent-up breath and

caught her father's eye. "Thank you, Daddy," she said, and he nodded. Never had she been so glad to have two such solid men in her corner.

Yet three hours later, at 2:00 a.m., she was still sleepless, staring into a darkness and a future she couldn't begin to fathom. Rose moved in her arms, then came awake with a violent thrash.

"You're squishing me, Momma!" she protested. "I can't breathe…"

Shannon relaxed her arms and kissed the nape of her daughter's neck, so soft and sweet and vulnerable. "I'm sorry, Rose, I didn't mean to, it's just that I love you so much. Go back to sleep."

Within three breaths, her daughter had done just that, but at daybreak, Shannon was still wide-awake.

CHAPTER SIX

THE DAY DAWNED bright blue and clear with a steady breeze out of the west that would keep the bugs down and the workers' spirits up. The threat of rain seemed distant. The entire band from the Dog and Bull showed up, as promised. Shannon had a big pot of coffee ready and she poured cup after cup as she scrambled three dozen eggs, fried two pounds of smokehouse bacon and made a stack of buttered toast. Her father drew her aside as the crew sat down at the table to eat.

"I can't pay those boys," he said.

"Don't worry about it, Daddy. We made a deal last night. They help us get the hay in, and I sing a few songs with them at their next gig. They have a band and they like my singing." He was still frowning as he ate his breakfast, but when Billy showed up, his eyes scanned the crowded table and he caught Shannon's eyes and grinned.

"Looks like we got us a real honest-to-God haying crew," he said.

Just then another vehicle pulled in to the yard. Ralph and Kitty Sayres climbed the porch steps. Kitty laughed at Shannon's expression. "I may be pregnant but I can still cook," she said as she waddled into the kitchen. Her husband carried a big box of groceries, which he set on the counter. "We figured we'd help out. Our hay's in, and Ralph just can't get enough of making hay, says it's his favorite chore."

This brought a big laugh from everyone. Shannon gave Kitty a hug. "Thanks," she said. "I appreciate it. There's plenty of eggs and bacon, Ralph. Pull up a seat."

"We've already et," Ralph said. He patted his hefty stomach. "The food smells great, but my wife's doc warned me about sympathetic weight gain, she says I can't eat twice as much because I'm not the one eating for two."

The men finished their coffee and stood from the table. Within moments the kitchen was empty except for Shannon, Rose and Kitty. Shannon watched them leave from the window over the kitchen sink. "We've never had such a big haying crew." She turned to give Kitty a grateful smile. "Thanks for coming. I don't know what to say. It's...overwhelming."

"We're glad to have you back, Shannon. Your daddy's one of the toughest men I've ever known, but he's had a rough time of it these past few years." Kitty was gathering the plates off the table and carrying them to the sink. "We felt bad about the pressure the town was putting on him over the turbines. That's just wrong."

"Last night was the first I heard about the wind project," Shannon said, running hot water into the sink. "But I knew as soon as I saw the ranch that my dad was having financial troubles. I can't understand why he's being so stubborn about something that could make his life a whole lot easier. The whole town will benefit from the project, and my father's holding everything up."

"Truth is, the town's pretty torn apart by it," Kitty said, clearing the last of the dishes off the table. "Landowners who stand to make big money on lease payments from the wind developer want the project to be built, but there are a lot of others who don't want to see the mountains around here covered with giant turbines and transmission lines. They don't want to live with the health problems or loss of property value. Some of the lodge owners who cater to tourists and hunters are really up in arms."

Shannon was swishing the soapy water around in the dishpan and paused at Kitty's words. "How do you and Ralph feel about it?"

"We thought we were the only ones against the project until your daddy spoke out at the first town meeting. Boy, he'd done his homework, too. He questioned every promise the wind developer made about all the jobs that would be created, about energy costs going down, taxes going down, life in Bear Paw getting better. He had information from a lot of other towns—the jobs and tax cuts are just temporary, property values plummet the closer to the wind turbines a person lives, and the health effects from low frequency sound are detrimental on humans and livestock, not to mention all the birds and bats those things kill.

"After he spoke, the battle lines were drawn in the dirt. Awful, really, how neighbor has turned against neighbor. I'd say the town's split pretty near half-and-half. Anyhow, when Billy Mac arrived on the scene, he gave the wind developers a whole passel of grief by standing with your father to lead this fight. I guess this same wind company wanted to put a project on the reservation.

"But the thing is, the wind developers have all the fancy lawyers and the government mandates for renewable energy on their side. They target small rural towns because they figure nobody can afford to fight them, and they're right."

Kitty stacked the dishes on the counter and picked up a clean dish towel to start drying the plates in the dish rack. "Steve Little's one of the landowners who signed a lease agreement with Patriot Energy. Conflict of interest? I'd say so." Kitty blew out her breath. "Sorry, I tend to get a little worked up over the subject."

Shannon rinsed a plate under the stream of hot water and added it to the drying rack. She glanced over her shoulder at Rose, who was brushing Tess. "Better let Tess have a nap, Rose," she said. "You brushed her yesterday."

"Momma, her hair needs to be brushed every day, just like my hair does."

"Well, she's old and she needs her rest, too."

Kitty laughed softly. "Your Rose is beautiful," she said. "How long're you planning to stay?"

"I don't know. At least until the hay's in. I've been away a long time. A lot's changed."

"Things do," Kitty said with a shrug. "I've gotten married and had two kids since you left. Both boys are in grade school now, and this one's my third." She patted her stomach fondly. "She was a complete surprise. We hadn't planned on another baby, but when Ralph talks about having a daughter, you should see his face light up. He can't wait to hold her."

"There's a special bond between fathers and daughters," Shannon said, thinking how hypocritical her words sounded, considering her strained relationship with her own father and the way Travis had treated Rose.

Kitty dried and stacked plates. "Your dad's sure glad you're home. He looks like a new man. He's missed you, Shannon."

"He thinks pretty highly of Billy."

"Billy's helped him out a lot. None of us ever believed Billy'd come back. All he wanted to do when he graduated high school was get out of Bear Paw, same as you. I guess we all think the grass is greener someplace else, and for you it sure was. You've done well for yourself, Shannon. We're all so proud of you. But I'm happy with my life here. I can't imagine living anyplace else."

Shannon gazed out the kitchen window and sighed. She wondered if she'd ever feel the contentment and sense of belonging that Kitty did. She wondered if she'd ever be *happy* again. "I'm surprised Billy's not married," she said.

Kitty laughed again. "You and all the rest of the gals in Bear Paw. He was the bad boy in the leather jacket that made all us go weak in the knees. High school quarterback and champion rodeo rider, with a chip on his shoulder the size of Texas because he was born on the reservation. He was mighty sweet on you for a while, as I recall, but then Travis came to town and the rest of your story was written in platinum records. Billy Mac didn't stand a chance."

Kitty shook her head, her expression becoming thoughtful. "Billy's just as handsome as ever, for certain, but he's lost that rodeo cowboy swagger and he keeps to himself. Maybe he's still coming to terms with what happened to him in Iraq. Must be hard for someone as athletic as him to come home injured. Ralph said Billy's vehicle was destroyed by a roadside bomb and he's the only one that survived. He won't be able to ride the way he used to… I notice you got some horses down in your corrals. Mustangs?"

"Delivered by the Bureau of Land Management yesterday. My dad and Billy gentle them for public adoption."

"Is there much money in that?"

Shannon shrugged. "Depends. I guess some of the horses sell for fairly high prices, depending on how much training they have. But Project Mustang isn't going to support this place, that's for sure. They'd have to saddle break ten a day, and the market for mustangs hasn't been that strong since Ford invented the automobile."

"Can we go riding today, Momma?" Rose asked.

"When the haying's done," Shannon replied. "Right now we got us some serious cooking to do for our haying crew. You can help, if you like."

"Beans and franks?" Rose scrambled to her feet, leaving Tess to her nap. "I like beans and franks, and so does Grampy!"

THE WEATHER HELD, and by noon they'd finished baling the first two fields, but Billy knew they were racing against time; he'd seen the mares' tails streaking across the sky.

Ralph's help had been invaluable. He was a stocky bull of a man, enormously strong, with an endless number of funny stories, something they all appreciated as the sweat stung their eyes and the morning wore on.

Shannon and Rose had driven out once to the fields midmorning in McTavish's rusty old pickup truck, taking a big cooler of ice water with lemon wedges floating in it and a bag of assorted granola bars. She handed them tall paper cups of ice water, and everyone downed them gratefully.

"You promised us cold beer," one of the band members teased.

"When you get the hay in the barn, you'll have all you want of that," Shannon said. "Lunch is ready whenever you are, and we're planning a barbecue tonight for when you're finished. Ribs and beans and coleslaw and fresh hot biscuits. Kitty didn't like the idea of spaghetti, and I have to admit, barbecue goes a whole lot better with beer."

She handed Billy the bag of granola bars and gave him a smile that made his heart skip a beat. "First haying job on this ranch where I haven't had to lift one bale."

They broke for lunch at noon. The kitchen table was heaped with stacks of sandwiches, bowls of corn chips, jars of pickles, pitchers of lemonade. There wasn't much talk, just filling empty stomachs and slaking the thirst that haying made so big. The band members and Ralph were covered with chaff and tired from lifting the bales, and Billy felt a little guilty that he'd been sitting on the tractor most of the morning, hauling the baler up and down the rows of hay.

One of the band members, Jeb, had strained his shoulder and was massaging it during lunch. "It's my guitar arm," he joked. "I'll starve if I can't play."

"You can drive the tractor when we go back out," Billy said. "I'll pitch bales this afternoon. I need to burn off the stack of sandwiches I just ate."

So it happened that Jeb was driving the

tractor and was halfway done with the third field when he drove over a rock that snapped the baler's axle. The machine slumped to one side. There was a collective groan from everyone as they gathered around to survey the damage. McTavish shook his head. "Bound to happen," he said gloomily. "Things were going too good."

"I didn't see the rock," Jeb said. "I'm really sorry."

"I know that, son. It's not your fault."

Ralph rubbed his jaw, squinting at the situation. "I'll go get my baling machine," he said. "Should've brought it this morning, we could have used both tractors and everything'd be baled by now."

"I can't ask that of you," McTavish said.

"You ain't asking. I'm offering," Ralph said. "Give me a ride to the house in the hay truck and I'll go get it. It'll take me an hour to get home, hook my tractor to the baler and get back here." They all looked at the dark cloud bank building over the wall of mountains to the west. "We're wasting time," Ralph said.

Billy knew it was hard on McTavish, accepting all this help in the first place. A self-reliant man, he was used to doing everything on his own, and right now he seemed mighty uncomfortable. Before McTavish could respond to Ralph's offer, Billy took matters into his own hands.

"Come on, Ralph. I'll give you a ride back. We sure appreciate the offer of your equipment," he said as he unhooked the broken baler from the old farm tractor, climbed onto the seat and fired it up. He didn't look at McTavish or listen when he started to protest.

Ralph hauled himself onto the running board and they set out at top speed, which for the old Moline, wasn't all that rapid. When they reached the house, Billy told Kitty and Shannon what had happened.

"How's my dad holding up?" Shannon asked. "He hates when machinery breaks."

"He'll be bringing down another load of hay pretty quick. You can check on him in person. I'm running Ralph over to his place to get his tractor and baler. We'll be back as soon as we can. We'll get 'er done before it rains."

"Sometimes it seems like bad luck is the only kind of luck on the McTavish ranch."

"There's six hundred bales in the barn already. That's not bad luck, Shannon, that's hard work."

"Speaking of hard work, I've been watching your mustangs all morning long," Shannon said. "They sure are pretty, but that little bay's going to be a handful. He's mighty wild."

"We'll get started on the mustangs soon as the hay's in the barn," Billy said, putting the truck into gear. "There's a lot riding on this contract. We told the BLM we'd have 'em ready for the adoption auction in four weeks."

Shannon stepped back as Billy pulled away, but not before he saw her skeptical expression. He passed the corral and spied the little bay she'd spoken of, the one that kept pacing the perimeter of the round pen with that wild expression in his eyes. Four weeks did seem a mite optimistic, but a much bigger contract was riding on this deal. In four weeks, that little bay mustang was going to be transformed into a saddle horse, along with the other five. He and McTavish could do it.

They had to. A ranch that couldn't hold its own wasn't a ranch, it was a failure headed for the auction block. Every little bit of income helped toward the taxes and expenses.

They had to prove to Shannon that this was a fine place to raise her little girl. The Mc-Tavish ranch used to be the most successful ranch in Bear Paw, and it could be again. The mustangs were the key.

SHANNON WATCHED BILLY'S truck until it was out of sight. Kitty and Rose came out of the kitchen and joined her on the porch. "Think they'll get back soon enough to beat the rain?" Kitty asked.

Shannon shook her head, disheartened. "Those thunderheads are getting mighty big. I'm worried about my dad. When machinery breaks, he's always been determined to fix it himself. He won't wait for them to get back."

At that moment, the big flatbed truck, loaded high with hay bales, lumbered into view. Shannon met the crew down at the barn. Her father was noticeably absent. Jeb was driving the truck.

"Your father had an idea how to fix the hay baler," Jeb explained before she could ask. "We dropped him off at the tractor shed to look for some parts."

"I don't see how he can fix a broken axle," Shannon said.

Jeb climbed down out of the truck and rubbed his sore shoulder. "Dunno. We'll get this load of hay in the barn and stacked, and then go see what he's up to."

Shannon returned to the porch and confirmed her father's stubborn behavior to Kitty and Rose.

"Pies are in the oven, and I'll get started on the ribs," Kitty said. "You go check on your dad, and Rose can help me set the supper table and get the ribs ready to barbecue. Want to help?" she asked Rose, who nodded vigorously.

"Can we have beans, too?" Rose asked. "Cowboys always eat beans."

"Of course," Kitty said. "Wouldn't be a cowboy meal without a pot of beans. Come on. The ribs have to cook long and slow, and they need to be basted often."

SHANNON COULD HEAR loud clanging and the banging of metal on metal well before she reached the shed but all was quiet when she arrived.

"Daddy?" She waited for her eyes to adjust to the dimness and then spotted his legs sticking out from under an ancient baler that hadn't been used in years. He had a big truck jack propping it up on one side. She felt a quick surge of frustration. Why did he have to be so stubborn? Why couldn't he just wait for Ralph and Billy to get back? "Daddy, come down to the house and I'll fix you some lemonade. You should rest awhile until Ralph returns."

"Can't move. My arm's stuck," he said, his voice taut. "Give me a hand here."

She crouched beside his legs. "Are you hurt? I can't see anything under there."

"The jack shifted and my arm got caught under the frame. Just jack it up a little more so's I can pull free." Shannon eyed the jack. It was at a bad angle. She braced one of her feet against the base of the jack to keep it from kicking out and lifted the heavy handle, pushing down until she heard the jack click, then repeated the motion. "Okay, that's good," she heard her father say tightly. "Hold 'er right there…"

His legs moved as he pushed himself forward a bit, then he slid out from under the baler and sat up, cradling his right arm against his chest. "Thanks," he muttered.

Shannon knelt down beside him. "Can you move your arm at all?"

"Not yet, but I'll be okay. Just give me a minute."

Shannon ignored him, peeling his rolled-up shirtsleeve back a little more. She drew her breath in sharply when she saw the maimed limb. "Daddy, your arm's broke."

"Just wrap it up, it'll be fine."

Shannon stood. "I'll bring some ice. That'll help with the pain and swelling. But then we're going to the hospital." She didn't wait to see him shake his head or hear his next argument. She ran out the open door of the tractor shed and sprinted all the way to the house.

At the hay truck she paused briefly to tell the haying crew what had happened. "Get the rest of the hay in, and then Kitty'll feed you. I don't know how long I'll be gone, but I owe you boys big-time and I'll sing at your next gig. Just say where and when."

Kitty's face fell when she heard the news. "Oh, Shannon, I'm sorry! I'll watch Rose for you."

"No need, she can come with me, but if you could just feed the crew when they've finished, I'd appreciate it. I'll be back as soon as I can, but it's a long haul to the hospital, and he's going to need a cast put on that arm. It'll probably be several hours. Don't wait supper on us."

Shannon retrieved the ice cube trays from the freezer as she talked, cracking the ice into a plastic zippered bag. "Rose, get your jacket, honey, we're taking Grampy to the hospital. He hurt his arm and they need to fix it."

She gave Kitty a hug before shepherding her daughter out to the car. "Thank you so much. I couldn't have managed without you."

The drive to the hospital in Cody took an hour, during which Rose was the only one who talked, and she talked nonstop. "Look Grampy, there's the house where Momma said we should be living," she chirped as they passed Billy Mac's place. "I like it, don't you? It's real pretty and I like how the creek runs right past it." Then, a few miles later, when they passed the general store, she read the sign beside the door out loud, working her way through the syllables. "Ice…cream… cones. Is that right, Momma?"

"That's right, Rose. Willard's General Store has everything."

Rose narrated the entire sixty-mile journey, reading every sign, counting every cow,
naming every horse and asking where every
side road went. The wait in the ER was mer-
cifully brief before the staff whisked her father off, grim and grumbling, to get X-rays
and have his broken arm set. Shannon and
Rose plopped down on some chairs in the
near-empty waiting room. "Will Grampy be
okay?" Rose asked.

"Yes, sweetie, he's going to be fine."

"He's real grumpy."

"Well, his arm and the baling machine are
both broke. He's grumpy, all right, but he's
going to be okay. The doctor will fix him up
and he'll be fine after a good night's sleep."

Even from inside the hospital they could
hear the long, loud rumbles of thunder. Shannon sighed. Well, they'd gotten six hundred
bales in the barn before the baler broke. That
wasn't bad. Matter of fact, that was really
good. And if it poured cats and dogs, they
could ted the field of cut hay again, dry it
out good and bale it when it was dry. They'd
need all the hay they could stuff into the barn
if they were trying for a big BLM contract.

Shannon sat up with a lurch. "Oh, no."

"What is it, Momma?"

She looked at Rose. "I forgot all about Project Mustang," she said. "Billy and your grampy have five wild horses to gentle in just four weeks, and now your grampy's hurt. Billy won't be able to do it on his own."

Rose slipped her little hand into Shannon's. "Don't worry, Momma," she said. "I'll help."

RALPH'S TRACTOR AND baling machine arrived at the McTavish ranch not long after Billy did. Ralph's tractor was a new John Deere that could travel at thirty miles per hour on the black road, and he pushed it getting back to the McTavish ranch. The thunderheads were boiling up black over the mountains and the breeze was picking up when Ralph started baling. The haying crew worked nonstop and flat out. Jeb drove the flatbed truck right behind Ralph's tractor, all hands working furiously to load and stack the bales on the truck as soon as they came out of the baler.

They got one last full load of hay on the flatbed and watched the sky turn green and dark as they headed for the barn. Bolts of lightning streaked down from the massive thunderheads. Jeb drove the truck right inside the barn and cut the ignition just as the clouds let loose with hail and rain. For a moment they all just listened to the wrath of the storm pounding the barn's steel roof, then they looked at each other and grinned. They were tired and covered with hay chaff, but they'd done it. They'd gotten the hay in, every last bale, and just in the nick of time.

It was a triumph that would have been celebrated with greater enthusiasm if Shannon and her father were there, but Kitty handed out the promised ice-cold beers and fed them a royal cowboy barbecue while the storm blew through.

Afterward, their stomachs groaning from all the good food, they took their beers out onto the porch and watched a magnificent sunset blaze over storm-washed Wolf Butte to the west. They all felt pretty good about the day, and were so tired the conversation was sparse, but no words were necessary.

Shannon arrived back at the ranch a good hour after Ralph, Kitty and the four band members had departed. Billy was sitting on the top rail of the corral when he saw her headlights come over the rise and descend into the valley. He slid to the ground and met her car up at the ranch house.

"The hay's in, all of it," he told them before either could ask. McTavish climbed out of the passenger seat, arm in a cast, and went inside without a word. Billy nodded to Shannon. "There's ribs and beans and salad and a whole apple pie waiting for you. We ate the other pie and almost ate the second one, too, but Kitty put her foot down. You hungry, Rose?"

Rose yawned as Shannon released her daughter's seat belt. The little girl climbed from the back seat, blinking sleepy eyes. "C'mon inside." He took her hand and led her up the porch steps and into the kitchen, where Tess slept curled on her dog bed in the corner, so deaf she never woke when they entered.

McTavish had gone upstairs. Shannon paused, listening to his footsteps in the hallway. "He's not in a very good mood," she apologized.

"Can't imagine he would be," Billy said. "He's nursing a broken arm, along with being worried about the hay and wondering how he's going to gentle those mustangs."

Shannon sighed, running her fingers through her hair. "Run upstairs and wash, Rose. I'll get supper on the table. Tell your grampy he should eat something." She looked at Billy and smiled. "Thanks for holding the fort. It was a miracle, everyone showing up like that and getting the hay in the barn. At least now you can feed those mustangs, even if you can't get them trained on time."

"Oh, we'll get 'er done. I was down there tonight talking to them. They're all excited about the idea of carrying people around on their backs."

Shannon laughed. "I bet they are. Did you show them your fancy belt buckle and tell 'em you used to be the best cowboy in the rodeo? Did you warn 'em that resistance is futile?"

"Nope. I fed them some excellent hay and gave them some clean, cool water. Their whole world's just been turned upside down. I don't blame them for thinking we're the enemy, but that'll change."

"You better hope so. Four weeks?" Shannon shook her head. "Daddy won't be able to help much, not with a broken arm." Rose came down the kitchen stairs without her usual bounce and sank into a seat at the table with a big yawn. "Where's your grampy?"

"He says he doesn't want any supper."

Shannon pulled the tray of ribs out of the oven, forked some onto a plate, put a spoonful of beans next to it, a plump biscuit to the side, and grabbed a knife and fork from the silverware drawer on her way toward the kitchen stairs.

Billy fixed a plate for Rose while Shannon went upstairs, but when he set it in front of her, she just yawned again, blinked up at him and said, "I'm not hungry, either."

Shannon came back down the stairs, holding the untouched plate of food and wearing a frown. She looked at Rose, sighed and set the plate on the table. "All this wonderful food Kitty cooked and we're too tired to eat it. Rose, go up and get into your jammies." Without a word of protest, Rose slipped out of her chair and climbed the stairs even more slowly than before. Shannon watched her out of sight and then gave Billy a rueful smile. "We're not very good company, arc we?"

"I'll get you a cold beer. Come sit on the porch for a while. You don't have to talk. Just sit and relax."

"That sounds great."

They sat side by side in the velvety darkness, looking out at the dark silhouette of the mountain range standing beneath a spangle of bright stars. Billy could hear the soft hoofbeats of the mustangs in the corral, restlessly pacing the perimeter of the fence, yearning for their freedom and for the band members that were lost to them forever. He felt a twinge of sadness at their fate. The West wasn't big enough anymore for herds of buffalo and wild horses. All the wild was being tamed out of it.

"There's no saving this ranch gentling mustangs for the BLM," Shannon said softly. "Billy, if Daddy doesn't let them put those wind turbines along that ridgeline, he's going to lose this place. Even if I had the money right now, which I don't, he's too proud and stubborn to accept my help, and if what Kitty told me today about that energy project is true, you're fighting a losing battle. The wind developer has all the money and all the lawyers and all the power behind them. She doesn't like the wind project, either, but she admits it's a hopeless fight."

"Maybe so, but a person has to fight for

what he or she believes in. It may seem like a David-and-Goliath type of battle to you, one we can't win, but we're going to try. And I have an idea that might keep this ranch on its feet without wind money."

Shannon sighed. "You're as crazy as my father."

CHAPTER SEVEN

"OUCH, ROSE! Quit kicking me," Shannon protested, struggling out of the depths of sleep to escape her daughter's vigorous thrashing. She opened her eyes, shocked to see that it was already morning.

She pushed up on her elbows, squinting toward the window. A light breeze stirred the curtain and dawn colored the sky beyond in shades of pale yellow, pink and violet. It was morning, all right, and here she was, lying abed on a struggling Wyoming ranch just like a rich, spoiled country-and-western singer from Nashville when she had an important job to do.

"Rose, time to get up," she said, throwing the covers aside and sitting up. Her daughter mewled in her sleep and pulled the covers back over herself. Shannon's bare feet hit the cool floor and she dressed in haste, wondering if her father was already up, if Billy was out with the wild horses.

She felt a sense of urgency as she swiftly washed up, brushed her hair back into a ponytail then grabbed her boots and descended the stairs. The coffee in the pot on the stove was still hot. She crept to the kitchen window and looked toward the corrals. Yep. Both of them were already out there.

She sat down, pulled on her boots, poured herself a cup of coffee and carried it with her as she walked toward them. Her father was standing outside the round pen, watching Billy work with one of the mustangs. She joined him, leaning up against the fence and taking her first swallow of coffee. The smells of fresh-cut hay, leather and horse manure, dust and morning dew mingled with the aroma of fresh-perked coffee. Ranch smells. She'd missed them.

"Morning, Daddy," she said. "How's your arm?"

He kept his eyes narrowed on the mustang that Billy was moving around the pen. "It's still broke."

"Probably half healed by now, tough as you

are." Shannon took another swallow of coffee. "I can help with the horses."

He looked at her, but this time she was the one who kept her eyes straight ahead, watching Billy work the dun-colored mustang first one way around the pen then the other. Billy still had a way of moving that caught her eye just as much as the beauty of the wild mustang did. "You haven't been around horses in ten years," he said.

"Neither has Billy, and he hasn't lost his touch. I watched Mom make magic with horses while I was growing up. Maybe some of her talent rubbed off on me." She turned her head to gaze up at him. "You have four weeks, Daddy. I'm offering my help."

They measured each other in the early morning light, then both looked to Billy and the mustang again. The first splinters of sunlight crept across the valley and turned a plume of dust kicked up by the mustang into a molten glow of fire. "I guess this means you're staying four weeks, at least," McTavish said.

SHANNON HAD ALMOST forgotten what it was like to be a rancher's daughter, but it all came back to her quick enough. She hadn't forgotten how to lug five-gallon buckets of water, clean stalls, brush horses, saddle and bridle them, and ride. Her first day working on Project Mustang was long and physically exhausting but very rewarding.

She used Sparky as her link to the dun mustang Billy had been working with, saddling the old gelding and then leading them both out of the corral. She took old Sparky and the dun for a long amble up beyond the tractor shed, down to the creek to splash in the water, something she knew all mustangs loved to do, then along the road that led to the ranch. She carried on conversations with both horses, sang a few songs and leaned over from time to time to let the shy but curious mustang smell her hand. She remembered words her mother had told her once.

"A horse doesn't care how much you know, Shannon, but they always know how much you care."

People do, too, Shannon thought as she rode old Sparky for the first time in many years, leading the wild mustang beside him. When she returned the mustang to the corrals, Billy was still there, working with another.

She handed him the lead rope to the dun, and he handed her the rope to another mustang he'd been working with. No words necessary. They exchanged a nod and a brief smile, and she reined Sparky around and started out again at a slow walk, teaching the second wild horse to follow along using a calm, steady cow pony who'd done it all. By ten o'clock she'd taken five horses for a walk, and the fiery little bay mustang was her last of the day.

"You're right about this one, he's tough headed," Billy said. "He struck at me twice and tried to bite. Better let me take him. Getting these mustangs used to a rider on horseback's the hardest part."

"Hand him over," Shannon replied, reaching for the lead rope.

She took two half hitches around the saddle horn. The rope was long enough to give the mustang some play if he spooked, but not so long he could pull Sparky off his feet. She nudged Sparky off at a slow walk. "Easy, now," Shannon said in a soothing tone to the mustang as Sparky plodded along. "We'll bring you down to the creek and you can splash like the others did. I know you're wilder than wild and wanting your freedom back, but sometimes in life we don't always get what we want."

It was plain this mustang wanted nothing to do with her or Sparky. He kept the rope taut, eyes wild and ears pinned to his head, as she towed him like an ornery mule toward the creek. He was a handsome horse with a thick, long mane and tail, a proud crest, bright eyes and a coat that reflected a brilliant shine where Billy had brushed him. He was built well and moved beautifully, but some of the mustangs were wild to the core and would never lose their rebellious spirit, and Shannon sensed this might be one of them.

He balked, reared and dragged all the way to the creek. It was a challenge maintaining control of him, but when Sparky plodded into the clear shallow water at the old fording place, the bay mustang's nostrils flared to take in the smell, his ears spooned toward the sound of the rushing stream and for a moment he forgot all about Shannon and Sparky.

The water mesmerized him. He pawed at it, sending plumes of spray flying. Shannon played out a little more rope and was so pre-occupied with watching the mustang that she never noticed the dark-colored SUV approaching on the ranch road until it stopped behind them and the driver hit the horn three times to get her attention.

The three short blasts on the SUV's horn threw the mustang into an explosion of motion. He reared, spun and jerked Sparky right off his feet. Old Sparky went down hard as Shannon threw herself out of the saddle, then he rolled onto his chest, trying to lunge to his feet when the mustang pulled him over again.

Shannon grabbed the saddle horn and, with her other hand, struggled desperately to unwrap the rope. It took what seemed long minutes to get them undone and the two horses free of each other. She caught only a brief glimpse of the mustang streaking up the bank, long rope snaking behind as he galloped away at great speed.

Sparky surged to his feet dripping with creek water. Shannon led him to the bank and was checking him over for injuries when she heard the rattle of loose stones above her. She looked up to see the driver of the SUV making his way toward them, his face a mask of concern.

"You okay?" he asked. "I didn't mean to spook the horse. Sorry about that."

Shannon bit back a sharp reply and ignored him. She stroked Sparky's neck and he rubbed his head against Shannon's shoulder as if reassuring her. She gathered the reins and lifted herself into the saddle while the man stood watching, his expression apologetic. He was dressed in urban cowboy attire, not a speck of dirt on his shiny brand-name boots. Midthirties, good-looking in a smooth, polished way. "I'm really sorry," he repeated.

"You should be. I'll never catch that mustang. He's probably in Utah by now." She lifted the reins and Sparky stepped out.

"Wait. Please! I was hoping to talk to you. My name's Tom Carroll and I'm the project supervisor for Patriot Energy, the company that's been permitted to build a wind project in Bear Paw."

Shannon drew rein briefly. "Mr. Carroll, I don't own this ranch. It's my father you need to speak with."

As soon as Sparky had reached the top of the bank, Shannon touched her heels to him and he broke into his easy rocking-chair lope, leaving Tom Carroll, project supervisor for Patriot Energy, standing beside the creek in his fancy Tony Lama boots, slack-jawed.

BILLY WAS WORKING with another mustang in the round pen when he heard the staccato hoofbeats of a running horse coming toward the corrals. The other five mustangs were on full alert when the bay came into sight, trailing the long lead rope behind him in midair. Ears flattened back, mane and tail streaming, he streaked right past the corrals and headed up toward the hay fields, ignoring the plaintive screams of the mustangs left behind in the corrals.

"Damn," Billy said softly, watching the mustang race past. He was thinking two things: first, that that horse could really run. And second, that all those years in Nashville had obviously taken their toll. Shannon had lost her touch. He leaned over the round-pen fence and waited for her to appear. Sure enough, a few minutes later, she came into sight. Sparky was jogging along and Shannon had her hat pulled down low over her eyes. Both of them were soaking wet. Behind her on the road and creeping cautiously along at a snail's pace was a black SUV.

Shannon rode right up to the pen and reined Sparky in. "Sparky got pulled right off his feet in the creek," she explained. "I had to let the mustang loose so he could get back up."

"You okay?"

"Fine." She indicated the SUV with a jerk of her head. "That's Tom Carroll from the wind project. Spooked the mustang with his car horn. Said he wants to talk to me, but I told him he needed to talk to my dad. I'm going in the house to change out of these wet clothes, then I'm heading off to look for that mustang."

"No need," Billy said. "He'll come back eventually. His buddies are in the corral and he's going to get lonely. I'll close the gate on the road soon as Tom Carroll leaves."

The SUV pulled up near the round pen and Carroll emerged. Billy turned away from him, walked to the center of the corral and began moving the mustang in circles, first one way, then reversing directions. He kept the horse's pace at a trot, but occasionally it would break into a lope, snaking its head and kicking out in protest before dropping back into the trot. Billy used a long carriage whip with a plastic bag tied on the end to keep the horse moving. He had only to flick the plastic bag and the mustang moved away from it, trotting as far from the man as he could get.

Tom Carroll leaned up against the rails. "Hello, Billy. That's a good-looking horse."

Billy ignored him, focusing his attention on the mustang.

"I came out here hoping to have a word with Shannon," Tom said. "I wanted to invite her to the chicken barbecue Patriot Energy's hosting on Saturday at the Grange Hall."

Billy rotated slowly in the center of the round pen, eyes following the mustang. "I'll be sure and tell her."

"And her father's invited, too, of course."

"All the barbecued chicken west of the Mississippi won't change McTavish's mind about your project. It won't change mine, either, for that matter. Not that you invited me."

"The barbecue starts at noon," Carroll said. "We've hired a band to play. Badlands, I think they call themselves." He pushed his spotless Stetson onto his head. "I heard Shannon McTavish sang with them the other night and made quite a sensation."

The mustang abruptly ducked his head, planted his forelegs and lashed his heels at the sky with an angry squeal. "That's it, work it out," Billy said softly. He shook the plastic bag on the end of the whip and the mustang jumped forward and began trotting in circles again.

"You're welcome to come, too, Billy," Tom said. "Everyone in Bear Paw's invited."

"Thanks, but I'm a beef eater."

Tom pushed off the fence and glanced toward the barn. "Maybe I should ask her myself. I have a feeling you won't pass any of this on."

"She's a busy lady," Billy advised, but Carroll paid him no heed.

SHANNON WIPED SPARKY down thoroughly with a towel after removing his saddle and bridle, making sure he hadn't been hurt in the fall. "You're the best, always were and always will be," she murmured softly to him as he stood patiently for her ministrations and nuzzled her gently when she'd finished. "Go find Old Joe and have a nap in the sun." She turned him out of the barn and watched as he ambled off toward the tractor shed, where Old Joe usually hung out.

"Shannon?"

She turned. It was Carroll.

"I wanted to apologize again for scaring your horse, and to make sure you were okay," he said. "That was a bad fall you took."

"I'll live. You shouldn't scare horses that way. We didn't hear you coming over the sound of the creek." Shannon used the towel to dry off the saddle she'd slung over a stall partition.

He nodded, shoving his hands into his jeans' pockets and hunching his shoulders. "I've learned my lesson. Listen, I came by to invite you and your father to a chicken barbecue at the Grange Hall this Saturday. There'll be information available on the wind project, and we've planned some fun events for the kids. Your daughter might enjoy it. Greasy pig contest, three-legged race, a magician with a monkey."

Shannon looked over her shoulder at him. "Magician with a monkey?"

Tom nodded. "Monkey's really good. Not sure about the magician."

"I'll think about it." When he didn't leave, Shannon paused again. "Is there something else?"

"Actually, yes. I haven't had much luck talking to your father about our wind project."

"There's not much I can do about that."

"Maybe you could talk to him."

"I do talk to him."

"I mean, about the wind project and how important it is to this town."

Shannon picked up the saddle that she'd slung over the stall partition and walked toward the tack room. "I just got back to Bear Paw a few days ago, Mr. Carroll," she said, returning the saddle to its proper place. "I haven't lived here for over ten years and I really don't know anything about your wind project, so I'm not the one to talk to my father about it." She hung the bridle on a hook and edged around Carroll as she exited the room. "As I said before, he's the one you need to be having this conversation with."

"I've tried. If he knew I was here he'd probably run me off at the end of a shotgun."

"Sounds like my father." Shannon started walking toward the barn door.

"The lease money would really help him,"

Carroll said, hurrying to keep up with her. "If you come to the barbecue you'll see the project maps and have a chance to ask questions. Your father's land could host quite a few turbines, plus the transmission corridor. We've already signed leases with all the adjoining landowners, he's the only holdout."

Shannon stopped and faced him. "I'll come to your barbecue because I should educate myself as to what's going on in Bear Paw. But just so's you know, I'm not going to try to change my father's mind about anything."

Tom nodded. "Fair enough."

SHANNON'S LEG HURT enough that she had trouble climbing the porch steps. Her father was standing in the kitchen doorway, watching her through the screen door. He pushed it open with his good arm. "What happened?"

"Sparky got pulled off his feet by one of the mustangs. He fell in the creek."

"You okay?"

Shannon nodded, flinging her hat onto the table with a discouraged sigh. "I'm fine, just a little wet and sore. Where's Rose?"

"She just ran upstairs to get something. Was that Tom Carroll I saw out by the barn?"

"Yep." Shannon met her father's gaze. "He wanted to invite us to a chicken barbecue at the Grange this Saturday."

"So he could spoon-feed you some wind industry propaganda, no doubt," McTavish said.

Rose's footsteps came down the stairs like scattershot. "Momma, look what Tess found outside this morning!" she said, thrusting her arms out and unfolding her cupped hands.

Shannon gazed down. "It's a dead frog, Rose."

"No, it's not dead, Momma, Tess made it hop. I picked it up and Grampy said I could keep it."

"Really?" Shannon took the limp green frog from Rose's hand. "Rose, this frog is dead. You can't keep it."

"But Grampy said I could!"

Shannon shot her father an exasperated look and at that moment the wall phone rang. She answered it, glad for the diversion.

"Shannon? Spencer Wallace. Sorry if I'm bothering you."

"Not at all, Spencer. I can't thank you enough for helping out with the haying. How's Jeb's shoulder?"

"Oh, he's fine enough to play a guitar. Listen, Patriot Energy's putting on a chicken barbecue at the Grange Hall this Saturday for the locals and they've hired us to entertain. Me and the boys, well, we were hoping you might sing a few songs with us. I mean, we understand if you can't, but we were just hoping…"

Shannon glanced at her father, then down at the dead frog lying belly-up in the palm of her hand. "I'd be glad to," she said. "I said I'd do that in exchange for you helping with the haying, and the gig couldn't be any closer to home than the Grange Hall. I'll see you on Saturday."

She hung up the phone, acutely aware of her father's accusing stare. "Rose, we have to bury this frog. It's dead."

"No, it's not, it's just sleeping," Rose said, her eyes welling with tears. "Grampy said I could keep it."

"That was while it was alive, but it isn't anymore."

"It's just sleeping, Momma. Give it to me, and I'll take it back to bed."

"Rose…" Shannon gave her daughter The Look as she held the frog out of reach. "We're going outside to find a nice place to dig a grave."

"No, you can't bury him. He's mine," Rose wailed, tears rolling down her cheeks. "Make her give him back, Grampy!"

"Are you planning on singing at Patriot Energy's chicken barbecue this Saturday?" her father asked over Rose's protests.

"I promised the Badlands I'd sing a few songs with them in exchange for them helping with the haying," Shannon said.

The kitchen door swung open and Billy came inside.

"Don't let her take my frog," Rose pleaded with Billy. "It's *my* frog. She can't take it. Grampy gave him to me!"

Billy quickly scoped out the situation, retrieved the dead frog from Shannon's palm and nodded to Rose. "Come with me, Rose," he said, extending his other hand. "We'll take the frog outside for a swim in the creek. Maybe the water will revive him. C'mon."

Billy led the still sobbing but hopeful Rose from the kitchen and Tess followed. Shannon looked at her father. "Tom Carroll wanted me to invite you to the barbecue."

"I bet he did."

"Daddy...maybe you should go. They're

going to have a lot of information about the wind project there."

"If you want to sing at their barbecue, go ahead, but don't be trying to convince me how to think or what to believe. This is *my* land. Nobody's going to tell me what I can and can't do with it. This wind project Tom Carroll's pushing on Bear Paw won't make a damned bit of difference to anything except their corporate bank account, and that's the truth. He knows it, he knows that I know it and he's wasting his breath trying to talk me into going along with his shell game. Once the federal subsidies dry up, these wind developers will blow away like tumbleweeds, leaving their mess behind them. You'd know that was true if you did some research."

Shannon sighed. "I need to take some aspirin, get into some dry clothes, make some lunch and then chase down that mustang." She started for the stairs but paused and looked over her shoulder at her father, who stood brooding by the kitchen door, arm in a sling and scowl on his face. "How does leftover barbecued ribs and beans sound, Daddy?"

BILLY TOOK ROSE down to the creek, where they squatted side by side on their heels as Billy held the frog in the water and let the current wash over it. Tess lay down beside Rose, who was peering intently at the frog in Billy's hand. "Is he waking up?"

"Not yet." Billy set the frog on a smooth wet rock at the creek's edge. "He seems unresponsive."

"He's not dead. He's just sleeping." Rose wiped her cheeks on her shirtsleeve. "I put him in my bed and he went to sleep."

"Where'd you get him?"

"Tess found him under the porch and Grampy said I could have him."

"Have you ever had a pet frog before?"

Rose shook her head. "Before we came here I had a goldfish."

"What happened to it?"

"It stopped swimming and floated, so Momma said the only way to wake it up was to put it in the toilet."

"What happened then?"

"It swam in circles and then it disappeared. Momma said it would find its friends when it got to the ocean."

"Huh." Billy splashed some water on the

frog. "Maybe we should try the same thing with the frog. Maybe letting it swim would wake it up."

"Do you think so?" Rose's big eyes were so full of hope that Billy felt a twinge of guilt.

"It might."

Rose thought about this for a few long moments. She picked the frog up very carefully, gave it a gentle kiss goodbye, then lowered it into the creek water and released it. The swift current whisked it away in a flash, and she stood, watching for as long as she could see it, which wasn't very long. She looked at Billy and her eyes welled with tears again, as if she weren't quite sure what just happened. "I think he was swimming," she said in a hopeful voice that trembled.

As he took her hand in his, Billy wondered how any parent explained the concept of death to a young child. "I think so, too," he said. "Let's go see what your momma's making for lunch. Maybe we can lend her a hand. She's worked hard this morning."

When they got there, Shannon was at the kitchen counter dressed in dry jeans and a flannel shirt, sleeves rolled back to reveal slim, strong forearms. "Lunch'll be a minute.

I'm heating up some of those ribs and some soup. Rose, you go wash up."

"My frog swam away, Momma," she said. "He went to the ocean to be with his friends."

Shannon gave her daughter a compassionate look. "I'm sorry you had to say goodbye to him. He was a very nice frog. Run upstairs and wash your hands."

Rose climbed the stairs slowly, clearly still sad about her frog. Shannon watched her out of sight, then glanced at Billy. "You held a frog revival?"

"I told her the water might wake it up, so she held it in the water until the current took it. It did sort of look like it swam away."

"That frog was dead. No amount of water was going to wake it up. You really shouldn't mislead her that way. It's important to be truthful with a child."

"Is that why, when you flushed your daughter's dead goldfish down the toilet, you told her it was swimming away to join its friends in the ocean?"

Shannon flushed, turned away from him and finished washing the coffee mug she was holding.

"How's your leg?" Billy asked. "I noticed you were limping."

"I'll live," she replied cooly. "Lunch'll be ready soon, maybe you could go find my father. He's out in the barn, probably, sulking because I agreed to sing at the Grange Hall this Saturday, but he'll get over it."

"You're singing at Patriot Energy's barbecue?" Billy felt the same jolt of betrayal McTavish must have experienced.

Shannon faced him, her chin lifting in defiance. "I made a promise to the boys in the band, and I'm delivering on it. That's why the hay's in the barn. Besides, there'll be information about the wind project there. I can educate myself like you said I should. Are you going to stalk off like my daddy did?"

Billy removed his hat, slapped it once against his leg, then shook his head. "Nope. I'm too hungry. But Shannon, think twice about the barbecue. Folks are angry, and there's no telling where that anger might come out."

"Billy, it's just a barbecue."

He shook his head again and left.

CHAPTER EIGHT

THE BAY MUSTANG ran west until the fence line turned him to the south, and then he ran until it pushed him to the east. The rope streamed out behind him as he ran, and the hated halter clung to his head. After running to the point of exhaustion he stopped in the shade of a cottonwood and rubbed his head against the tree trunk, trying to rid himself of the contraption.

If he could find a place with no fence, he knew he could find his way home. The fence line was all that stood between him and his old way of life. When he had rested enough that the wind dried the lather of sweat on his body, he trotted along the fence, looking for a way through or around it.

And then he heard something. Soft, measured hoofbeats approaching from behind. He spun around and backed up two quick steps. His hind foot stepped on the trailing rope and jerked him to an abrupt stop.

"Sunk'ituya," a human voice said. "That fence will not stop you from running forever, but that rope will."

The two legged with the deep voice spoke to him from the back of a small spotted horse. The mustang snorted his alarm as the spotted horse approached. He jerked his head against the rope that was now anchored firmly by his hind hoof and wrapped around his lower leg. He was caught and didn't know how to free himself.

The two legged stepped down from the spotted horse and moved toward the mustang. He trembled as the two legged approached and slowly extended a hand. "Easy, *mithakhola*, I will not not hurt you. I will free you so you can fly away."

The hand smelled of sage and sweetgrass and sunshine and something herbal and strong. The mustang drew the mingled scents into his lungs, and when the hand touched him, he flinched but remained still. The hated harness binding his head was being loosened. In a heartbeat it fell away and the pressure of imprisonment was gone.

The mustang whirled in one movement and tore off at a gallop, the rope tangling around his hind leg for one jump, two, before it fell off like the bindings on his head and he was free! He lowered his head and put on a strong burst of speed to outrun the two legged, and then stopped at the crest of the knoll and whirled around to look behind him for pursuit, head high and nostrils flaring.

The two legged was watching him and raised his arm, the rope and halter dangling from it.

"Oyuskeya unpi, mithakhola, tanyan omani," the deep voice called out. "Freedom, my friend. Have a good journey." Then the two legged climbed back onto the spotted horse and returned the way he had come.

The loneliness built within the mustang until he could stand it no longer. He whinnied plaintively at being left behind, then followed the two legged on the spotted horse.

SHANNON WALKED OUT onto the porch to find her father. She was halfway down the steps when she spotted him near the machinery shed with another man. Billy came out onto the porch behind her and said, for her benefit, "My grandfather, Henry Crow Dog."

She stopped short and looked back at him, surprised. "From the reservation?"

"He comes to visit your father from time to time, usually when the tribal police are looking for him. Lets himself through the gate that backs onto BLM land."

"But how did he get here? The reservation is over a hundred miles south, as the crow flies. And why would the tribal police be after him?"

"Henry lost his driver's license years ago. Usually he gets caught driving into town or something and they want to throw him in jail for a few days to teach him a lesson. So he saddles his horse and rides over. He and your father like to share the tobacco. Bet you didn't know your father smokes the pipe with an outlaw Shoshone."

"Nothing my father does would surprise me."

"Whatever you do, don't ask him to stay for lunch," Billy warned. "He's like a stray cat. Feed him once and he might never leave."

Shannon walked to meet them, sizing up Billy's grandfather. He was shorter than her father, but just as wiry and strong looking, dressed in worn jeans, scuffed boots, a flannel shirt and a dark leather vest. He wore a flat-crowned black hat with a colorfully beaded hatband over long black hair streaked with gray, and he didn't look like a grandfather.

"Lunch is ready," she called with a wave of her arm when they were in earshot. "I'll set another place."

Henry Crow Dog raised his own arm in response and even from a distance Shannon recognized the rope and halter he held in his hand. Shannon felt her stomach drop. Had the wild horse gotten hung up on something? Was he dead? How else could Henry Crow Dog have gotten the halter off that mustang?

"Henry found the mustang that ran off," her father said as the two came to a stop in front of her. "He was hung up by the back fence line, so Henry took the halter off and the mustang followed him back here."

Shannon hid her surprise and stuck out her hand. "Shannon McTavish. Thank you. That mustang doesn't much like the idea of being saddle broke."

"Smart horse," Henry said, shaking her hand.

"I hope you'll have lunch with us. You're welcome to put your horse in our corrals. We have plenty of hay. Billy can take care of him for you." She shot a glance over her shoulder. Billy was still standing on the porch wearing a stony expression, hands on his hips. She got the distinct impression he and his grandfather weren't on good terms.

"My horse is already turned out with your horses," Henry said. "That mustang was trying to find his way home. He doesn't want to be civilized."

"We're not all that civilized around here. Seems like he should fit in just fine," Shannon said wryly.

Henry nodded to his grandson as he climbed the porch steps. "Billy," he said.

"Grandfather." Billy nodded in response but his stance never changed and his expression remained aloof.

"I heard you bought some land from McTavish so I came to see it."

"Nothing much to see," Billy said.

"Come inside, Henry," Shannon invited him. "Rose, help me get lunch on the table."

Five minutes later the men had removed their hats, washed at the sink and chosen their respective chairs. A big platter of ribs, a pot of leftover beans, a bowl of coleslaw, a basket of Kitty's wonderful biscuits and a pitcher of cold sweet tea crowded the center of the table. Shannon had put cutlery and plates on the table as well as a generous stack of paper towels. She sat down between Rose and her father, her chair legs scraping loudly in the silence of the kitchen. She glanced around the table. All eyes were fixed on their own plates. The silence stretched out.

"This looks good," McTavish finally said, breaking the awkward moment.

"Kitty Sayres cooked all of this for the haying crew. I can't claim credit. All I did was heat it up." Shannon picked up the basket of biscuits and started passing it around the table. She followed it with the pot of beans, the bowl of coleslaw and, finally, the platter of ribs. Food eventually filled the plates and the pitcher of tea filled the glasses.

"So," Shannon said to Henry as she distributed the paper towels around the table. "How'd you get the halter off that mustang?"

Henry paused with a fork full of beans halfway to his mouth. "I unbuckled it."

Shannon wanted to ask a whole lot more

questions but he was eating, so she concentrated on her own plate and wondered why Henry and Billy were at odds with each other. What had happened between them? She noticed her daughter hadn't touched her food. "Rose, eat your lunch."

"I'm not hungry, Momma. I want my frog back."

"Your frog is gone. Now eat."

"Did I make him go to sleep when I put him in my bed?"

Shannon poured herself some iced tea. "No, sweetie. It wasn't your fault. Your frog wasn't asleep, he died. It was just his time, that's all. You had nothing to do with it. Try to eat something. These ribs are delicious."

"But he's not dead. Billy said the water would wake him up so he could swim away. He saw it, too. He swam away, we both saw it!" Rose's lower lip trembled. She was close to tears.

"Rose, we have company. We're not going to discuss the frog any further. No more tears. Eat your lunch."

Henry pushed from his chair and reached for his hat from the wall peg. "Death is part of the Great Mystery of the Creator, and your daughter needs to understand that it is okay to cry, because only when the tears flow do we begin to feel a connection to all things, and it is that connection with all things that makes us strong." Without waiting for a nod from Shannon, he looked at Rose. "Can you take me to where you last saw your friend?"

Two huge tears spilled over and ran down Rose's cheeks. "Yes," she sniffled.

"Good. Then we will go to that place and send him on his spirit journey."

A surge of indignation propelled Shannon to her feet. "Rose should eat first."

Henry put his hat on. He held Shannon's gaze for a long moment. Shannon slowly sat back down. Henry shifted his gaze to Rose. "Ready?"

Rose nodded. She slid off her chair and walked to the kitchen door, and the two departed together. When the kitchen door banged shut behind them, Shannon looked first to Billy, then to her father.

"I can't believe that man just took my daughter away without asking!" she said.

Billy broke a biscuit in half. "Henry might not have a driver's license, but by the time he's finished with his smudging ceremony,

Rose will know all about 'Skan and the spirit journey and the meaning of the frog totem. Let him teach Rose about the Great Mystery. His lesson will be better than mine, and a whole lot more helpful. Could you pass the butter, please?"

JUST AS BILLY had predicted, Henry stayed for an entire week, bunking with Billy in the cook's cabin and helping out with the mustangs, not because he was asked, but because he enjoyed working with horses. Shannon grudgingly pardoned Henry's proprietary behavior with her daughter, mostly because Rose had instantly bonded with Henry and to protest their friendship would only create more friction in a household that had enough internal conflicts already.

She helped Billy and Henry with the mustangs, tolerated her father's surliness as he struggled with both his broken arm and his daughter's perceived disloyalties, and cooked endless meals for the hungry crew. Three meals a day took quite a bit of prep work and planning, all the while keeping one eye on Rose, so Shannon was looking forward to the chicken barbecue at the Grange, not to mention a day without cooking and cleaning.

And there was no denying that she was also looking forward to singing again.

Saturday dawned clear and cool, an early August morning that held a hint of fall. Shannon slipped out of bed, careful not to wake Rose, and opened the window wide so she could lean her forearms on the sill and admire the sunrise.

She'd forgotten how quiet Wyoming mornings could be, and this day had begun with a hush, as if the entire valley was holding its breath, listening to the stillness of the mountains. Not a breath of wind was stirring.

Then she heard a meadowlark sing the first beautiful salutation to the sunrise. Moments later a raven flew over with a loud swish of wings, spied her standing at the window and veered aside with a startled croak. One of the mustangs whinnied down at the corrals. She wondered if it was that restless young bay who wanted to go back home.

A movement out by the barn caught her eye. Billy. Already up and working. Not surprising. Sometimes it seemed as if he hardly slept. He'd been withdrawn and downright glum since his grandfather had arrived, leaving in his truck after working all day to go stock shelves at Willard's or spend a few hours alone at his house, pounding nails until darkness brought him back to the ranch again. Occasionally he missed supper, but Shannon guessed it was the only time he had to himself, with Henry Crow Dog sharing the little cook's cabin.

Shannon washed, dressed and started a pot of coffee down in the kitchen. She was surprised her father hadn't already put the coffee on himself. He was usually an early riser, but Tess was the only one in the kitchen, wagging her tail when Shannon paused to stroke her head. Shannon pulled on a light jacket and walked out to the barn, where Billy was throwing a few bales of hay down out of the loft to feed the mustangs.

She helped him lug the bales out to the corrals, break them apart and throw the flakes of hay inside. The wild horses were coming along nicely after a week of handling. No longer did they shy to the far side of the corral when the humans approached with the hay. The bay was the only holdout, distrustful and wary whenever Shannon and Billy were around, but he trusted Henry, which galled Shannon to no end. It galled her, too, that he called the horse Khola, which he explained was short for *mithakhola*, which meant *friend*.

"What does that wild horse see in your grandfather?" she asked as she and Billy leaned against the corral fence and watched the mustangs jockey for position.

"Annoys you, doesn't it?" Billy said. He was chewing on a piece of hay, hat pushed back, forearms dangling over the top rail.

"Yes," Shannon admitted. "I've tried so hard to make friends with him and he wants nothing to do with me. The horse, I mean, not your grandfather."

"Henry pisses me off, too," Billy remarked casually. "Not because of that mustang and not because Rose worships him, but because he disowned my mother when she had me out of wedlock. Chased her right out of his life when she was young and scared and alone and in love with the wrong man. So because she had nowhere to go, she went and married that wrong man."

"Your father?"

Billy nodded. "He was an abusive alcoholic. I was born on the rez but my mother moved from there because my father was white and had a house close to town. But he didn't have a heart, and he sure as hell broke my mother's."

Billy tossed the piece of grass to the ground. "Still, if I'd grown up on the rez, I wouldn't have gone to your high school. You wouldn't have been my lab partner. Guess you could say that meeting you was the silver lining to Henry Crow Dog kicking my mother out of his house when she was just sixteen years old...even though you broke my heart when you wouldn't go with me to the prom."

"I did no such thing," Shannon retorted. "You had more girlfriends than you knew what to do with. Are your parents still alive?"

"My father died of liver failure while I was in the Marines and my mother sold his house and moved back to the rez. Housing's really short there, so she moved in with one of her widowed sisters, my aunt Mary. Henry asked Mary and my mother if he could move in with them when his current wife kicked him out, and they both said no. So now he comes here, wanting to move in with me." Billy uttered a short laugh. "What goes around comes around."

"What will you do?"

He shrugged. "Don't know. What do you say to your grandfather when he wants to move in with you because he has no place else to go?"

Shannon watched Khola, who was watching her with a pensive expression on his beautifully wild equine face. *Khola*. Now she was calling him by that name.

"When I left here with Travis ten years ago, my father disowned me, but he took me back when I came home again. Maybe that's what family does, even when they don't want to. Speaking of my father, I better go check on the coffee. I started it before coming out here. Daddy wasn't up yet, which is unusual for him." Shannon pushed away from the fence and started for the house.

"You still planning on singing at the barbecue today?" Billy asked as she started away.

"Yep," she said, casting a smile over her shoulder. "You should come, even if you don't want to. I can really put on a show."

THE COFFEE WAS DONE. Shannon carried a cup with her as she tapped on her father's door. When there was no response, she opened it and poked her head inside. "Daddy?"

His bed was neatly made. She drew a breath and released it. Relief. Why did she always imagine the worst? He'd been fine at supper the night before, if still a little peeved with her about singing at Patriot Energy's barbecue, but he hadn't died in the night. He was just up and about before her, not unusual. What was unusual was that he hadn't made the coffee. She went back downstairs and started breakfast.

She'd told the band members she'd be at the Grange Hall at eleven, which gave her five whole hours to work with Khola. She was determined to win the horse over. She was her mother's daughter, after all, and this horse whisperer stuff should run in her blood.

She was draining the bacon on the sideboard when Billy came into the kitchen. He poured himself a mug of coffee and glanced around the kitchen. "They're both missing in action," he commented before taking his first swallow. "Henry and your father, along with two horses. They've flown the coop."

Shannon turned from the stove, spatula in hand. "On the day I'm singing at the wind developer's barbecue. How very interesting. What do you suppose they're up to?"

Billy shrugged. "Robbing a bank, probably. I wouldn't put it past Henry, and your father could use the money."

Shannon laughed. "Somehow I can't see the two of them pulling off a bank robbery, especially with my daddy riding a very old horse and sporting a broken arm. How many eggs?"

"Three," Billy replied, leaning his hip against the counter. "You ever wonder how your life might've turned out if you'd gone to the prom with me instead of Travis?"

Billy's question caught Shannon off guard. She cracked the eggs into the hot fat one after the other. "No."

Billy nodded slowly. "You ever thought about that kiss we shared on this porch?"

Shannon spooned the hot bacon fat over the egg yolks. "I've thought about it from time to time," she said, feigning indifference.

"Good thoughts?"

"You only wanted me because I was the only girl that ever turned you down."

"That's not the only reason."

Rose chose that moment to descend the stairs, one step at a time, still clad in her pajamas.

Shannon handed Billy his plate of eggs and turned to her daughter.

"Sweetie, today we're going to a barbecue, and you're going to see a magician with a real live monkey! Doesn't that sound like fun?"

"Can we go now, Momma?"

"I have to work with the horses for a bit. Do you want to keep me company?"

After working with Khola for a few hours, Shannon hurried to get herself and Rose ready for the barbecue. At eleven, she took Rose out to the car, securing her into the back seat. "Wait here a minute, while I tell Billy we're leaving," she said. She found Billy in the barn, filling two water buckets from the spigot.

"We're off," she said.

He straightened, shut the water off. "Leave Rose with me. I'll watch her."

Shannon shook her head. "I promised she could come. She'll be fine, I can keep my eye on her while I'm singing, and there'll be neighbors and friends there. I know just about everyone in Bear Paw. Sure you won't come along?"

"Shannon, those neighbors and friends you're talking about, a lot of them are really mad at your father for not signing the wind farm lease."

Shannon heaved a tolerant sigh. "I understand not everyone's on board with this energy project, but Bear Paw's a tight-knit community. Nobody's going to hassle me about how my father feels about wind power, and they sure aren't going to hassle Rose. It's a barbecue, Billy, a fun family event in a little town. We're not singing at some redneck bar on a Saturday night for a bunch of drunks.

"I left some sandwiches in the refrigerator for you and the monkey wrench gang, should they decide to return. Keep working with those mustangs and stop worrying about us, we'll be fine," Shannon said in parting.

Five minutes later she and Rose had left the brooding Billy behind and were headed for town. Shannon had the radio turned up and was singing along to country-and-western music, warming up her vocal chords. She used to do that every day and it was time to get back into the swing of things. She was feeling really good about herself for the first time in ages. This was her first gig since the divorce. Maybe she'd been too hasty in thinking the responsible thing to do after splitting up with Travis was to give up her singing career. Maybe she could find a way to keep singing and be a good mother.

Three miles past Willard's General Store and just a mile from the Grange Hall, her cell phone rang. She switched off the radio, pulled the car over and fumbled in her purse to retrieve it. Reception was spotty through here but it was good enough that she could hear Billy's voice.

"What if Travis shows up?" he asked. "By now everyone knows you're going to be singing at the Grange Hall today. I'm coming into town to pick up Rose." And either Billy hung up on her or the call went dead. Shannon sat for a few moments, thinking about what he'd just said.

She'd forgotten all about Travis.

CHAPTER NINE

THE GRANGE HALL parking lot was crammed with vehicles, mostly pickup trucks but a few sedans and station wagons. Kids swarmed everywhere. The smell of mesquite hardwood chips and chicken barbecue flavored the air. Billy could hear the nasal twang and guitar strum of the Badlands band in the background, out where the big tent was pitched.

Shannon was here somewhere. He'd spotted her car parked on the side of the road in a long line of vehicles that couldn't fit into the Grange parking lot. All he had to do was find her and pick up Rose. There was every possibility Travis would show up at this free concert. Billy cursed himself for not thinking of it before Shannon left for town.

He made for the band platform, nodding to familiar faces. Patriot Energy had set up a table with project information on it on the outer edge of the big tent that had all the long banquet tables and chairs under it. There were big maps on easels and brochures and pamphlets, and a few townspeople were perusing the offerings and displays. Billy passed by the table with a nod to the fresh-faced young rep who was answering questions, and, in Billy's opinion, greenwashing the naive residents of Bear Paw with the false promises of wind power. He didn't spot Tom Carroll, and for that he was grateful, as he threaded his way through the people crowded around the bandstand.

He heard Shannon call his name and spotted her beside the bandstand, holding Rose's hand. His heart gave a thump at the beauty of her smile when she recognized him. She raised her arm in a beckoning wave and he altered course to meet her. "Thanks so much for coming," she said when he drew near. "I never thought about Travis being here, but you're right. If you could take Rose home and keep an eye on her, I'd owe you big-time."

"That's why I'm here," Billy said. "C'mon Rose. Let's go."

Rose looked at her mother. "You said I could see the monkey magician."

"I'm sorry, Rose, but Billy came to pick you up and you have to go now."

"But Momma…!"

"I'll take her to see the magician, then we can go home. I won't let go of her hand. Where's this dude and his chimp hanging out?" Billy said.

"There was a crowd of kids over beside the Grange Hall," Shannon said.

"Okay then, Miss Rose, let's go find the monkey and the magician."

Shannon gave her daughter a hug and then hugged Billy, a brief gesture of gratitude that sent him into the stratosphere. He felt his face flush as he took Rose's hand in his and turned toward the Grange Hall just as the band ended their song. A spattering of applause trailed off as Spencer Wallace spoke into the mic.

"And now it's my great honor to introduce, as if any of you needed the introduction, Shannon McTavish, one of Bear Paw's very own, who's dazzled the Nashville scene for the past ten years the same way she's going to dazzle all of us today. Shannon?"

Billy paused to watch her ascend the steps to the bandstand, take the guitar that was offered by Spencer and step up to the mic wearing that same beautiful smile that she'd flashed him so brightly.

"Thank you, Spencer, and thank all of you for being here today to enjoy this wonderful barbecue. I've been away for ten years but that's made coming back home all the sweeter. I'd almost forgotten how beautiful this valley was, and what waking up to a Wyoming morning did for the soul."

"All our souls would rest a whole lot easier if your father would just quit screwin' us over!" a man bellowed from the back of the crowd.

"McTavish should sign the lease," another added in a belligerent tone of voice. "He needs to get on board and quit holding this wind project up."

"Ain't fair, one man putting the brakes on something that could help all of us feed our families and bring in tax dollars for this town," a third pitched in.

The crowd at the bandstand milled restlessly, nobody looking at anybody else. Billy's hand tightened on Rose's as he scanned the crowd for the three hecklers, but they were hidden way in the back. "C'mon," he said

and started tugging Rose toward the bandstand. After five steps he picked her up and
carried her in his arms and pushed through
the crowd.

"I've heard about this energy project, and
I realize it has a big impact on the residents
of Bear Paw," Shannon said in a calm voice.
"I'm not here to dispute the pros and cons of
wind energy. I'm here to sing with Badlands.
My daddy has a right to run his affairs as he
sees fit, and unless I'm in the wrong town, if
someone told any one of you what you could
or couldn't do on your land, you'd blow your
tops. I realize you're all here at the invite of
the wind company to enjoy a free meal and
listen to some good music, but if you think
bullying me can get him to change his mind,
you don't know Ben McTavish very well."

"Which side are you on, Shannon?" a man
called out. "If you're here today, you must be
for the wind project. Am I right?"

Billy had reached the bandstand. He carried Rose up the stairs and handed her to a
startled Spencer Wallace. "Hang on to her
for a second, Spence," he said. Billy walked
up beside Shannon and, as diplomatically as

he could, moved her aside so he could speak into the mic.

"Is Tom Carroll here?" he said, anger tightening his words. "Anyone seen him? No? Funny, isn't it? I haven't spotted hide nor hair of him, either, which is strange because he's the project manager for Patriot Energy, and this is his party. He should be right handy, but my guess is, he didn't want to be around when the hecklers he hired started harassing Shannon McTavish. Am I right?"

He scanned the crowd and nobody would meet his eyes. "Who shouted those questions from way in the back? Come on up here and let's talk face-to-face. We're all neighbors, aren't we? Step right up here, we're real interested to hear what you have to say about all this."

Nobody came forward. Shannon was trying to regain the mic so he plucked it off the stand and held it in his hand. "How much were you fellas paid?" he called out. "Don't be bashful, we all want to know." The crowd was beginning to break up and wander off. "If the rest of you are embarrassed by this, you should be," Billy challenged them. "More than a few of you have harassed Ben McTavish over the past six months, including Bear Paw's mayor. Shannon McTavish shouldn't be wasting her talents singing for the likes of you."

"Billy!" Shannon protested. *"That's enough!"*

Billy put the mic back into the stand and before she could reach for it he took her by the hand and tugged her off the bandstand, pausing to scoop Rose away from a slack-jawed Spencer Wallace. "Sorry, Spence, you just lost your lead singer."

"But I promised!" Shannon struggled to twist from his grasp.

"You're not singing for this crowd," Billy said, pulling her down the steps behind him.

"Billy Mac, you let go of me!"

Billy paused at the foot of the steps and rounded on her, anger tightening his voice. "Listen to me, Shannon. Rose isn't safe here, and neither are you. If you want to stay, I can't stop you. But I'm taking your daughter home." He released her hand and headed for his truck, reasonably sure that as long as he had Rose in his arms, Shannon would follow.

He was right. She stalked behind him, stiff with anger. When he reached his truck he stopped short with a soft curse. All four of his tires had been slashed and the truck was sitting on its rims. Shannon stared.

"I have to hand it to you, Billy. You sure know how to make enemies," she said, then dug in her jeans pocket for her car keys. She started down the line of vehicles parked beside the road until she reached her own, where she unlocked the doors, buckled Rose into the back seat and climbed behind the wheel. Billy stood uncertainly beside the car until she powered her window down and said, "I don't have all day and you have four flat tires. Get in."

SHANNON WAS SO upset she had trouble getting out of the parking spot, nearly hitting the vehicle in front of her and then the one behind. Her hands were shaking and she kept them clamped around the steering wheel so Billy wouldn't see. For a few minutes they drove in silence, then she had to vent or explode.

"You had no business interfering like that," she burst out, hoping he didn't hear the tremble in her voice. "That was my first real gig since my divorce, and you ruined it."

"You were set up," Billy said. "Tom Carroll planted those hecklers in the crowd to rattle your cage so's you'd run home to daddy and get him to sign the wind leases."

"You have no proof of that whatsoever," Shannon shot back. "You're just trying to poison me against the project and against Tom Carroll."

"Did you recognize any of those voices?"

"I've been away for ten years, Billy, there's probably a whole slew of newcomers I wouldn't recognize."

"In Bear Paw? Nothing much ever changes around here, including the population."

"If you'd just've stayed out of it, I could've handled them," Shannon said. "They were all talk, they weren't going to throw rotten eggs."

"Or slash truck tires?" Billy countered.

Shannon blew out her breath. "You okay, Rose?" she asked, glancing in the rearview mirror at her daughter.

"I didn't see the magic monkey, Momma," Rose said in a small voice. She didn't understand everything that had just happened back at the Grange Hall, but she knew it was bad.

"I'm sorry, sweetie, but we had to leave early." Shannon shot Billy a brief dark look. "We'll do something fun when we get home."

"Like what, Momma?"

"Like pack our bags and get out of Dodge," Shannon muttered under her breath.

"That's extreme," Billy said.

"Is it? You can fight against that wind project till hell freezes over and everyone hates you, if that's what trips your trigger. Frankly, I think you're both crazy for fighting something that could be so beneficial.

"Coming home was a bad idea. I thought Bear Paw would be a good place to raise my daughter, but I was wrong. I brought Rose back here to try and rebuild my life, to mend fences with my father, to find some peace and healing, and instead we landed in the middle of a war zone. Rose deserves better than this. She didn't even get to see the magician and the monkey!" Her voice trembled with anger and she realized she was on the verge of tears.

"I'm sorry," Billy said.

"Me, too," Shannon choked out. "But maybe it was for the best. I have friends in California that have been asking me and Rose to come visit. Maybe it's time we did."

"I never figured you for a quitter," Billy said.

"*Quitter?* This isn't my fight, Billy. Don't drag me into it."

She turned onto the ranch road, driving beneath the magnificent sign her mother had designed, driving past the house that should have been hers but wasn't, through gates that sagged on rotten fence posts, along the rutted dirt road full of potholes and choked with weeds, and suddenly she wanted nothing more than to leave this shabby place populated with small-minded, vindictive ranchers and farmers.

When they topped the knoll that overlooked the ranch buildings, Shannon felt the bottom drop out of her stomach. They were still a quarter mile from the house, but that was close enough for her to recognize the sheriff's vehicle parked in front of it and the uniformed sheriff standing on the porch.

"Oh, no," she said.

THE SHERIFF DESCENDED the porch steps to meet Shannon as she hurled herself out of the Mercedes. "What's happened?" she blurted out before the sheriff could utter a word. "Is my father okay?"

The sheriff glanced at Billy as he exited the sedan, then redirected his expressionless gaze to Shannon. "Far as I know," he said. "I just arrived here a few minutes ago. I have a few questions I'd like to ask him."

"About what?" Shannon demanded.

"Is he here?" the sheriff asked.

Shannon rounded her shoulders defensively and shoved her hands into her pockets. "He went off early this morning."

"Do you know when he'll be back?"

"He didn't say."

"Was he alone?"

"We weren't up when he left," Billy pitched in before Shannon could respond. "We can give you a call when he gets home."

The sheriff nodded. "Appreciate that." He handed Shannon his business card with his cell number.

"Can you tell me what this is about?" Shannon asked, glancing at the card.

"There's been some vandalism of Patriot Energy property," the sheriff replied. "A meteorological tower was pulled down over on Wolf Butte. That's across the valley from here, isn't it?"

"Yes," Shannon conceded, glancing toward Wolf Butte.

"There were hoofprints around the tower. Tom Carroll from Patriot Energy called this morning to report the vandalism. He gave me some names of ranchers who oppose the project and your father's headed the list. Was he on horseback when he left here?"

"My father has a broken arm," Shannon said. "I doubt he was out toppling towers before dawn."

"Maybe not, but if he could get a saddle and bridle on a horse with just one arm, it's not impossible," the sheriff responded stonily. "If you could have him give me a call when he gets back?"

"I will, and if you're driving through Bear Paw, sheriff, you'll see an old blue truck parked beside the road near the Grange Hall with four flat tires. That's Billy Mac's truck. His tires were slashed while he was taking my daughter, Rose, to see the monkey and the magician at the chicken barbecue. I had to give Billy a ride home. You might want to check into it."

The sheriff climbed into his Ford Explorer, nodded curtly and sped off in a cloud of dust. Shannon scowled after the departing vehicle, shoving the sheriff's card into her pocket. She turned to take Rose out of the car. "Go inside, Rose, and see if Tess needs to come out for a pee," she said.

When her daughter had climbed the porch steps and disappeared inside, Shannon glared at Billy. "I hope you have enough money saved up to spring for Dad and Henry's bail, because as far as I'm concerned, they can both rot in jail for pulling that tower down."

She turned on her heel and followed Rose into the kitchen, letting the door bang shut behind her.

RATHER THAN STAY and face Shannon's wrath, Billy drove McTavish's old truck back to town to hunt up four used tires he couldn't really afford and find the junkyard man, who had a flatbed tow truck. Fortunately, Slouch didn't have much of a social life and he lived at the junkyard. Billy found him sleeping on a couch in his office, which was a tiny alcove inside the Quonset hut. Unshaven, disheveled and wearing greasy jeans and a T-shirt promoting pit bulls, he followed Billy to the Grange Hall and winched Billy's old Ford truck onto the flatbed.

"Somebody don't like you," Slouch remarked as he chained Billy's truck down.

"More than a few somebodies, probably," Billy remarked, nodding toward the gathering at the Grange Hall. "Patriot Energy's hosting a barbecue today if you want to grab a free plate of food."

Slouch brightened. "I can always eat something," he said and wandered off.

Billy figured he had some time to kill while Slouch sated his appetite, so he headed toward the marquis tent and the long banquet table where Patriot Energy had a display of maps and wind energy information. A small group of townspeople were perusing the information when Billy arrived.

Billy had never met the young man staffing the table, who was eager to answer all of Billy's questions about the size and scope of the project and point out on the maps where the turbines would be located. "One hundred seventy-five turbines in all, running along this ridgeline, then over on this one to this butte here…" the staffer said, running his finger along the higher elevations that defined the valley's boundary and paralleled the Bear Paw River.

"What kind of turbines?"

"They're Gamesas, rated at two megawatts

per turbine, and they're almost six hundred feet tall," the young staffer said with pride. "They'll generate enough clean energy to power over seventy thousand homes."

"We don't have seventy thousand homes here in Bear Paw, maybe four hundred if you count the hunting camps," Billy commented. "What's the actual capacity factor of these turbines, and how much of the energy is lost in transmission? Isn't it quite a bit, when you're talking hundreds of miles? Wouldn't it make more sense to put these machines near the population centers rather than way out in the boonies?"

"There's more space out here, and the power will be sent to other states to fulfill their renewable energy mandates," the staffer said, avoiding Billy's questions. "The transmission corridor's going here..." The staffer's finger traced a dotted line on the map that ran across the McTavish ranch.

"Huh," Billy said. "Are these plans permitted yet?"

The staffer hesitated. "Patriot Energy's well into the process. We held this barbecue so we could introduce local residents to the project and answer questions."

"Well, if it ain't Billy Mac," a loud, boisterous voice accompanied a vigorous slap to his shoulder. "Watch out for this one," he warned the staffer. "Billy here hates renewable energy, ain't that right, Billy? You'd shoot this whole project down if you could. Hell, between you and McTavish, you're doing a mighty good job at keeping the wheels from turning. Don't give him any of your free chicken barbecue, he don't deserve it, and besides that, you'll never win him over with your barbecue sauce, it's terrible."

"Boyd," Billy greeted the well-built middle-aged rancher with a nod.

"Heard your truck tires got slashed," Boyd Bannon said, knocking his tan Stetson back with his wrist and smoothing his sandy colored mustache. His blue eyes crinkled at the corners. "That's a real shame."

"I needed new tires anyway," Billy said.

"Me'n the boys are sharing a few drinks at the Dog and Bull. If you dare to join us, I'll stand you to a beer. We'd like to talk to you about a proposal we leaseholders want to make to McTavish. We'd invite him, too, but we heard he was busy pulling down Patriot Energy's met tower." Boyd shook his head.

"Damn shame you dragged Shannon McTavish out of here today. You sure know how to spoil a good party."

"I'd say those hecklers Tom Carroll planted in the crowd made a pretty good job of that," Billy said.

"Well, Billy, if you want to hear what we have to say, we'll be at the Dog and Bull. Might be worth your while to stop in. Folks around here are getting mighty tired of McTavish's attitude."

Boyd turned and walked toward his pickup truck and Billy watched until he vanished into the crowd. Slouch chose that moment to reappear, balancing a paper plate heaped with food and a large paper cup filled with lemonade.

"You should get some of this, it's pretty good," he said around a mouthful as he headed for the flatbed. "You're going to need some tires on that truck of yours."

"Figured you might have some used ones I could buy."

"Come on back to the yard with me and we'll have a look. Dang, I hate to leave, that band's not bad, and I could sink another plate of food. Who'd you say was throwing this shindig? An oil company?"

"Wind company."

"Wind company. Huh," Slouch said as he wrenched open the flatbed's door and carefully placed his plate of food and cup of lemonade in secure positions. "Well, their chicken's okay, but their barbecue sauce stinks."

SHANNON WAS DETERMINED to be gone before her father or Billy returned. She threw her suitcase on the bed and was cramming both her own and Rose's clothing into it when Rose came upstairs.

"Momma, why are you packing our things?"

"We're leaving, Rose. We've visited long enough."

"You mean, we're leaving Grampy?"

"Yes."

"And Billy?"

"Yes."

"And Henry Crow Dog?"

"Rose, we can't stay here forever."

"Why not? Grampy likes having us here, and I really, really like Grampy and Billy and

Henry Crow Dog. Is it because you're mad about what happened today?"

Shannon straightened with a sigh. "I'm upset about what happened today, yes, but it's more than that. I want to visit California. I think we'd both have fun there."

"I have fun *here*, Momma." Rose's face was getting red. She was close to tears.

One of the mustangs whinnied shrilly from the corrals and Shannon glanced out the window. The mustangs were staring up behind the machinery shed where, after a few moments, a man on horseback with one arm in a sling rode into view. "Damn," she cursed beneath her breath, torn between being relieved her father was okay and mad she hadn't made her escape before he got back.

"Grampy's home!" Rose cried out, then wheeled and clattered down the stairs. Shannon looked at the suitcase lying open on the bed, hastily stuffed with the remnants of what used to be an endless wardrobe. She sat down on the edge of the bed and buried her face in her hands.

Billy had humiliated her today in front of the entire town, her father was wanted by the sheriff for destroying a meteorological tower, Travis Roy was in the area trying to snatch Rose from her, and as if all that wasn't enough to deal with, she was caught in the middle of an ugly conflict between energy company proponents and a handful of people who stood in opposition—chief among them, her father and Billy. She'd come home seeking refuge, and ended up in the middle of an unholy mess.

"Grampy!" She heard Rose's young voice cry out as her daughter ran across the yard toward her grandfather. Shannon pushed to her feet, brushed her hair off her face with both palms and held them there as she stood and watched from the bedroom window.

Her father swung out of the saddle, turned to the little girl and swept her up with his good arm. Rose hugged him around his neck and across the distance Shannon heard Rose say in her high, piping voice, "I love you, Grampy, and I wanna stay. Please don't let Momma take me away from here."

Shannon groaned. Her father had unsaddled Sparky by the time Shannon reached the barn. With one arm he'd handily loosened the cinch and pulled the saddle off, heaving it atop the fence rail. He did the same with the bridle, hooking the crown over the saddle horn.

Freed, Sparky shook himself like a big dog and then rubbed his head against her father's shoulder. He slapped Sparky's neck with affection and brought him a measure of oats from the barn, holding the bucket while the old horse ate. He paid no attention to Shannon, but made sure Rose stayed by the corral fence, away from the mustangs.

"Ten miles is too far to ride an old horse like Sparky," Shannon said when the silence between them had built up to the point of implosion.

Her father cast her a questioning glance, but didn't respond. He waited until Sparky had finished the oats in the bucket and wandered off to have himself a good roll in the grass, then returned the saddle and bridle to the tack room and headed toward the house. Only then, with Rose still dogging his heels, did he speak. "Rose tells me you were packing to leave. Were you planning to say goodbye?"

"What difference would that make to you? You left here this morning without telling anyone where you were going or when you'd be back. Where's Henry Crow Dog?"

"She said you were going to California."

"The sheriff came by earlier. Said he wanted to ask you a few questions about some equipment belonging to Patriot Energy that had been vandalized over on Wolfe Butte. Daddy, did you and Henry Crow Dog pull down one of their meteorological towers?"

Her father climbed the porch steps and walked into the kitchen without answering. He drew himself a tall glass of water at the kitchen sink and drank it down, then drank a second glass. Shannon stood with her arms crossed, her spine rigid and anger boiling her blood. "Go upstairs, Rose," she told her daughter.

"I don't want to."

"Rose!"

Her daughter turned and reluctantly climbed the stairs. When she was out of sight, Shannon let her anger out. "Where'd you go with Henry Crow Dog this morning, Daddy?"

Her father's eyes met hers and didn't flinch. "Henry's gone back to the reservation. I rode with him a ways."

"The two of you didn't pull that tower down before Henry headed south?"

"That damned met tower's been flat on the ground since May, probably earlier."

"And how would you know that?"

He patted his shirt pocket and withdrew an envelope, handing it to her. "Photos taken this spring by one of Henry's friends on the rez. They've used Wolf Butte for generations for tribal ceremonies. There was a pivotal battle fought there a long time ago between the Shoshone and the Crow, and some of their dead are buried up there."

"I know all that, Daddy. I grew up here, or have you forgotten?"

He ignored her jab. "When they went up there for the ceremony this spring, the meteorology tower was on the ground. Henry brought the photos with him when he came to visit, not because of the met tower, but because he knows Wolf Butte was special to your mother. The pictures are date-stamped, in case you're wondering, and he has plenty of witnesses to back up the facts."

Shannon slipped the photos out of the envelope and studied them. All three showed the tower from various angles, crumpled in a tangled heap of metal on the ground, but the focus of the photographs seemed to be a cairn of stones, a shrine built for some ceremonial purpose, she supposed. Perhaps to honor their dead warriors.

Henry's people and several saddled horses were scattered in their ceremonial tribal regalia in the background. The sky was blue, the grass was just greening up and there were patches of snow on the ground. The date stamp on the back of each photo read May 15.

"Had Henry Crow Dog heard about the wind project and the turbines planned for Wolf Butte?"

Her father shook his head. "Wind developers don't advertise in advance. The fewer people who know about a project, the fewer people protest. They try to operate under the radar. They came in well over a year ago, got most of their leases lined up first, then started the permitting process. Henry thought the met tower on Wolf Butte was a cell phone tower, but he knows about the wind project now."

"Did he give you these photos today?"

"Yep. Handed them to me right before we parted ways. Never mentioned them to me the entire time he was here."

"You'll need to show them to the sheriff," Shannon said, handing the photos back to her father along with the card the sheriff had given her. "His phone number's on that card."

He uttered a humorless laugh. "Quite a co-incidence that Tom Carroll calls the sheriff today of all days to report that I tore down his met tower. Speaking of which, you're home mighty early from singing at his taxpayer-funded barbecue."

Shannon shoved her hands in her jeans pockets and lifted her chin. "Not by choice," she said. "Billy dragged me away."

"Good for Billy. You're too good to be singing for that bunch of snake-oil salesmen."

Her father turned away from her and walked out the kitchen door, letting it slam shut behind him. Shannon blew out her breath and felt something brush against her leg. Tess gazed sightlessly up at her. Her muzzle might have been white with age and her eyes milky blue with cataracts, but her tail still wagged with unflagging devotion and her fidelity brought tears to Shannon's eyes.

She knelt down, wrapped her arms around the frail bones of her loyal old friend and let the tears come.

CHAPTER TEN

BILLY HELPED SLOUCH replace the tires with a matched set he'd found in his endless stacks out back of the Quonset hut. They had good tread and Slouch gave him a good price.

It was handy that Slouch had a vehicle lift and did mechanical work, as well. He told Billy it was fine to leave McTavish's truck there, they could pick it up anytime. By three that afternoon Billy was driving his own truck back through Bear Paw, past the Grange Hall, where the barbecue was winding down, past Willard's General Store.

He pulled in to the Dog and Bull parking lot, which was filling up early with Saturday spillover from the barbecue. He sat for a moment, engine idling, wondering how wise it was to risk getting his tires slashed twice in one day, but Boyd Bannon's comments had rubbed him the wrong way. How could he not show up at the Dog and Bull after being challenged in public that way?

He cut the ignition and climbed out of the truck. It wouldn't take long to find out what Boyd and his boys wanted him to tell McTavish. Then he'd head home and try to patch things up with Shannon. He pushed through the door of the Dog and Bull. The bar was full, the jukebox was blaring and the first person Billy recognized wasn't Boyd Bannon.

It was Travis Roy.

Travis was holding court at center stage, signing autographs and chatting with several of the patrons, most of them pretty young women. He was wearing his signature black Stetson with the fancy silver conch hatband, blue jeans and a dark leather jacket. When he saw Billy, he finished signing the back of a placemat and started toward him. Billy edged through the crowded room, ignoring a hail from an unseen Boyd at the back of the room.

"Stay away from Shannon, Travis," Billy said when they'd come face-to-face, speaking loudly over the noise, his blood up. "She told us about the restraining order. If you show up at the McTavish ranch again, I'll call the sheriff and have you arrested."

"Whoa. Easy, Billy." Travis raised both hands in a gesture of mock surrender. "I'm not here to make life hard for Shannon. I've done enough of that already," he said. "I have something for her and Rose. Something real important. All I want to do is make sure they get it. I heard she was going to be singing at the Grange today so I came into town, thinking if I talked to her in a public place she'd feel safe, but you dragged her away before I got there."

Travis pulled an envelope out of the inner pocket of his jacket. "I'd appreciate it if you'd deliver this to Shannon."

Billy eyed him suspiciously. "Why should I?"

"Because it contains a lot of money. Shannon walked out on everything she worked so hard for all these years. She didn't want anything out of the divorce, told her lawyer she just wanted to expedite the process. I didn't argue because I was sure she'd change her mind and take me back, but she didn't. And I don't blame her. I made her life hell for years." Travis held the envelope up. "I sold our big house in Nashville and all the fancies. The cars and the yacht we never used, the villa in Tuscany. This is her and Rose's share of the proceeds, and she earned every penny of it. I can't change the past, but I can make sure she and Rose have a comfortable future." He extended the envelope to Billy. "Would you see she gets it?"

Billy hesitated for a moment longer, then reluctantly took the envelope.

"Appreciate it," Travis said. He gave Billy a nod and then walked toward the door, ignoring the clamor of requests for his autograph. Billy glanced down at the envelope in his hands. Travis had written one word across the front of it—*Shannon*—and underlined it three times.

Billy folded it in half and tucked it carefully into his shirt pocket, fastening the button just as Boyd Bannon slapped his shoulder hard enough to knock him off balance for the second time that day.

"I took the liberty of ordering you a drink, Billy. C'mon, sit for a minute. We got a proposal we want you to take to McTavish."

At the table, four of the biggest landowners in Bear Paw were sharing a drink. A fifth chair had been drawn up to the table and Boyd gestured for him to sit, then nudged a shot glass full of whiskey in front of him.

Boyd dropped into his chair and leaned forward on his elbows. "No point beating around the bush. You know how we feel about McTavish blocking this wind project, so I'm not going to rehash any of that," Boyd said, lifting one hand in a cautionary manner. "McTavish and I go way back. We went to school together. He's a hard-working man and I got nothin' against him. He's had a rough string of luck, and I sure didn't wish it on him, but when he stands up in front of God and country and acts like he's the moral compass of Bear Paw, that's where I draw the line."

Boyd's voice intensified with emotion. "Let me be clear. I don't give an owl's hoot if these wind turbines ever produce one drop of electricity, all I care about is the lease agreement I signed with Patriot Energy that promises me a big chunk of money every year." The other landowners nodded in agreement. "I got kids to feed, taxes to pay, college tuition for my daughter. You know how expensive it is to send a kid to college? So I don't give a damn if this whole green energy thing is nothing but a big scam, like McTavish preaches. I don't care. I want that lease money. I *need* it.

"Now, here's the thing," Boyd continued, rapping his knuckles on the table for emphasis. "I own Wolfe Butte. When McTavish wanted to scatter his wife's ashes up there because that's where she released her rehabbed eagles, I went along with it. She was a good woman, and he told me how much she loved that spot. But I draw the line at McTavish going up there to haul down a met tower to protest the wind project." Boyd sat back in his chair. "That's vandalism, Billy, and it's against the law."

"You got proof he did it?" Billy said.

"Proof? Tom Carroll called me to report it first thing this morning. I went up there myself to check it out. Only way to get up there was on horseback because the road washed out this spring. Sure enough the tower was down."

"Any witnesses that McTavish pulled it down?"

"Who the hell else would do it? He's the ringleader of the turbine opposition, and the only one who lives within riding distance. When the sheriff went out to his place to ask about McTavish's whereabouts, he wasn't there. That's all the proof I need. So here's the deal, Billy. We'll agree not to press charges against McTavish if he signs on with the project."

With one finger, Billy pushed the untouched glass of whiskey back to the middle of the table and rose to his feet, picking his hat off the table. "Here's something for you to think about, Boyd. The only clear line of sight to the met tower on Wolf Butte is from McTavish's porch, and even there it's hard to see because of the distance.

"You said yourself the only way you could get up on Wolf Butte to check it out was by horseback. Tom Carroll's never been on a horse in his life. Which means he knew that met tower was already down. One of the project's pilots probably reported it during an aerial survey and Tom figured today was a good day to make a big public fuss about it." Billy pulled on his hat and started to leave, then paused. "I don't suppose you know who slashed my tires, Boyd?"

Boyd surged to his feet, his face tight with anger. "I can think of about two hundred people who'd like to have done it," he said, "and when I find out which one of 'em it was, I'll shake their hand. It's gonna get worse for you, Billy."

Billy nodded. "I expect it will, Boyd."

He turned and walked out the door of the Dog and Bull. As he headed for his truck he spotted Travis Roy being corralled against the side of a shiny late-model black F-350 diesel crew cab by a group of young women. Billy was mad enough that he didn't pay any attention to the men gathered on the far side of his own truck, sharing a bottle in a paper bag. It was a common enough sight in the parking lot. One of them motioned to him as he reached for his door handle.

"Hey, mister," the one holding the paper bag said. "Looks like one of your rear tires might be a little low on air."

Billy released the handle with a quiet curse and walked around the front of his truck. The man holding the bag pointed to the rear tire while the other three shifted restlessly. One of them let out a nervous giggle. He could hear the hiss of air and see the tire was well on its way to being flat. He had a pretty good idea how it got that way.

"Looks like you're having some real bad

luck today," the bag holder said, and then he grinned. As the others started to snicker, Billy felt anger sear through him like a wildfire. He was going to enjoy wiping the grins off of all their faces.

He threw the first punch and put all his weight behind it. The right cross was a doozy that lifted the bag holder off his feet, wiped the sneer off his face and sent him crashing into his three friends. Billy dove after him, wanting nothing more than to tear all of them to shreds, but as it turned out, they weren't nearly as drunk as they'd first appeared, and when the smoke cleared, it was Travis Roy and his clinging entourage of female fans who saved Billy's bacon.

THERE WASN'T A shred of sympathy in the sheriff's eyes when he looked Billy up and down ten minutes later. "Looks like you got the worst of it," he remarked. "What happened here?"

"This man attacked us, sheriff," the bag holder whined through a wad of bloody paper towels he was holding to his nose. "We was only trying to help him out by letting him know he had a flat tire, and then he just attacked us. Broke my nose, I think. Bastard went crazy on us."

"You boys want to press charges?" the sheriff asked.

"Hell, yes," the bag holder said. "I mean, he broke my nose, didn't he?"

"Sheriff, if I could just say something here?" Travis Roy, standing next to Billy, interjected in his smooth-as-honey, slick-talking drawl. "I was nearby when all this went down, and it appeared to me straight off that these boys were doing something illegal out here. Firstly, they were drinking liquor out of a paper bag, and secondly, they were messing with this man's vehicle. I saw one of them cut the sidewall of his rear tire with a hunting knife just before he came out and caught them at it. All this man did was try to defend his property from being vandalized by these rednecks. If anyone should be pressing charges, it's Billy Mac."

Billy wasn't sure he was hearing things right. He wiped his eyes with his forearm and spit out a mouthful of blood. It was all he could do to remain on his feet. He had no idea who'd hauled him up off the ground and didn't remember all that much of the fight, but he knew for damned sure he hadn't won it.

"He's right, sheriff, we saw it, too," a gushing female voice piped up. "Travis Roy went right to the rescue. I've never seen anything so brave in my entire life! If Travis hadn't stepped in like that, this man would be dead by now, beaten to death by these hoodlums, I'm sure of it. One of them hit this man over the head with that bottle they were drinking. They were kicking and hitting him while he was down on the ground. They were trying to kill him. It was awful to watch!"

"That right?" the sheriff commented, unimpressed.

Billy stood unsteadily on his feet, listening to Travis Roy being elevated to hero status. His fan club had no doubt taken photos of the whole altercation with their cell phones, soon to be sold to all the gossip rags. He wiped more blood out of his eyes and felt a hand close around his upper arm.

"I'll drive Billy home, sheriff," Travis Roy said. "It's the least I can do, seeing's he rescued my ex-wife from a potentially life-threatening situation at the Grange Hall today. You should keep a closer eye on these thugs. Book 'em for slashing tires and drinking in a public place and harassing Shannon

McTavish when she was just trying to entertain this Podunk town. Bear Paw used to be a decent, law-abiding place. Not anymore."

"Yeah, Travis is right, this town really stinks!" his groupies echoed. The sheriff hooked his thumbs in his gun belt with a scowl but didn't say a word as Travis steered Billy over to his shiny black F-350 crew cab and helped him crawl into the passenger seat. Billy was too punch-drunk to speak and wouldn't have known what to say, even if he could. Travis Roy, the alcoholic wife abuser, had just rescued him from a brutal beating, had prevented the sheriff from detaining and possibly arresting him, and was now driving him back to the ranch.

How would he ever explain any of this to Shannon?

SHANNON SAT ON the edge of the bed, staring at her open suitcase and the jumble of clothing hastily packed inside. She didn't know what to do. Should she stick it out on the ranch or head for California? She'd never been more confused, more undecided about anything in her entire life. She was furious with her father for riding off without telling anyone where he was going, and equally angry with Billy for literally dragging her off the stage at the Grange Hall barbecue. He had a helluva nerve treating her that way in front of half the town. Then again, he'd only come into town in the first place to make sure Rose was safe. And someone had slashed his tires.

One moment she was adding the last of their clothes to the suitcase and the next she was thinking she should unpack their things and wait till the dust had settled.

Rose crawled into her arms and wrapped her own arms around Shannon's neck. "I love you, Momma. I love you so much. But if we leave here, it'll go back to the way it was before. You'll be gone all the time and I'll never see you. Don't take me away from here, Momma. Can't we please stay with Grampy and Billy and Tess?"

What Rose said was true. In Nashville, Rose had been under the supervision of a full-time nanny while Shannon was on the road or practicing with the band or in the studio writing songs. These last few weeks she'd spent more time with her daughter than she had in the past six years. Isn't that why she'd vowed to give up her singing career after the divorce? Was it possible for her to be a good mother and have a successful career? Other mothers managed to do it. Why couldn't she?

Rose didn't want to leave and the truth was, Shannon didn't want to leave, either. She still loved this valley, these mountains, this land. And in spite of everything that had passed between them, she still loved her father and always would.

The feelings she had for Billy were another story. One moment he infuriated her, the next she was grateful for his help. And there was no denying she was still attracted to him. But how could she stay after the way he treated her today?

"Rose, we'll come back, I promise. We'll drive to California and walk on the beaches there and maybe see whales and sea lions, and we'll visit my friends and we'll be together every minute, just like now. I know you don't understand why I need to get away from here, but it's not forever. We'll visit again. I promise."

"What about Tess? What if she dies before we get back here? What if Grampy dies?"

Shannon hugged her daughter close. "They

won't," she said, knowing it was a promise she shouldn't make.

"Momma, can you leave me here? Grampy and Tess need someone to take care of them."

Shannon groaned and stood from the bed. She heard the approach of a vehicle and moved to the window, leaning her forearms on the sill. A cloud of dust marked the vehicle's approach. It was a big fancy black truck that slowed to a stop when it reached the barn. Shannon frowned as the passenger-side door opened and Billy climbed out. He said something to the driver, then closed the truck door and started toward the cook's cabin, walking slow and all bent over like an old man. The fancy black truck make a snappy U-turn up by the barn and headed out the ranch road. Shannon felt her heart stop when she caught a glimpse of the driver's profile through the open window.

Travis!

She whirled from the window and bolted from the room, descending the kitchen stairs two at a time. "Billy!" she shouted as she burst out the kitchen door and raced down the porch steps. *"Billy!"*

He ignored her, reaching the cook's cabin

at the same time she did. She caught his arm, halting him, her blood running cold when she saw the shape he was in. He could barely stand, and Billy was a strong, tough man. "Who did this to you? Was it Travis?" He stared mutely at her for a few moments, as if trying to process her words. She turned him gently toward the ranch house. "Never mind," she said. "You can tell me later. Come inside."

In the kitchen she ordered Rose upstairs, but her daughter defied her. "Momma, we can't leave now 'cause Billy needs us, too!"

Shannon filled a basin with warm water and added a squirt of iodine to it. Armed with several clean dishcloths, she sat Billy down at the table and went to work. Everything she did must have hurt, but he was stoic. Rose stood at his knee and touched him reassuringly. "Momma, don't forget his hand. It's all bloody."

Sure enough, Billy's knuckles were raw. "Looks like you got in a few licks before you lost the battle," Shannon said grimly. The water in the basin darkened. She changed it for clean, added another dollop of antiseptic and went back to work. "Some of these cuts need stitches, and you could have a concussion, internal bruising, broken ribs. I'm taking you to the clinic, and the sheriff should be told about this."

"He already knows," Billy said. Those were the first words he'd spoken, so soft she barely heard them.

Shannon heard her father's footsteps climb the porch steps. The kitchen door opened and closed. Her father came to an abrupt stop and gave Billy a steely-eyed stare. "Was Boyd Bannon behind this?"

"No," Billy said. "It was just a stupid fight outside the Dog and Bull."

"Daddy, I'm taking Billy to the clinic to get him checked out. Can you watch Rose?"

"Of course I will."

"Travis brought Billy back here," Shannon said. "Drove right up to the barn in a big fancy black pickup truck, bold as brass. He might return."

"He won't if he knows what's good for him," McTavish said.

Billy fumbled with his left hand to unbutton his shirt pocket. He pulled a folded envelope out and laid it on the table top. "Travis had nothing to do with what happened to me. He wanted me to give you this. Said it was important."

Shannon felt her entire being recoil from the envelope. She shook her head, holding the dishcloth in her hands over the basin and wringing the bloody water from it. "I don't want anything from Travis." She leaned toward Billy and dabbed at the cut on his temple. "This gash needs stitches."

"Tape will do," Billy said.

"*Stitches*. Daddy, I'll pick up something for supper at the big grocery store near the clinic and be back as soon as I can." Shannon carried the basin of bloody water to the sink and poured it down the drain. Her hands were trembling. The kitchen was like a scene out of a war movie, her father with his arm in the cast and sling, grim faced and sinister, and the battered and bloodied Billy looking like death warmed over.

"I'll take care of Grampy and Tess while you take Billy to the doctor, Momma," Rose said.

Shannon felt her eyes sting with tears. "I'm sure you will, Rose."

TWENTY-THREE STITCHES and multiple X-rays later, Shannon and Billy departed the clinic. Billy was bruised and battered but there were no internal injuries, broken bones or concussion. The doctor was stern. "Complete bed rest for at least a week."

"I'll see to it," Shannon assured him. She stopped at the big grocery store to fill the prescription for painkillers the doctor had written for Billy, and to pick up supper. But as they headed for home, Billy sitting silent in the passenger seat, she wondered how successful she'd be at keeping him off his feet.

All thoughts of taking Rose and heading to California had been dashed by this latest catastrophe. There were the mustangs to gentle, and with Henry Crow Dog gone and her father and Billy out of the picture, that task would now fall completely to her. Could she pull it off before the BLM picked the horses up? Could she hire someone to help? Who? Half the town of Bear Paw now hated the McTavish clan, and the other half…? Well, she could ask Ralph and Kitty Sayres if they knew of any potential recruits.

She glanced at Billy's profile as she hit cruising speed. "What happened, Billy?"

she asked. He'd been silent on the way to the clinic, not responding to several of her attempts to find out what had been behind the fight. She hoped he might be more talkative on the pain meds. "Who picked a fight with you?"

For a long moment she thought Billy was going to ignore her again, but he made a sound somewhere between a moan and a sigh and rubbed the back of his head with his hand. "I started it."

"*You?* Why? And what the hell were you doing at the Dog and Bull, today of all days? After that scene at the Grange Hall? Billy, why would you go there? That's just asking for trouble."

"Boyd Bannon wanted me to meet him there, said he needed me to deliver a message to McTavish."

"*Boyd Bannon's* behind this? I've known him and his family all my life. What was the message?"

"Boyd had nothing to do with the fight. He wanted to tell me that he wouldn't press charges against McTavish for pulling the met tower down on his land if your father signed the lease agreements with the wind company."

Shannon's laugh was abrupt and incredulous. "Daddy didn't pull that tower down. According to my father, it's been down for months. So if it wasn't Boyd, who were you fighting with in the parking lot?"

"Doesn't matter, Shannon. Doesn't matter how it started or what was behind it. Travis saw it. He broke it up."

"Travis?" Shannon's grip tightened on the wheel. "So that's why he brought you back to the ranch."

"I couldn't drive my truck. Someone gave it another flat tire while I was in the bar."

"Does that 'someone' have anything to do with you picking that fight?"

"There were three or four someones."

"And naturally you thought you could whip them all." Shannon blew out a frustrated breath. "I'm grateful he brought you back to the ranch, but Travis better not come back."

"He won't. That envelope he gave me has money for you and Rose."

"He thinks a little money can ease his conscience?"

"He told me he sold the house and some

other stuff. He said it was a lot of money, and he wanted you to have it because it was yours. He said he didn't want to make any more trouble for you."

Shannon drove in silence, thinking. She was glad her hands were wrapped around the steering wheel. "The last two years with Travis were awful," she finally said, speaking quietly in a voice that shook. "He wasn't just drinking. He was into drugs. I don't even know what kind. His mood swings were unpredictable. Rose was scared to death of him, and so was I."

"It's over now, Shannon. You don't have to live like that anymore."

"But he came here, don't you see? He followed us. He could've wired that money. He could have had his lawyer mail a bank check. He didn't have to come here himself. Daddy ran him off once. He knows he's not welcome, and he knows there's a restraining order against him." Shannon's heart was pounding. She was filled with a kind of paralyzing fear that Billy would never understand. "Where can we go where Travis won't find us?"

"It doesn't matter if he finds you here. Your

father and I will protect you—always. You don't have to be afraid anymore."

Despite the state he was in, Shannon believed him. And for the first time in years, she started to let her fear go.

CHAPTER ELEVEN

WYOMING WINDS HAD always blown through Shannon's world. They were as constant as the seasons. Strong and gusty in winter, steady and cool in summer. She'd watched eagles soar on their updrafts and ravens play and tumble on the turbulent currents.

Now, sitting here in this special place that she hadn't visited in over ten years, she pressed her back against the sun-warmed ledge, drew her knees up to her chest, looked out over the valley and let the clean, cool Wyoming wind fill her soul with its wild freedom.

She should be working with the mustangs. She should be checking on Billy in the cook's cabin. She should be with Rose and her father, helping clean up after supper.

Instead, she'd shouldered her guitar and hiked up onto the ridge behind the ranch house, to the ledge where the mountain lion used to bask in the afternoon sun, not far from the secret cave where ancient petroglyphs traced mysterious figures across smoke-darkened walls. This had always been her special place to hide out from the world.

She hadn't unpacked her guitar from the trunk of the car since she'd arrived back in Wyoming, and the case was covered with road dust. She opened it and her guitar lay there like King Arthur's sword embedded in stone. Would it still feel the same in her hands? Would she still be able to make her magic, write her songs and give music to the lyrics?

She drew a deep breath and closed the guitar case. She didn't dare touch it. Didn't dare try. Didn't want to know if everything inside of her had died the day she'd walked away from Travis.

Instead, she withdrew the envelope from her jacket pocket. Unfolded it slowly and forced herself to look at the handwriting on the face of it. The sun was sinking below Wolf Butte to the west. The sky was aglow with all the colors of a Rocky Mountain sunset and the scenery surrounding her was heart wrenchingly beautiful, but Shannon could only stare down at the envelope in her hand and wonder if she had the courage to open it.

Travis had played this game many times in the past two years. As soon as he realized he'd crossed the line, he'd beg, make promises that he was going to change, give up the drugs and the alcohol, go into rehab…and he would. He would. He'd be good for a while. Really good. But then, invariably, he'd slide back into the abyss. He'd go out drinking with "the boys" after a gig and their lives would become hellish again.

But that was then. Shannon realized things were different now. She and Travis were finally divorced. Their marriage was really and truly over. Travis had told Billy this envelope held money for her and Rose. A lot of money from the sale of their big, fancy mansion. But she wondered at his true motivation. Had it been so he could start over afresh, without all the memories of their life together surrounding him, same as she was doing? Or was this just another ploy to try to win her back?

The envelope scared her. Somewhere deep down inside of herself, she feared her own weakness. She feared he'd be able to talk her into coming back, because he'd done it before. He knew she was weak and played on her sympathies. He knew he held that awful power over her. But that was then. Things were different now.

She was stronger now.

Shannon blew out her breath, lifted her eyes to the horizon, the rugged wall of mountains to the west. The brilliant colors of the sunset. The sun was gone but the colors remained, bands of bright gold, violet and red. Darkness would come quickly. The days were getting shorter. Where would she be when the snows came? Here, in this valley, with her father and Rose and Billy? Where would she be?

An overhead movement caught her eye. A bald eagle soared above her, banking in big circles, descending gradually. The colors of sunset reflected brightly off its white head and tail as it banked to the east, then vanished until it circled again. Shannon felt her breath catch as the eagle dropped lower and lower over where she sat, mesmerized by a bird with a wingspread wider than a man was tall.

Was this eagle a sign from her mother? A spirit animal sent to give her the strength she needed to decide her own future? She watched until the majestic raptor abruptly broke from the downward spiral and winged purposefully toward Wolf Butte, then disappeared into the sunset.

Shannon watched until the eagle had vanished from her sight. A curious calm flooded through her and she drew a deep, steadying breath. She couldn't give up singing. She'd thought she could, but today at the Grange Hall, when she climbed up on the bandstand, she'd realized it was still a huge part of her life, a huge part of who she was.

She *had* to sing. She *needed* to be up on that stage in front of a big crowd of people. She wanted to feel the way she used to feel after a concert, with the crash of applause still ringing in her ears, the whistles still echoing, the music still lifting her onto a high so incredible nothing compared to it. She couldn't give that up. Why did she have to?

She could sing without Travis. They'd put on an incredible show together but she could fly solo, and so could he. She could do this. She could raise her daughter and live a grounded, normal life. She could write the songs and sing them. Maybe not on the scale she used to, but she could do it. She was going to make this work. She was never going back to Travis, no matter what he said or did. No matter what kind of power he had held over her in the past, things were different now. She was free of him. And it felt good. It felt great.

Shannon looked down at the envelope. Her hands were no longer trembling. She was no longer afraid. She was stronger now. She slid a fingernail under the flap and pried it open. Drew out the Wells Fargo bank check. Read her name on it, printed mechanically in official Wells Fargo ink. *Shannon McTavish*. Saw the amount in print, the words jumping out at her, then registered the endless number of zeroes. Stared as if the check was some sort of illusion that would vanish the moment she blinked. She drew a slow breath, in and out, but was still breathless.

She tucked the check back into the envelope, slid the envelope inside her jacket pocket and zipped it carefully shut. She'd told Billy that she didn't want anything from Travis, but she'd changed her mind. She'd worked hard for that money. This was Rose's legacy, too. She thought about her father's shoddy ranch house and how it hadn't been updated in decades. She thought about the worn-out furniture, the 1950s kitchen appliances, the roof that needed shingling, the fences that needed mending, the ranch road that needed grading, the farm machinery that needed replacing. She remembered her mother sticking wish lists on the refrigerator with magnets. Photos of beautiful kitchens. Renovated rooms. All the things she wanted but knew she'd never have.

With this money, Shannon had the power to change things now. She had the power to give Rose a good future, a good education. From this day on, even if she and Rose didn't stick around, life was going to be a little different on the McTavish ranch. She only wished her mother was still alive to see her dreams turned into reality.

Shannon opened her guitar case and lifted her guitar out of it for the first time since leaving Nashville. She tuned it, tucked into it, played a few chords. Then a few more. And before too long, the music and the words found each other, and sitting in her special place, she created a new song that seemed to come out of nowhere, as if by magic, the same way the eagle had. She hadn't lost her touch. Things were different now, but that much hadn't changed. Her life as a singer and songwriter wasn't over.

Relief and joy and power flooded through her. She looked out at the mountains, at the beauty that surrounded her, and realized that her life was really just beginning.

BILLY SAT OUTSIDE the cook's cabin on a big old stump he used for splitting firewood. Darkness was gathering in the hollows, the sky was a deepening violet color and the mustangs were pacing up in the corral, walking around the perimeter over and over, as if they could walk themselves back to their wild haunts. He heard a nighthawk and wished he had a shot of whiskey to dull the pain of breathing. Tomorrow would be better, but right now he felt just like he'd been kicked and beaten senseless. His own fault, too. He deserved every ounce of the pain.

He wondered where Shannon had gone when she walked up the ranch road, guitar case in hand, head ducked, deep in thought. Was she still planning on leaving?

He couldn't blame her. Bear Paw had been torn apart by the energy company. Friends and family members no longer spoke to each other over the contentious project. The town she remembered and had come back home to was no more. All that remained for her was an old, run-down ranch on the edge of nowhere, and a man from her past who'd stolen her dream of building a house beside the creek where she could raise her daughter.

Worst of all, he'd ruined her solo singing debut by dragging her away from the Grange Hall today. She was angry with him and had every right to be. She'd take Rose and go west, and maybe, just maybe, if she got lucky, she'd find what she was looking for.

When Shannon came back to Bear Paw, her unexpected arrival had been like a ray of bright sunshine on a cloudy day, a windfall that filled the hollow space inside him, a space so big that not even owning his own piece of land and building his house on it had filled it.

He'd had nothing to offer her in high school, and realistically, he had nothing to offer her now, but it didn't stop him from hoping she'd stick around. And it didn't stop him from imagining what it might be like if she one day shared the feelings he had for her. It didn't stop him from wondering what their kids might look like and thinking about how Rose would love having a brother or a sister to grow up with.

It didn't stop him from remembering that one sizzling kiss they'd shared in high school.

Footsteps came from behind the tractor shed and Shannon walked into view, still deep in thought, holding her guitar case in one hand and never glancing in his direction. She climbed the porch steps of the house and disappeared inside. The screen door banged shut behind her. He could hear father and daughter conversing in the kitchen. They talked for a few minutes. Was she telling McTavish she was leaving in the morning? That would wreck him. Shannon might never believe it, but McTavish enjoyed having his daughter and granddaughter around.

Billy sat until the voices in the kitchen were silent and the darkness had thickened until the horses in the corral were just moving shadows without form. He was about to push to his feet and go inside the cook's cabin when the screen door opened again, and Shannon descended the porch steps. She walked straight over to where he sat, carrying a bottle in one hand and two glasses in the other.

"Did you take that pain pill like the doctor ordered?" she asked him.

"Didn't need it," he replied.

"Figured you'd say as much. I bought a bottle of hooch in that big grocery store. Thought you might like a snort to take the edge off."

Shannon looked around, spotted another stump and handed him the bottle and glasses, struggling to drag the stump over next to his.

Billy glanced at the label on the bottle. Ten-year-old Talisker. No ordinary bottle of hooch. But then, Shannon was no ordinary gal. She retrieved the bottle, poured him a generous shot, did the same for herself, then nested the bottle between their two stumps and touched the rim of her glass to his. "Cheers," she said, and with a lift of her arm and toss of her head, she downed the entire shot in one big swallow.

For a moment she sat paralyzed as the whiskey burned its way into her stomach. Her eyes watered and she blinked back the tears. Then she gasped, coughed, picked up the bottle and poured herself another slug.

"I'm going to call Kitty Sayres tomorrow

and see if she knows anyone who'll help us with these mustangs," she said in a whiskey-seared voice, setting the bottle between them again.

Billy tasted the Talisker. It stung his bruised and broken mouth but was as smooth as honey going down. "No need. I'll be on my feet again by then."

"You'll do exactly what the doctor told you to do, Billy Mac. Bed rest for one week." She shook her head with a sigh. "Henry Crow Dog sure picked a mighty poor time to ride off into the sunset."

"Henry helped out while he was here. Earned his keep."

"Suddenly he's your favorite grandfather?"

"He helped with the horses. We wouldn't be nearly so far along if he hadn't pitched in. He has his faults and they're mighty big ones in my world, but nothing's black-and-white."

Shannon took a more cautious sip from her glass and leaned back against the cook's cabin. "I guess you're right about that," she said. "And he did give Daddy the photos that proved he didn't pull down Patriot Energy's tower."

Billy gave her a sharp look. "*What* photos? Who took them?"

"Every spring the tribe holds a ceremony up on Wolfe Butte to commemorate a battle that was fought there."

Billy nodded slowly. "When I was young I went to a couple of those ceremonies."

"This past spring, when they had their ceremony, they took photos."

"That's not something my people do."

"Well, somebody did. They're date-stamped this past May, and all three photos show the tower collapsed and crumpled in the background. The subject of the photos wasn't the tower, it was a pile of stones on top of the butte."

"I don't remember a cairn up there, but I haven't been up to the butte in over ten years. Maybe the elders built something to honor the fallen warriors. But why would Henry Crow Dog give those photos to McTavish?"

Shannon shook her head. "Daddy didn't say and I didn't ask, but I'm sure glad he did. They'll clear my father of any wrongdoing yesterday. So I guess I owe your favorite grandfather a big thank-you. And you're right, nothing's black-and-white, and none of us is perfect. I've screwed up so many times I've lost count. Made some really bad choices. But things are going to change now, things are going to be different."

Billy took another small swallow. The liquor stung his mouth again but the slow burn of whiskey in his belly eased the pain.

"I have to sing again," Shannon said. "Writing songs and singing them is who I am and I can't walk away from it. I thought I could but I can't, so I'm going to do things different this time. I called my agent. He says the band'll back me up on my next solo gig. That's nice of 'em. I love those guys. My agent wants to get me back to Nashville for my solo debut. Wants me to cut my first single and get back out there in front of God and country before everyone forgets who I am. He's right, but I'm going to do it my way."

"How so?"

Shannon sighed. "I haven't figured it out yet. But Rose doesn't want to go back to Nashville. She wants to stay here."

"What do *you* want?"

The silence stretched out. Shannon finished off her second shot of whiskey. Drew her breath in and held it for a long moment before releasing it with a rush.

"I want it all, Billy. Is that so bad? I want to sing. I want to write and record songs. I want my child to grow up on the ranch. I want a successful career and I want to raise my daughter right."

She turned her head to look at him. "I opened the envelope from Travis. I'm going to use the money to set up a trust fund for Rose and fix this place up the way my mother always wanted it to be. Daddy won't care, he'd be happy living in a tent or teepee, but it'll be my tribute to her. After that? I'll figure out my career and how I can make it work without moving back to Nashville.

"But right now I'm just going to sit here and drink whiskey." She snatched the bottle out of his hand and poured herself another shot. "It's not bad stuff if you can get past the awful taste and the terrible burn." She took a swallow of her third shot and extended the bottle to him. "So tell me, Billy, what do *you* want out of life?"

Billy took the offered bottle and rested it on his knee. He didn't have to consider his reply for long. "I used to think all I wanted to be was a rodeo star. The best bronc rider in the West. Back in high school I had it all figured out. I was on my way to the big time. I had all the pretty girls, too, except for one, but she was way out of my league. Shannon McTavish wasn't interested in some half-breed Indian off the rez."

"I told you that wasn't the reason," Shannon said. "You said it yourself, you had all the girls, and I didn't want to be your next conquest. But I enjoyed having you as my lab partner." She shot him a sidelong glance and a slow grin. "Chemistry class was something I really looked forward to."

Billy shook his head. "You broke my heart when you ran off with Travis. All my dreams were dashed, so I gave up on my rodeo career and joined the Marines."

"You can't lay that at my feet, Billy Mac," Shannon protested. "You walked your own path. We both did, and we both paid for it in our own ways."

"It was a rough one for both of us." Billy poured himself another shot of Talisker. "I came back a changed man, changed in all the wrong ways. Someone who could barely ride a horse or cope with day-to-day life. Hell, I wasn't even sure I wanted to be alive. Then I ran into your father when I was stocking shelves at Willard's, and we got to talking. He needed some money in a hurry to pay his back taxes, I needed a place to call my own. That was my first big break, buying that piece of land.

"But I tell you what, Shannon, working with these mustangs is what really turned me around. For the first time in forever, I wake up and I'm glad to be alive. And that got me to thinking about all the soldiers who get mustered out with their heads all messed up like mine was. I want to start a mustang camp for combat veterans. I'd teach them how to work with these wild horses and gentle them for the adoption program. With your father's help, I think we could turn a lot of veterans with PTSD around."

"That's a good idea," Shannon said, nodding thoughtfully. "I like it."

"And there's something else I really want." He looked her straight in the eye. "I want you to stay. I'm hoping you can find a way to have your career and raise your daughter right here and be happy. I'll sell you that piece of land back, if you want it. You can finish building the house however which way you want, or tear it down and start over. Rose can catch the bus right where you used to wait for it. You can have your dream back again, Shannon. It still belongs to you. You can go to Nashville and cut your records and put on your concerts—just so long as you always come back home. That's what I want."

She regarded him for a long, somber moment, then shook her head. "Look at you. You've just been beaten to within an inch of your life by a bunch of Bear Paw's rednecks, and you talk about me and Rose being happy here."

"Bear Paw's as good a place as any to raise your daughter, Shannon. It's the wind project that's torn the town apart."

"That's not going to change, not as long as my father refuses to sign the lease agreement. This town's a powder keg waiting to explode, all over a bunch of wind turbines. If this energy project generates money for the local landowners and the town, I don't see the harm in it, and I don't understand why my father's so dead set against it.

"These neighbors are his friends, or at least, they used to be. He needs the income from the wind leases, same as they do. He's living on canned beans and franks and driving the same old pickup truck he was driving ten years ago. I could make things easier for him here, but he wouldn't accept my money. He's too proud."

"McTavish is a man of strong principles. He knows the right and wrong of things."

Shannon gave a snort of laughter. "My father's a stubborn, opinionated old cowboy, but I'll say this much for him—he stands by his principles. Nobody'd ever be able to buy his vote, even if he was starving to death. And by the way, you're just like him."

"I take that as a compliment."

"Don't. I think you're both crazy."

"Crazy about you, that's for sure, even if you are way out of my league."

"I wish you'd quit saying that." Shannon rose to her feet. "Keep the bottle. It's time to tuck Rose into bed."

"You could come back afterward," Billy said. "Watch the stars shine down with me."

She smiled, a sweet curve of lips in the gathering twilight. "You really need to get some rest."

"What I really need to do is kiss you." The

words came easy, after a few shots of Talisker 10.

"That might hurt, cowboy."

"I'm tough."

For a moment he thought she was going to leave. Just walk away and leave him sitting there like a rejected fool. But she didn't. She bent over him, her fingertips touching his shoulders, her lips barely touching his. The gentlest of kisses, and far too brief. But he took her good-night kiss as a very good sign.

CHAPTER TWELVE

THE ONLY THING that could have possibly made waking up the following morning any worse would have been the sound of a rooster crowing before dawn. When Rose tugged on the coverlet to wake her, Shannon opened her eyes and closed them immediately with a groan. She hadn't had a hangover in ages. Whiskey was the devil's drink and she swore she'd never touch it again.

"Momma? Grampy sent me up to check on you. He says the coffee's ready and it's time to get up. Are you sick?"

"Go tell your grampy I'm taking a shower and I'll be down soon." After Rose left, Shannon forced herself out of bed. The hot shower brought her to life but her stomach was still roiling when she descended the stairs into the kitchen. Her father was washing up the breakfast dishes one-handed.

He didn't acknowledge her when she crept

down the stairs into the kitchen. His back was a silent rebuke. Her father was sixty years old, yet even with a broken arm he could still outwork her. His years as a stuntman had toughened him in ways she couldn't even begin to imagine. If he knew she was suffering from a hangover, he'd never let her live it down. Shannon murmured a good morning, quietly poured herself a mug of coffee, and carried it onto the porch, where Rose sat beside the sleeping Tess, brushing her.

"She likes it, Momma," Rose said. "She doesn't even open her eyes."

"Just be real gentle with the brush, honey. She's old."

Shannon sat on the edge of the porch, dangling her feet, nursing her pounding head and sipping hot coffee. No sign of life at the cook's cabin. Was Billy still asleep? He'd been brash last night, asking her for a kiss the way he had, his mouth all broken and bruised, his body hurting. Yet he'd wanted a kiss, and she'd given it. He'd said he wanted her to stay, enough to sell her back the place of her dreams, but could she live out on the edge of nowhere and make her career work? Should she return to Nashville, where she

knew the ropes and had all the right con-
nections? And what about Rose? And Billy?
And her father?

The screen door opened and her father
stepped onto the porch. He walked over to
where she sat and poured a splash of something into her mug of coffee. When she
glanced up, startled, he showed her the little bottle of pure vanilla extract. "There
hasn't been any liquor stashed around here
for years, but there might be enough alcohol
in the vanilla to help that hangover," he said,
then turned and went inside. Shannon stared
after him, speechless.

She heard the sound of hoofbeats and
looked toward the corrals. Dust rose into the
dawn, turning red in the sun's rays. The mustangs were moving as if someone had entered
the corral. Sure enough, she saw the shadowy
figure of a man through the dust. Billy, out
working with the horses when he was supposed to be in bed. Shannon sighed. He was
just as stubborn and pigheaded as her father.

"Stay with your grampy, Rose. I'm going
to help Billy with the mustangs," she said,
pushing to her feet and carrying her mug of
coffee and her aching head toward the cor-

rals. Billy had already saddled Sparky and Old Joe. He was in the corral, shaking out a loop while the mustangs circled warily. The rope snaked out and the mustang's quick duck proved futile. Within moments the gelding was tethered to the corral fence and Billy was coiling the rope to catch another horse. His movements were stiff but he was still a better hand with a rope than most cowboys.

"I don't suppose anything I say would make you get back in bed," Shannon commented.

He cast her a sidelong glance. "Oh, I don't know about that. I can think of a few things."

Shannon flushed. Was he grinning? Hard to say, as he was angled toward the horses. "You need to rest up and heal, Billy Mac."

"Talisker 10 doesn't seem to agree with you, Shannon McTavish."

"All I have is a hangover. You're the one with the broken bones."

"There's a lot riding on this government contract," Billy responded, watching the circling mustangs as he started building his loop. "If we make good with this batch of mustangs, they'll keep these corrals full all year round. Figured we could take a little ride with a couple of them before settling down for some round pen work."

"I'm sure a little ride would be just the ticket for your battered body."

"Old Joe's a smooth-gaited horse."

"Old Joe's so old he's apt to drop dead on you and crush all your bones," Shannon replied.

"You want to work with Khola today?" Billy asked, ignoring her comment as he built the loop and studied the milling horses. "He'll be the toughest to gentle, but Khola's the best of the bunch. Bet you could race him at the fair this fall. There's a big purse for the winner. He's little, but he's fast. Never saw any horse burn trail like he did the other day." Billy dabbed the rope over Khola's head as neatly as if he'd done it a thousand times, which he probably had. He patiently persuaded the reluctant bay to step up to the corral fence.

Shannon held her hand between the rails so Khola could smell her. "That race is suicidal and Khola's being shipped out for adoption with the rest of the bunch." She sighed. "Sad, isn't it? All he wants to do is go home."

"Being adopted is better than getting shipped

to France and served up in a fancy restaurant." Billy handed Shannon a dandy brush. "He could stand a good grooming."

Shannon opened her mouth to say she needed more time for the caffeine to kick in, but she shut it again and climbed through the fence rails. Khola shied away from her when she reached her hand toward him, backing away until the snub line brought him up short.

She spoke to him until his ears came forward and some of the fear left his eyes. It might have been ten years since she'd been surrounded by horses, but Shannon hadn't forgotten. She moved slowly, quietly, talking all the while, and within minutes Khola had let her slide her hand up his forehead and rub between his eyes.

"What a good horse you are," she crooned, and when she started brushing his neck, he stood taut and trembling, but gradually began to relax. With the dried mud brushed off his coat and his long, thick mane painstakingly untangled, the young bay mustang had begun to gleam like a polished gemstone.

"You're a handsome boy, Khola," she praised him. "We'll take another ride this morning and this time maybe we won't go for a swim."

Billy was working on grooming the other mustang he'd roped while the four remaining horses watched cautiously. McTavish came out of the ranch house and walked with Rose up to the corral.

"We're going to walk these two mustangs around before breakfast," Billy said.

McTavish nodded. "Me 'n' Rose'll hold the fort."

"We'll take care of everything, won't we, Grampy?" Rose said, reaching for her grand-father's hand, and McTavish took it.

THE WEEK PASSED in a blur of hard work for Shannon, rising at dawn to a hurried break-fast, meeting Billy out at the corrals before breakfast and working with the mustangs all day while McTavish and Rose held the fort. Shannon rediscovered muscles she'd forgot-ten she had, and at the end of the day, dust covered and sweaty, she cooked supper as best she could, but nobody complained about the fare.

Sometimes, as she stood over the hot stove stirring a pot of beans or frying up burgers, she'd have a flashback to her big gleaming stainless steel and granite air-conditioned Nashville kitchen. Of waltzing in to pour herself a glass of wine and ask the chef when dinner would be served before heading back to the studio.

As she stood in her father's sweltering kitchen, dressed in faded blue jeans and a T-shirt, hair pulled into a ponytail, up to her elbows in dishwater, she'd flex her shoulders to ease the ache and bite back a laugh at how much her life had changed in the space of just a few short weeks.

As the heat of late August intensified, it became the routine to take Rose down to the creek after supper for a cooling dip in the Bear Paw. Sometimes Billy would head off to his home site to spend a few hours working there, or he'd go help Willard unload deliveries and stock shelves at the store to make some extra money.

But he always returned before dark to sit outside the cook's cabin and watch the last colors of sunset stain the big Wyoming sky. She'd join him there, and they'd sit side by side sharing cold beers and making occasional small talk about how the mustangs were coming along. Once or twice Shannon had brought along magazines to show him pictures of kitchen and renovation ideas for the ranch house, hoping for more feedback than her father provided, but mostly they just sat in silence, content to share each other's company.

On Friday evening, Shannon had just put Rose to bed and gone outside to watch the sunset with Billy when the sheriff drove up. He didn't spot Billy and Shannon sitting outside the cook's cabin because he was too focused on climbing the porch steps to rap on the kitchen door. Shannon rose to her feet, and without a word to Billy, crossed the yard and climbed the porch steps just as her father appeared. Before the sheriff could state the reason for his visit, Shannon spoke.

"Hello, sheriff. Did you come here to tell us who vandalized Billy Mac's truck?" she asked point-blank.

The sheriff's eyes flicked over her briefly, then he turned his attention to McTavish. "Ben McTavish," he began. "Boyd Bannon and Patriot Energy have filed trespassing and criminal mischief charges against you for pulling down the met tower on Wolf Butte.

Because that tower was valued at more than a thousand dollars, this could be a potential felony charge, with a potential sentence of ten years in prison and ten thousand dollars in fines, but Patriot Energy is going easy on you. I'm here to serve the papers."

He stated this in a hard, flat tone of voice, pulling a sheaf of papers from his jacket pocket and extending it toward McTavish.

Shannon intercepted the delivery by stepping between them and squaring off with the sheriff. "My father had nothing to do with that tower on Wolf Butte being torn down," she said. "Didn't he already tell you that? Daddy, show the sheriff the photos. They'll prove you weren't on Boyd's land last Saturday."

"I don't believe I will," McTavish said quietly. "Let them file their charges against me. I'll see them in court."

"Daddy. *Please*. Just show the sheriff the photos. There's no need to let this go any further."

"Keep out of this, Shannon." Her father's voice cut like a whip. Shannon closed her mouth and stepped aside. The sheriff extended the papers again, and McTavish accepted them. The two men nodded curtly to each other, then the sheriff turned and descended the porch steps.

"Why, Daddy?" Shannon asked, rounding on her father. "Why make things worse than they already are?"

"Boyd's the one who's making things worse," her father responded, tossing the papers on the kitchen table. "If he thinks this'll bring me to my knees and force me to sign the lease agreement, he's dead wrong."

"Boyd used to be your friend," Shannon said, a flush of anger warming her blood. "You'd always help each other out during hard times. When Mom was sick and they had that collection jar at Willard's to help us with her medical expenses, it was Boyd who stuck a check in there for a thousand bucks. A thousand bucks! Remember, Daddy? He and his entire family came to the funeral, and they helped pay for it, too. The whole town did. *Remember?*"

"Things've changed around here. Boyd's turned against me. He's all about the money now. This wind project's corrupted him and half the town."

"Maybe so, Daddy, but it's changed you,

too. You used to care about your neighbors, and now you're looking forward to dragging them into court."

"Boyd's the one that's filed the trespassing charges against me."

"You could stop this foolishness by showing the sheriff those photos that prove your innocence!"

"The only person I have to prove my innocence to is the judge."

Shannon wanted to vent her anger and shout her way past her father's bullheaded obstinance, but Rose was asleep upstairs, so instead she stormed down the porch steps and ran to the cook's cabin.

Billy sat in calm silence exactly as she'd left him. She plopped into her seat with an angry huff, staring straight ahead, heart hammering. "The sheriff just served my father with legal papers charging him with criminal property damage for tearing down Patriot Energy's tower, and he wouldn't even show the sheriff the photos that Henry gave him. He could get ten years in prison for this if convicted!"

"They can't convict him for something he didn't do," Billy reassured her. "They have no proof that anyone tore that met tower down. The wind could've blown it down, that's happened more than once. As long as he has those photos, and as long as Henry backs him up, he'll be fine. Don't worry about it. McTavish's dander is up, that's all. They're trying to force his hand so he'll sign the lease. He wants to teach them a lesson."

"It's a foolish lesson. I'll go talk to Boyd myself first thing tomorrow and tell him the truth of it before they decide to duel it out with pistols."

"Let them resolve this matter between themselves," Billy advised.

"The way you worked it out with the vandals who slashed your tires? No, I'll go over to Boyd's and still be back in plenty of time to ride Khola. Tomorrow's the big day—I'm going to give him his first ride, come hell or high water."

Billy gave her a cautious look. "You really believe he's ready?"

"Yep, I do," Shannon replied with a whole lot more conviction than she felt.

HER FATHER WAS already up with coffee made the next morning, and Shannon drank her first mug contemplating the pastel colors of the quiet dawn from the porch steps. Because it was Saturday, she fixed a real breakfast for them. Scrambled eggs and bacon, toast and juice. Breakfast was the one meal she could cook half-decently.

"I'm going into town to run a few errands," she commented when her father, Billy and Rose were seated at the table. "I'll be back for lunch. Anyone need anything?"

Billy gave her The Look, which silently cautioned, "Don't meddle with Boyd Bannon." She ignored it. Rose brightened and sat up straight in her chair.

"Can I go, too, Momma?"

"Of course you can. I'll buy you an ice cream at Willard's."

"Even if it's still morning?"

"Even if," Shannon promised.

It wasn't until they were on the road to town that Shannon thought about how she'd handle having Rose along if her conversation with Boyd became confrontational, but she doubted it would. Boyd Bannon was an old family friend. She'd clear up this foolish misunderstanding about the met tower and everything would be okay.

Hair in a ponytail, wearing jeans, a Hard Rock Cafe T-shirt and low-heeled riding boots, she drove the ten twisting miles to Boyd Bannon's place.

Shannon was taken aback by how run-down Boyd's place looked when she pulled in to the yard. The Bannon ranch house used to strike her as being quite grand—a two-story sprawling structure with three matching dormers across the front and a porch with fancy newel posts.

Now it looked as weary and unkempt as her father's place. There were cattle, she'd spotted them on the drive in, but not many. And not a single horse. The haying equipment parked out by the barns was almost as old as her father's. A white pickup truck and a small blue sedan were parked in the shade of a big cottonwood to one side of the house. A planter sat on the porch blooming with geraniums and petunias.

"Come on, Rose," Shannon said, taking her daughter's hand to give herself the courage to climb the porch steps, knock on the door and talk to the most influential rancher in Bear Paw.

When the door swung inward, Shannon

instantly recognized the woman who stood before her. Ten years had changed her, but not that much. She was a little thinner, had a little more gray hair, but she was still the attractive, capable woman who had raised five kids and worked as hard as her husband to keep their ranch afloat while always being what the cowboys would refer to as "a real lady."

"Hello, Mrs. Bannon," she said.

"Shannon!" Eva Bannon's expression was a mixture of glad surprise and apprehension. "Boyd's not home. He left for town about half an hour ago. You must've just missed him on the road in."

"That's okay. I wanted to come by to say hello and introduce you to my daughter, Rose," Shannon said with a genuine smile. "Rose, this is Mrs. Bannon. She used to baby-sit me when I was your age. She and my momma were good friends, and Mrs. Bannon made the best gingersnap cookies in the whole wide world."

"Hello, Rose," Mrs. Bannon said, shaking the little girl's hand. She opened the door wide. "Come inside. I have some of those very same gingersnaps in my cookie jar and a pitcher of homemade lemonade in the ice box. I heard you were in town again," she said to Shannon. "Your father must be glad."

"Well, that's up for debate," Shannon laughed as Mrs. Bannon showed them into the tidy kitchen, about twenty years more modern than her father's, sat them at the table, and poured tall glasses of real home-made lemonade and offered a plate of her legendary gingersnaps. The lemonade had just the right tartness and the gingersnaps made Shannon close her eyes with a rapturous sigh. "Just like I remember," she said. "Try a cookie, Rose."

"She's a lovely child."

"I've been blessed," Shannon said, watching Rose nibble a cookie. "Good?"

Rose nodded. "Good, Momma. Better than yours."

Small talk ensued and the visit became almost a normal social call, but when Rose left the table to pursue a calico cat that strutted through the kitchen, Mrs. Bannon reached out and took Shannon's hand in her own. "I'm sorry about what's happened."

"Me, too. I was hoping to talk to Mr. Bannon about it. My father didn't do anything to that met tower up on Wolf Butte. He has photos that prove the tower was already down back in May, but he's so stubborn headed he wouldn't show them to the sheriff last night."

Eva shook her head. "It's hard times here, Shannon. Cattle prices are down and grain prices are sky-high because of government ethanol mandates. That's driven the price of everything else through the roof. We're hanging on by our fingernails trying to put the kids through school and hold on to the ranch.

"When this wind company came to town and talked about the money and jobs, we believed it was our saving grace. They met with all the big landowners, your father included. Boyd signed the lease. He doesn't give a hoot about renewable energy, but he'd do anything to keep this ranch afloat and to keep our youngest daughter, Miranda, in college. She's a sophomore at Wyoming State, majoring in microbiology.

"She's smart, and she won a generous scholarship that helped her with the first year. But if we don't get that turbine money, she'll have to drop out. All she ever wanted was to be a pediatrician and work with young kids. Boyd and I did all we could to help her. We'd do anything to help our kids."

"So would I," Shannon said softly, gazing to where Rose sat cross-legged in the next room, playing with the cat. The soft rhythmic tick of the Regulator clock on the kitchen wall filled a silence that the two women shared, each deep in her own thoughts.

"Boyd's not a bad man, Shannon," Eva continued. "He's just desperate. We need the money from those leases. I understand how your father feels about the wind turbines being built on Wolf Butte. Your mother loved that butte. That's why your father spread her ashes there."

Shannon felt a jolt of shock. *"What?"*

"He asked Boyd if he could, and of course Boyd agreed. This was four or five years ago. I thought you knew."

Shannon shook her head. "When I left, her ashes were still in his bedroom."

Eva nodded. "She was the love of his life."

"Yes, she was," Shannon said softly, remembering all the good times, how devoted her parents were to each other and how they'd surrounded her with love like a warm blanket. "He never recovered from losing her." She suddenly understood the reason for the cairn of stones that had been the focal point in the three photos that Henry had given her father. That shrine had been built in honor of her mother.

"My mother loved those eagles. The turbines will kill the eagles and destroy their habitat. Patriot wants to build the turbines right along Wolf Butte, the very same place my father spread her ashes. I think I finally understand why he's so dead set against this project."

She spoke slowly, thoughtfully, gazing at Eva Bannon but seeing the lone eagle that had circled above her at sunset the evening she'd opened Travis Roy's check. "There's no way I'm going to change his mind about this wind project."

"I know," Eva said. "They used to be best friends, Boyd and your father. That's the worst tragedy of all. This energy project has torn Bear Paw apart, and it'll never be the same place it was. Friends and family see each other in town and cross the street to avoid having to speak to each other. What happened to you last Saturday at the wind company's barbecue was unforgivable."

She sat in silence for a moment, then squared her shoulders. "Boyd's at Patriot

Energy's office this morning, if you want to talk to him about the photos. He had a meeting with Tom Carroll and one of the project's lawyers. Their office is on Main Street where Eddie Polk's barbershop used to be. There's a flag in the window. Very patriotic of them." She met Shannon's surprised look with a thin smile. "I did a little research of my own when Patriot Energy first came to town. Boyd's no fool. He knows this project will scar the land he loves forever and take away his control of it. But we need the money, Shannon. That's the bottom line. It's all about the money."

"I understand, and I appreciate your hospitality, Eva, and everything you've done for my family over the years," Shannon said, rising to her feet. "You were as good a friend to my mother as Boyd was to my father. I'm sorry things have turned so bad between them."

Eva stood. "They say time heals all wounds, and I hope that's true, for all our sakes. It was good to see you, Shannon. We're so proud of you and all you've accomplished."

Shannon impulsively hugged the strong, slender woman, eyes stinging with tears. "Thank you," she whispered past the painful cramp in her throat, and minutes later she was buckling her daughter into the back seat of the car and heading for Bear Paw. The fences may never be mended between her father and the Bannons, but she had to try.

CHAPTER THIRTEEN

BILLY MAC SPENT the better part of the morning working with the mustangs while McTavish watched. The only horse he avoided was Khola. The little bay warily watched everything Billy did with the other mustangs. When McTavish asked him why he kept passing Khola by, Billy explained as best he could.

"Shannon's taken with that horse," he said. "She's worked real hard with him, and he's a real hard horse to work with. Wilder than the rest, skittish and jumpy. He's finally to the point where he trusts her, and she got the saddle on him yesterday without too much fuss. She wants to be the first one ride him."

"That's foolish talk," McTavish said bluntly. "You climb aboard that horse before she gets back. Take the edge off him so's she doesn't go and get herself killed trying to prove she's as good as her mother was. Shannon might be a great country-and-western singer, but she's no horse whisperer."

"Don't sell her short. She's done a great job with these horses. She's worked hard ever since she got home."

McTavish tossed a grass stem into the round pen. "I know it."

"We're lucky she's stuck around."

"I know that, too." Voice lower now, edges softened by emotions McTavish struggled to keep hidden.

"She'll skin me alive if she finds out I rode her horse," Billy said. "That's no joke."

McTavish plucked another stem of tall grass with his good hand and gestured with it to make his point. "She'll get over a big mad, but broken bones take a long time to heal. Besides, that horse belongs to the BLM and they'll be picking him and all the others up pretty quick."

"Wouldn't hurt to keep a few younger horses around the place," Billy suggested.

"That's foolish talk, too. Hay burners is all those useless critters are. Two old hay burners is enough."

"Khola's fast. Fastest horse I've seen, and I've seen a few. He could win that race at the fall fair and that prize money would keep us in beans and franks all winter long. It's about time a McTavish won that race again."

McTavish laughed. "You're dreaming now, son. But get that saddle onto him and show me what he can do. Then we'll talk."

THE DRIVE INTO town took half an hour, mostly because Shannon drove the dirt roads slowly, practicing what she'd say to Boyd Bannon.

"Momma, why are you talking to yourself?" Rose interrupted from the back seat.

Shannon blew out her breath. "Because I'm rehearsing what I'm going to say to a man who's very mad at us."

"Why's he mad, Momma?"

"Because your grampy's standing in the way of something he really wants. Something he really needs."

"Why's Grampy being so mean to him?"

"He's not, sweetie, not really. Your grampy's just standing up for something he believes in, but Mr. Bannon doesn't believe in the same thing."

"You mean, like God?"

"Sort of. Money can have that same effect on people."

"We have to talk to Grampy and make him stop being mean."

"Well, the thing is, Mr. Bannon's being mean to your grampy, too."

"Then they both have to stop being mean to each other."

"You're right, Rose." Shannon glanced in the rearview mirror and smiled at her child, a child who believed all of life's problems could be solved by simply stating the obvious solutions. "That's exactly what I'm going to tell them."

PATRIOT ENERGY'S OFFICE was housed in a narrow brick building tucked between the hardware store and the gas station. The window fronting Main Street needed washing, and the large flag that had been tacked over it, just beneath the Patriot Energy sign, had come unfastened at one upper corner.

Shannon took Rose's hand in hers and paused outside the door for a brief moment to collect her thoughts, then opened the door and stepped inside, pausing while her eyes adjusted to the dim interior. There were no staff present in the front office. A large desk dominated the room, with a big office chair behind it and several metal folding chairs scattered in front of it. Four easels were set up on the right-hand side of the room, displaying large land maps liberally studded with small red pins.

Shannon stepped closer to study the maps, searching for her father's land. She was surprised to see that even though he wasn't a participating landowner, his property was covered with red pins. Roads had been drawn on the map, running along the ridgelines and connecting the red pins to each other. She counted the pins on her father's land. "Fifteen red pins, five blue," she murmured aloud. She followed the line of red pins onto Boyd Bannon's land and counted twenty more, five of them on Wolf Butte. The pins weren't all on ridgelines, some were in the valley, too. Between all four land maps, there were scores of little red pins signifying the one hundred and seventy-five wind turbines proposed by Patriot Energy.

"Wow," she breathed, trying to picture the iconic beauty of their valley and mountains transformed into an industrialized landscape of transmission lines and wind turbines, the night sky studded with blinking red lights atop towers as high as skyscrapers.

The door in the back of the office opened suddenly, startling her. Tom Carroll stepped into the room, followed by Boyd Bannon. Both men halted abruptly, surprised to see her. Carroll was the first to recover. He crossed the room and stuck out his hand. "Shannon. I was hoping you'd stop by. We need to talk."

"Yes, we do," Shannon agreed, cooly ignoring his outstretched hand.

Carroll dropped his hand and flushed. "I'm sorry about what happened at the Grange on Saturday, and I'm sorry about the charges we were forced to file against your father."

Shannon looked over Carroll's shoulder. "Mr. Bannon, I just came from a visit with your wife. She helped me to understand why my father was so dead set against this wind project. My mother's love for that place on Wolf Butte and for the eagles she rehabilitated… She told me you allowed my father to spread her ashes there. That was kind of you, and I'm grateful."

"Your gratitude doesn't change anything," Bannon said, stepping around Carroll with his tough-man swagger. He *was* tough, too.

He was as tough as her father, and Shannon knew it. "Your father trespassed on my land and tore down a met tower. Those charges will stick."

"That's why I'm here. We have proof that the tower was already down in May. Date-stamped photos."

Bannon barked a harsh laugh. "No judge and jury would ever believe those photos were real. He's bluffing, and I'm calling his bluff. You can call it blackmail if you want, but if he doesn't sign on with this wind energy project, we're not dropping those charges. I can guarantee it."

Shannon gripped Rose's hand so tightly that her daughter made a noise of protest. She relaxed her grip, but her nerves were drawn taut. "Mr. Bannon, I understand why you need the lease money, but my father didn't tear down that tower and there's a whole tribe of Shoshone who'll testify to that in a court of law."

"That's a bunch of cow manure," Bannon said. "Your father's friends with the people of the tribe. They'd say anything for him."

Shannon fought to keep her cool. "The Shoshone hold a spiritual gathering up on

Wolf Butte every May to commemorate a historic battle they fought there against the Crow. This past May one of them took photos of a shrine built of stones to honor my mother. They called her Eagle Woman. *Biagwei'yaa Wa'ipi.* They took the photos to show my father how they had honored her by building the shrine. In the photos, you can see the tower had already collapsed."

Boyd Bannon's face darkened. "One way or the other, this wind project's being built, and the sooner your father learns to live with that, the better off we'll all be."

SHANNON WAS STILL shaking with anger when she stopped at Willard's for Rose's ice cream and a few groceries. Rose made a beeline for the ice cream freezer, standing in rapturous admiration of the frozen treats tucked inside the glass-topped chest. It would take her a few minutes to make her choice, giving Shannon time to shop. She fumbled in her jeans pocket for the list she'd scrawled at the breakfast table, but her stomach was churning and the last thing she felt like doing was shopping for groceries.

She pushed the little cart up and down the

narrow aisles, wondering who the best lawyer in the area was. She could ask Willard. He'd know. She'd feel him out about the wind project, too. She wondered which side of the fence he was on, since he wasn't one of the big landowners who stood to gain annual lease payments from the wind company.

But when she asked the cashier at the checkout counter if Willard was around, the teenage girl with a freckled face and friendly smile that showcased a mouthful of braces shook her head. "Gone fishin'."

Shannon placed the groceries on the counter. "Come on, Rose, hurry up and choose your ice cream. This train's about to leave the station."

There was a coffee can on the counter, a hand-lettered sign taped around it asking for donations for the Hewin family, who'd lost their entire hay crop in a barn fire. Shannon remembered when a similar can had been on this counter to raise donations toward her mother's medical bills. She fished through her purse and stuffed three twenties into the can. "When was the fire?" she asked the girl.

"Two nights ago. They lost their hay barn

and their chicken house, but nobody was hurt. Just the chickens."

"Did they have insurance?"

A head shake. "Couldn't afford it. There's a spaghetti supper at the Grange Hall tonight to raise money. Starts at five, one seating. Ten bucks a head. I helped my mother make the spaghetti sauce last night," she added proudly.

"We'll be there. Thank you." Shannon paid for her groceries and Rose's ice cream bar, corralled her daughter and carried her bags out to the car.

Her morning mission hadn't taken nearly as long as she'd anticipated. There'd be plenty of time to feed everyone lunch and spend the afternoon working with Khola.

It was the only thing she could think of that would take her mind off the mess her family and this town was in.

BILLY QUICKLY REALIZED he'd made a big mistake. Khola had been born in the high desert of Nevada and knew how to run. And run he did, hoofbeats drumming like machine-gun fire on the hard dry soil, kicking up a trail of dust that rose into the hot summer air. Billy had no control over the mustang whatsoever and could only hope the bay ran out of steam before he reached the back fence line. That fence should turn the bay gelding and keep him from running right over the top of the Rocky Mountains.

Knowing Shannon was going to attempt to ride the mustang that afternoon, he'd decided McTavish was right, and it was a good idea to take the edge off the horse before she returned. But he hadn't expected the explosion of rebellious power underneath him the moment McTavish opened the corral gate. Three tremendous stiff-legged leaps were followed by a pitching fit that nearly sent Billy to the moon several times before morphing into a series of jackrabbit jumps. He heard McTavish let out a cowboy whoop behind him as the mustang pinned his ears back, flattened out and hit top speed. Within moments they'd left the ranch buildings far behind.

After several miles at a full gallop, the mustang showed no signs of tiring. He was sure-footed, even at a dead run, a tribute to his wild upbringing. Billy got swept up in the exhilaration of the ride, temporarily forgetting all about the fact that Shannon would probably be headed back home soon. Forgetting all about how mad she'd be if she found out he'd ridden her horse. Forgetting all about how long it took a sweaty horse to cool down and how he'd never be able to hide the evidence of his betrayal.

As Khola approached the rear fence line, he veered gradually in response to Billy's shift of weight and subtle pressure on the rein. His speed slowed as Billy rode him in a big arc that would head them back toward the ranch. The mustang was snorting now at every stride, big powerful snorts as his lungs worked like bellows after his blistering run.

Billy brought his speed down, little by little, to a canter, then a trot and finally a fast walk. Head tossing, neck arched, sidestepping in impatience, the horse behaved as if he was just getting ready to start a race, not heading for the winner's circle. Billy was filled with giddiness from the wild ride, and he threw his head back and let out a heartfelt cowboy yell to match McTavish's. The mustang sprang forward and Billy reined him in, grinning broadly.

"Easy, Khola. You've run your race. We'll stop at the creek when we get to it and you can splash your heart out. You've earned a swim." He stroked the lathered shoulder as the gelding jogged along, chin tucked to his chest, still trying to work the bit out of his mouth.

When they reached the Bear Paw and were almost within sight of the ranch buildings, Billy guided him down to the edge of the creek. Khola plunged into the water without hesitation, wading out belly deep, dipping his muzzle into the swift, clear water for a brief drink. "Not too much, you're all hotted up," Billy cautioned.

The mustang's head shot up, ears pricked toward the ranch road, and Billy saw the approaching plume of dust that signaled Shannon's return. "Well," he said with resignation, "I guess we're about to find out how mad a McTavish woman can get."

Shannon's car came into sight. They spotted each other at the same moment. The car braked to an abrupt stop. Shannon emerged from the vehicle, walked around the front of it and stood for a moment, staring as if she couldn't believe what she was seeing, because she probably couldn't. Her chin came up, her hands went to her hips and even from nearly sixty feet he could see the sparks flying from her Scots/Irish eyes.

"Billy Mac! *What the hell are you doing on my horse?*"

SHANNON WAS SPITTING MAD. She marched to the edge of the creek and confronted man and horse. "You have no right whatsoever to be sitting on the back of that mustang!" she challenged him. "You knew I was going to ride Khola today. How could you do this to me? I trusted you!"

Billy pulled his hat brim lower over his eyes until all she could see of him were the rugged planes of his jaw, which were covered with dust and stubble. She took two steps into the creek and, standing knee-deep in the cold water, reached for Khola's reins. "I'll never forgive you for this. *Never!* Get off!"

"Shannon…"

"Don't *Shannon* me!" she snapped. "Take Rose back to the ranch and watch her, you owe me that much. I've had a terrible morning and you've just ruined the rest of my day. Get off my horse. I'm taking Khola for a ride."

Billy moved the mustang a little closer to

shore before stepping out of the saddle into water that was knee-deep. "You might want to give him a little time to settle down," he cautioned, handing her the reins. "Yourself, too."

Khola jerked his head up, unsettled by Shannon's turbulent emotions, but she was too angry to heed Billy's words or the horse's body language.

"You better let me walk him out of the water for you," Billy said.

"The last thing I need is your help," Shannon snapped. She waded deeper into the creek, pulled Khola's head toward her as she put her left foot into the stirrup and took a firm grip on the saddle horn. The current was swift, tugging hard at her lower leg. Just as she was making her swing into the saddle, Khola shied violently out from beneath her.

There was a moment of shocked disbelief as she hung in midair, then she hit the water with an undignified squawk and went completely under. She struggled to her feet to see Billy lunge for, and miss, the trailing rein as Khola surged out of the creek in a powerful spray of water and take off up the bank, bound once again for the high desert of Nevada.

Shannon pushed wet hair out of her eyes and staggered a few steps closer to shore, fending off Billy's attempts to help her.

"Don't you touch me, don't you *dare* touch me, Billy Mac, do you hear me? I hate you!" she raged. "You rode my horse, and now look what you've done. All those hours of work I put into him, down the drain! None of this would've happened if you'd just left him alone!"

Billy said nothing, just stood on the bank, watching her sputter with anger as she dripped water, which made her even angrier. "Don't just stand there, go find him!" Tears mixed with water on her face and Shannon didn't want Billy to know that she was crying. She never cried and was only crying now because she was spitting mad.

She brushed past him and started for the car, squelching cold water out of her boots at every step. When she slid behind the wheel and slammed her car door, Billy was still standing in the same spot on the edge of the creek, standing in that handsome cowboy slouch she remembered from high school, thumbs hooked in his belt, hat brim pulled over his eyes. He looked appealing as hell, which made her madder than ever.

"Curse that man!" she burst out. She'd thought she could trust Billy, thought he trusted and respected her. Had she been wrong?

SHANNON WAS MAKING a stack of ham-and-cheese sandwiches when her father drove up to the ranch house. Billy wasn't with him, so she figured they'd found the runaway horse and Billy had somehow managed to catch him. She hoped he had a long, hot walk back to the ranch. She hoped he got blisters on his feet. It gave her pleasure to think of him struggling to lead that spirited and rebellious mustang for several miles.

Moments later her father came onto the porch, removed his hat, dusted it against his pants leg, paused a little longer than he normally did, then came into the kitchen. "We found him, he was fine, pacing along the fence line. Didn't even break a bridle rein."

"Billy's leading him home?"

"Nope, riding him. Should be here pretty quick, they were moving right along."

Shannon had changed out of her wet

clothes but her hair was still damp, which was all that kept her from smoking with anger as she cut the sandwiches in half, stacked them on a platter and set it on the kitchen table with a solid thump that toppled several sandwiches onto the table. She left them lying there. "He had no right to ride that horse," she fumed, returning to the kitchen counter to mix up the iced tea. "No right!"

"He was following orders," McTavish said curtly, washing up at the kitchen sink. "I *ordered* him to take the kinks out of that horse before you got back, so's you didn't break your neck."

Shannon's spine stiffened as she squared off with her father. "You told him to ride Khola, fully aware of how hard I'd worked with that horse, how much time I'd put into him, how much I wanted to be the first person to ride him? You knew how much it meant to me, and you *ordered* Billy to ride him?"

McTavish reached for a towel. "I ordered him," he said. "And as long as Billy Mac works for me, he follows my orders."

Father and daughter locked eyes. Shannon had always lost these battles with her father, but her blood was hot. "You had no right to do that."

"I had every right. This is *my* ranch. Those were horses *I* was contracted to gentle for the BLM adoption program, and you're my daughter. My only child. I lost your mother. I'm sure as hell not losing you, too. Not to a two-hundred-dollar mustang." He tossed the towel on the kitchen counter. "If you don't like that, too bad, but I'm not backing down. You haven't ridden a horse in ten years. You picked the snuffiest bronc in that bunch to try and gentle, and you're not up to it. Not yet, and maybe not ever."

Shannon carried the pitcher of iced tea to the table and set it down hard enough to cause it to splash over onto the toppled sandwiches. She whirled to face her father. "Have I ever done *anything* that pleased you? Have I ever *once* measured up to the legendary McTavish clan? The horse whisperers, the stunt riders and movie doubles, the mountain men and the railroad tycoons? And oh, by the way, were you ever planning to tell me where you scattered Mom's ashes? Did I really have to find that information out from the *Bannons*? I loved her, too, Daddy, or have you forgotten that?"

Shannon's voice was choked with emotion and the tension that filled the kitchen was broken by Rose, who came clattering down the kitchen stairs. "Billy's home!" she said, and raced out the door. Tess struggled up from her bed, stiff with arthritis, and followed after her. Shannon stalked out of the kitchen, following daughter and dog to the corral where Billy was unsaddling Khola. There was just enough time and distance to let most of the anger drain from her.

"You stay out of the corral, Rose," Shannon cautioned her daughter before ducking between the rails and walking up to the bay mustang. She let him smell her, then rubbed her hand over his shoulder and scratched his withers until he relaxed and allowed her to slide her hand up, smooth his long forelock over to one side of his face and rub between his eyes. "I'm sorry, handsome boy," she murmured, ignoring Billy, who was rubbing the sweaty horse down with a rough towel.

"He's a helluva lot more than just handsome, Shannon," Billy said, as if they hadn't just had an explosive encounter. "This horse can really run. Only problem is, all he wants to do is run clear to Nevada."

Shannon gazed into the mustang's dark, intelligent eyes. "Be careful what you wish for," she murmured. "All I wanted to do was get back home when my world fell apart, and look where it got me." Shannon ran her fingers through Khola's long, thick mane, untangling it. To Billy she said, "My father just told me he ordered you to ride Khola and you had no choice in the matter."

"He's wrong about that. I had a choice," Billy said, draping the damp towel over the top rail. "I may work for your father but I'm still my own man. This horse is worth all the work you've put into him, Shannon, and if you hadn't done such a good job, I'd probably be a heap of broken bones right now, lying out there somewhere waiting for the vultures to find me.

"He's come a long way, but Khola's still a stick of dynamite waiting to explode, and I didn't want you on him when he did. So I followed McTavish's orders because he was right. On the one hand I'm real sorry I stole your thunder, but on the other hand I'm glad

I did. I said I'd protect you, Shannon, and I keep my promises."

Billy's eyes caught and held hers, and she couldn't look away. He was close enough to reach out and close one hand on her shoulder. His grasp was warm and firm. "I can live with you being mad at me, and I can even live with you telling me you hate me, but I don't think I could live without you."

Shannon's anger drained away, leaving her tongue-tied. "I don't hate you," she said, small voiced. "I wanted to be the first to ride him, that's all."

Billy gave her shoulder a gentle squeeze. "You'll ride him, Shannon. First thing tomorrow morning. That race at the fall fair is only a month away, and this horse is going to win it for you. When he does, he's going to put these McTavish mustangs back on the map."

CHAPTER FOURTEEN

SHANNON'S SUGGESTION OF going to the spaghetti supper didn't raise much enthusiasm at the lunch table. "It'll be good food for a change," Shannon prodded, setting a glass of milk down in front of Rose. "I'm not much of a cook, and the Grange Hall suppers are legendary."

"Your food's just fine," Billy said around a mouthful of sandwich, and her father grunted in agreement.

"This spaghetti supper's for a good cause," she said, sitting down and picking up a sandwich half. "The Hewins lost their barn and their entire hay crop and all their poor chickens, and they didn't have insurance."

"I'll donate money to the cause, but I'm not going," her father said bluntly.

"But Daddy, you're a member of that Grange."

"Not anymore, he isn't," Billy said, reaching for another sandwich. "Patriot Energy donated fifty grand to the Grange to fix up the building, and most of the Grange members have signed leases with the wind company. Safe to say, most of the Grange members aren't too fond of your father right now."

"Well, you two can stay here, but I'm going."

"Can I come, too, Momma?" Rose asked, wearing a milk mustache.

"Best you stay here with me and Tess," McTavish said. "We'll watch a movie after supper and make popcorn."

"Really?" Rose forgot all about the spaghetti supper.

"I'm going to get in touch with Spencer Wallace and the Badlands and suggest doing a benefit dance at the Grange Hall next Saturday," Shannon announced.

"How much money can one small town raise?" McTavish said. "Everybody who gives a hoot will be at that spaghetti supper tonight."

"That's right, and they'll be at the dance next Saturday, too," Shannon said loftily. "And if we advertise it on the radio, the turnout could be big."

"You'll definitely get the entire population of Bear Paw," Billy said.

"Don't forget the Morton brothers," her father added.

"If they all show up, that might just cover the cost of the radio ads," Billy calculated.

Shannon flushed. "Make fun of me all you want, but every little bit helps. Eat your sandwich, Rose. Oh, by the way, Daddy, I went to talk to Boyd Bannon this morning. I told him about the photos and asked him to drop the lawsuit. He refused, so it looks like we're going to have to find you a good lawyer."

McTavish and Billy stopped chewing and stared at her. "No lawyers," McTavish said. He reached for his glass and took a big swallow. "I'll make my own defense."

"If it's a poor one, you could end up getting ten years in prison," Shannon said.

"Then I'll be damned sure to make it good."

AFTER EVENING CHORES were done and she'd fixed a simple supper for her father, Billy and Rose, Shannon changed into a clean pair of jeans and a short-sleeved blouse, put on her best boots and belt, brushed her hair, applied lip gloss, mascara and a spritz of perfume, and called it good. She kissed Rose goodbye and was on her way to the car when she saw Billy approaching from the cook's cabin. He'd cleaned himself up and made a brave attempt at shaving, something he hadn't done religiously since being stitched up at the clinic. He was carrying his good hat in his hand and arrived at the car the same time she did.

"Thought I might be able to hitch a ride with you," he said.

"To the spaghetti supper? You're going?"

"I was told it's for a good cause."

Shannon beamed. "Climb aboard."

As they passed Billy's house beside the creek, he said, "I meant what I said about this place, Shannon. It's yours if you want it."

Shannon shook her head. "Every day I change my mind about staying or leaving, and today was a bad day. It hurt like hell, hearing from Mrs. Bannon this morning about my mom's ashes. Why didn't my own father tell me? Why didn't *you*? My mother used to stand at the kitchen sink long after the dishes were done, watching the eagles and hawks ride the updrafts along Wolf Butte.

That's a favorite hunting ground for them and she loved watching them soar. That's why she released the rehabbed eagles there, that and the sheer drop-off that helped them get airborne. But my father probably told you all that when he explained why he put her ashes up there."

Billy shook his head. "He never talked about it. I heard it from Bannon myself just a while ago and I figured you already knew."

"You mean, in all the time he's been fighting this wind project, you never understood the reason why he didn't want turbines being built up there?"

"If he spread your mother's ashes over the butte, that may be one reason why he wants to protect that place, but there're a whole slew of other reasons. It'll be bad for the rivers and mountains, the wildlife and the people who have to live near the turbines."

Shannon's eyes narrowed skeptically. "If wind power's as bad as you make it out to be, why's the government pushing it so hard?"

"Because big business controls the government, big oil and foreign countries own a lot of these wind LLCs, and because right now, these wind projects are the biggest and best tax write-off going for companies making hefty profits. The wind industry's about a whole different kind of green than you're thinking of, but don't take my word for it. Do your own research. The information's out there."

"And the Grange members?"

"When landowners sign lease agreements, they essentially sign a gag order forbidding them from discussing any lease information with anyone else and from complaining about the project. But your father never signed any agreement with them, so he was free to say what he wanted."

"And I bet he did," Shannon said.

"He announced at his very last Grange meeting how much Patriot Energy had offered him. Nearly started another range war, because every rancher and big landowner present had signed up for a whole lot less money than what Patriot Energy offered your father."

"So that's when he quit the Grange?"

"I'm surprised they didn't tar and feather him on the spot. And that's the hell of it. No matter what happens, nothing will ever put the town of Bear Paw together again."

Shannon shook her head. "You're wrong. This town has always been about neighbor helping neighbor. Events like tonight are proof of that, and that's why it's so important for me to do all I can to help the Hewins. Speaking of which, we better get going. I'm so hungry I could eat a horse, and when the food runs out at a Grange Hall supper, they stop serving."

The Grange Hall parking lot was full, and a slow-moving line of people had formed at the door. Shannon and Billy joined the queue, exchanged polite nods with others waiting in line, and eventually filed into the hall, ponied up their donations, and filled their plates at the buffet line. Shannon was looking forward to eating good food prepared by good cooks.

The thick, meaty spaghetti sauce smelled wonderful and there were fresh homemade yeast rolls, several types of salads and, on a separate table, a delectable array of homemade pies. Her mouth was watering as she dropped into a chair and eyed the bounty, and her stomach growled with anticipation. She twined sauce-laden spaghetti around her fork and was lifting it to her mouth when a deep, familiar voice said, "Surprised to see you here, Shannon. Figured your father would've advised you not to come, since he's not a Grange member anymore."

Shannon lowered her fork and looked up at Boyd Bannon, who stood on the other side of the table with his wife, Eva. Both held plates of food. Eva was wearing a pained expression. "You're welcome to sit here with us," Shannon said, indicating the chairs across from them. "We don't have anything that's catching, and if my father's behind on his Grange dues, I'll make that right. He's always supported the Grange, you know that. And this supper's about raising money for some folks who need it. That's why we're here."

Talk around the long tables quieted as people listened in on the conversation. Boyd Bannon glanced around at the expectant faces and he grew a little taller, a little more self-righteous. "This wind project's about the same thing, Shannon. It's about bringing money to people who really need it. Helping them through hard times. A lot of those hardworking people are in this Grange Hall right now, probably wondering why it is you care so much about the Hewin family and so little about the rest of us."

Billy started to rise out of his chair and Shannon put her hand on his arm.

"Mr. Bannon, you have a right to your opinion, and as a fellow American I defend that right. But there's a time and a place for everything, and maybe this isn't the best time or place to discuss this. Right now I want to tell you how much I appreciate the open-handed friendship you've extended to my family over the years. Life is short, and good friendships are precious."

She hesitated for a moment, struggling to find the words, but when she continued, her voice was steady and clear, and loud enough that every curious ear heard what she had to say.

"Folks around here've always struggled to make ends meet. Living on the edge of dead broke's a way of life for most. But you found it in your heart to help my family out when we needed it so badly. That's what makes Bear Paw such a special place. We may disagree on lots of things, we may fight and feud and carry grudges, but when the going gets tough, we pull together and help each other out.

"That's why we're all here, to help a family who just lost a lot. So, Mr. Bannon, and all the rest of you who might think Billy and I don't belong here tonight, I'm just asking that we set aside our differences and join together in the spirit of community, because I'm looking at a plate of amazing food that's way better than anything I've prepared since taking over cooking duties at my father's ranch. I may be able to carry a tune, but I sure can't cook, and right now I'm starving. So let's eat. We can fight and feud later."

The ripple of laughter that spread through the Grange Hall at Shannon's concluding words dissolved the tension that filled the room. Boyd Bannon gave Shannon a grudging nod and moved with his wife to sit at the next table. Shannon picked up her fork again and cast a sidelong glance at Billy, who was looking back at her with an expression she couldn't fathom. "What?"

He shook his head. "Nothing."

"No, really. What?"

"I was just thinking I'd like to buy you a drink at the Dog and Bull after supper."

"Really?" Shannon tilted her head to one side and studied him for a moment. "I might just let you, under one condition."

"What's that?"

"You promise to dance with me just once."

"Just once? Is that my limit?"

"The limit's completely up to you."

"Then I'll do my best to dance you off your feet."

Shannon grinned. "You're on, cowboy."

THE DOG AND BULL was packed. Shannon barely had time to have a quick word with the band members about the fund-raiser as they set up their equipment. "Our schedule's free that afternoon," said Spencer. "We don't start playing here until 7 p.m. It'd be great a great honor for us to be your backup band for such a good cause."

"If you could announce it tonight so word starts to get out, I'll put the radio ads together and get them on the air," Shannon said. "I figured an open-air concert staged around the bandstand outside the Grange Hall would work best. That way the crowd can get as big as it likes. We'll play for donations and give the proceeds to the Hewin family. Thanks, boys. It *is* for a good cause, and I really appreciate your help. The Hewins will, too."

Shannon joined Billy at the table he'd found toward the back of the room. Her heart jumped as he rose to his feet at her approach. In denim jeans and a plain but clean blue chambray shirt, he wasn't the fanciest dressed cowboy in the room, but he was the handsomest by far. She sat down as the waitress arrived and plunked two frosty mugs of draft beer, a pitcher of ice water and two glasses in front of them.

"Looks like my first solo concert's next Saturday afternoon, and if we don't get more than half the population of Bear Paw, I'll be a little disappointed," Shannon said, filling their water glasses.

"If you advertise your concert on the radio, you'll rope in so many they won't all fit in town. And if they each pony up ten or twenty bucks to hear the best and most beautiful country-and-western singer ever born, you'll have built the Hewin family a new hay barn and filled it with hay. You're more famous than you know."

"Everyone wants a piece of you when you're famous," Shannon said wryly. "It's who wants you when you aren't that really matters."

Billy raised his beer to her. "Famous or not, you'll do to ride the river with."

Shannon picked up her beer and touched the rim of her mug to his. She gazed into Billy's eyes and forgot all about being mad at him for riding Khola, because right at this moment she wanted him to kiss her like he'd kissed her all those years ago. She wanted to know if that kiss could possibly live up to its ten-year-old memory, and she had a feeling it would.

The band finished tuning up their instruments and launched into their first song. Shannon rose to her feet and reached her hand out to Billy. "C'mon, cowboy, you promised me a dance." When they reached the dance floor and he took her into his arms, Shannon felt like she'd finally come home.

THERE WERE TIMES, after being torn to pieces by that roadside bomb in Iraq, when Billy had wished he'd died with his buddies, because being alive was like living in hell. Now, as he held Shannon McTavish in his arms, he got his first taste of what heaven must be like.

He forgot about his bad leg, the hardware in his skull and the long months of rehab before his honorable discharge. He forgot about everything except the fact that he was dancing with the girl of his dreams.

She started out with her fingers curled around the edge of his belt, one hand lightly resting above each of his hips, keeping a safe distance between them as they felt each other out on the dance floor. The first song had a quick, snappy beat that kept them moving right along. She could dance, all right. She knew all the moves, but then, she would. She was country through and through.

They moved with the other couples, and their first few dances together were textbook country-and-western. But four songs later, when the band transitioned into a slow number to give the dancers a breather, he drew her into his arms. He bent his head over hers and breathed in the sweetness of her hair, savored the feel of her slender, graceful body moving slowly with his. It had taken him ten years to get to heaven, but now that he was here, he didn't want the moment to end. When the song was over, she kept her hand in his and pulled him back to their table.

"I need a break," she said, draining her glass of ice water before sinking into her chair. "You might be able to outdance me, Billy Mac, and that's saying something."

Billy wanted to tell her how much it meant to him, just being here with her tonight, but couldn't find the words. He could never find the right words when he needed to. They all ran off into the sunset. "I'll get us a couple more beers," he said, picking up their empty mugs and making his way to the crowded bar.

He groaned inwardly when he recognized Tom Carroll and Holly Duncan sitting at the bar, two fruity mixed drinks in front of them.

"Billy," Tom said when he spotted him.

"Tom," Billy replied. He nodded to Holly, then said to the bartender, "Two more drafts here, Al."

Holly gave him a cool up and down. "I guess you're a real cowboy, after all."

"How's that?"

"You can dance the two-step like nobody's business," she replied. "Takes a real cowboy to do that."

"And here I thought being a cowboy was all about the tough stuff, like riding broncs, mending fences and herding cattle," Billy said, digging into his jeans pocket for a twenty to hand Al as the other man slid the two drafts onto the bar. "The two-step's easy."

"Maybe you could teach me a thing or two about those *easy* dance steps of yours," Holly suggested, stirring her drink with a little red plastic straw. "I'd like to learn more than just the basics."

Billy stuffed the change Al gave him into his pocket after leaving a tip.

"Maybe Tom could help you out. I'm kinda busy right now. Thanks for the beers, Al."

"Something you should be aware of," Tom Carroll said as Billy picked up the two mugs. "The access road to Wolf Butte's going in on Boyd Bannon's land. Construction starts on Monday. The transmission line's being re-routed around the McTavish spread. There's no stopping this project now, and McTavish's going to have a front-row seat from his ranch house. Too bad he's not getting any of the benefits, but that's his choice. Thought you'd want a heads-up, so you could prepare him."

"That's mighty good of you, Tom." Billy nodded curtly, turned away from the bar and moved through the crowded room as the heat of anger scorched his blood. If he hadn't had two beers in hand, he'd have flattened Tom Carroll and probably have spent the rest of the night in jail.

Shannon gave him a questioning look when he returned to the table. "Something wrong?"

"Nope." Billy set the beers down just as the band started gathering on the stage again after their short break. They picked up their instruments and started to play "Any Way the Wind Blows." Billy looked at Shannon and forgot all about Tom Carroll, Holly Duncan and the Badlands' poorly chosen song.

He extended his hand and her smile lit up his world as she reached to take it. She accompanied him back to the dance floor and stepped into his arms. To hell with Tom Carroll and Boyd Bannon. Shannon was the windfall who'd made his life worth living again, and if all he ever had of her was this one night, he wasn't about to waste a single moment.

IT WAS LATE when they left the Dog and Bull. Shannon was tired yet happy as they left the saloon, and she hadn't felt happy in a very long time. "Tonight was fun," she sighed, sinking deeper into the passenger seat as Billy pulled out of the parking lot. She hadn't even thought about it, how he'd taken the keys from her, opened her car door, helped her in, then taken his place behind the wheel. Now she studied at his profile and said, "You're a real gentleman, Billy Mac. I'm so tired I can't see straight, I drank three beers, which is three more than I usually have, and you're politely making sure I get home safe."

"Your father'd fire me if you didn't," Billy replied.

She laughed softly. "You danced me under the table tonight. I had a really good time. Thank you." She watched the road ahead of them unwind in the headlights. When he turned off the main road and drove beneath the McTavish Ranch sign, Shannon felt a sharp pang and her eyes unexpectedly flooded with tears. "We can never go back, can we?" she said.

"Everything changes, Shannon."

Shannon brushed her wet cheeks with the palms of her hands. "I just wish some things would stay the same. I just wish there was someplace I could go where everything was the way I remembered it. I wish I could see my mother again and share with her all the things I wanted to tell her over the years. She would've loved Rose so much. I never had a really close friend, but I could talk to my mother about anything. After she died, I felt so alone. My father and I never had that sort of closeness. I still can't believe he didn't say anything about spreading my mother's ashes on Wolf Butte."

"Don't be too hard on him. You've only been back a little while. Takes time to catch up on ten years."

They drove on in silence and were passing Billy's homestead on the Bear Paw when Shannon said, "If I took you up on that offer about the house and the land, what would you do? Where would you live?"

"I'd bunk in the cook's cabin until McTavish kicked me out or until I bought another place. The important thing is that you stick around. Your father's going to need you in the coming months, and not just because his arm's broke. I ran in to Tom Carroll at the bar tonight and he warned me they've rerouted the transmission corridor in order to bypass your father's land. The road's going in up on

Wolfe Butte, and they're starting construction on Monday. There'll be a lot of bulldozing and blasting, and you'll be be able to watch it all of from your front porch. Your dad's going to take it pretty hard."

"So that's why you looked so dark when you came back with our beers," Shannon brooded, connecting the dots. "You think Daddy'll do anything rash?"

"You mean, guns-and-bullets stuff? Not while you and Rose are here. He has too much to live for now."

Shannon considered this for a few moments and sighed. "Well, home isn't quite the peaceful sanctuary I thought it would be, that's for sure. But on the bright side, Rose loves being with her grampy. And I love being with you."

WHEN THEY PARTED ways at the McTavish house that night, it was an agony for Billy to tip his hat politely and, like the gentleman she thought he was, say, "Thanks for dancing with me tonight, Shannon. I'll see you bright and early tomorrow morning." He handed her the car keys, turned away and started toward the cook's cabin.

"That's it?" she asked indignantly. He stopped and turned. "That's it?" she repeated. *"Thanks for dancing with me tonight, Shannon? I'll see you bright and early tomorrow morning?"*

Before he could respond she closed the distance between them, reached up, pulled his head down and kissed him. It was a kiss like he hadn't experienced in ten years. The intensity of the first kiss they'd ever shared ignited between them again as they embraced under a blanket of stars. It seemed as if they were the only two humans in the universe, and he forgot all about how far out of his league she was, how he'd vowed to keep his distance, to respect the boundaries between their two worlds. He was a half-breed, she was a country music star. The two didn't mix. Couldn't mix...

He pulled away. "Shannon, we can't do this." He caught her hands in his.

"Yes, we can. I've wanted this for ten years. Don't stop now. Please don't stop."

"You waited ten years, we can wait a little longer. You need to give yourself some time to think things through."

"Isn't ten years enough time to do that? I

made mistakes in my past and Travis was the biggest one, but right now I'm trying to figure out my future, and I want you to be a part of it, starting right here and now. I need you to want to be with me, not push me away."

"Shannon, I've wanted to be with you from the first time I laid eyes on you, waiting for the school bus with your guitar slung over your shoulder," Billy said. "But back then all you wanted was to make it big in Nashville, not to be the wife of a rancher living a hardscrabble life. I don't blame you for the choice you made. You were on your way to being a star, and I was a nobody. And the truth is, I still am. You've been through a lot and you need to give yourself time to figure out what it is you really want. And I need to know I'm the only man you want to be with, not just a stand-in until something better comes along."

He heard her draw a sharp breath, then without another word, she jerked her hands out of his, spun around and disappeared into the night.

CHAPTER FIFTEEN

SHANNON SPENT THE night tossing and turning. She woke her daughter so often that Rose began to protest.

"Momma, you're kicking me again!"

She rose before dawn, took a long hot shower while her daughter burrowed beneath the covers and slept. She wiped the steam off the bathroom mirror and stared at the young woman with the dark tangle of wet hair, the grave eyes, the solemn expression.

"Billy's right," she said softly to her reflection. "You need to figure out what it is you really and truly want. So tell me, Shannon McTavish. What do you *really* want? Is it fame and fortune as a country-and-western singer? Or is it a life here on this backwater ranch with a good man? A man who'd make a good father for Rose?"

Her reflection stared back at her, carefully considering her words. For a long time there was no reply, and then came the answer, straight from the heart.

"I want a family for Rose."

The moment she spoke the words aloud, a great weight lifted from her shoulders.

She exited the bathroom in a cloud of steam, dressed in clean jeans and a flannel shirt because the morning was cool. The smell of fresh coffee wafted up the kitchen stairs and she descended them in stockinged feet, carrying her boots. Her father was just pouring his first cup. It was 5:00 a.m. and the sun was rising over Wolf Butte.

"You missed a great spaghetti supper at the Grange Hall last night, Daddy," she said, pouring herself a mug of strong brew and bending to pat Tess as she passed by the old dog's bed on her way to the kitchen door. Tess pushed to her feet and walked stiffly behind Shannon as she stepped out onto the porch to breathe the cool morning air. The old border collie descended the porch steps slowly and went off on her morning rounds. Shannon heard her father come out behind her as she gazed at the butte and took her first sip of coffee.

"Glad you had a good meal. You got home late," her father said.

"Yep. We went dancing at the Dog and Bull. Thanks for watching Rose." She glanced sidelong at him, then looked back at the mountains. "Daddy, if the wind turbines went up along Wolf Butte and you had to look at them every day from this porch, would you want to stay here? Would you consider moving someplace else?"

Her question brought an abrupt laugh from her usually taciturn father. "Where would I go?"

Shannon shrugged. "I don't know. We could find another place where there were no energy projects planned. British Columbia's beautiful, and I'm sure we could buy a big property up there."

Her father studied her sharply. "Why are you talking about this? What did you hear last night?"

Shannon gripped her mug with both hands, ignoring the heat. "Tom Carroll said that Patriot Energy rerouted the transmission lines in order to bypass your land. The project's moving forward. Construction starts tomorrow on the access road up Wolf Butte."

McTavish said nothing, but his jaw muscles corded as he gazed at the butte. She figured he must be picturing the mammoth wind turbines scraping the sky with their enormous blades, defiling a place he and the Shoshone had long held sacred. A place where the eagles soared and where he'd spread his wife's ashes. He turned abruptly and went back inside the kitchen, the screen door banging shut behind him.

BILLY WAS ALREADY at the corrals grooming one of the mustangs when Shannon arrived, carrying her second mug of coffee in one hand and a thermos in her other. He wasn't sure what to expect after last night, but he was fairly certain things were going to be mighty awkward between them. He couldn't have been more wrong.

"Morning," she said, giving him an amiable smile. "Brought you some coffee and told my dad about the road construction starting on Wolf Butte tomorrow. I'm making breakfast and I expect you to be there. We'll train the horses afterward. We have some important things to talk about as a family." She set the thermos of coffee down outside the corral, turned on her heel and returned to the house.

Billy stared after her, still holding the currycomb and brush in his hands, completely confounded. He finished brushing the mustang and poured himself a slug of coffee from the thermos. The caffeine helped clear his head. She'd said they had to talk about things as a family. What did that mean, exactly? Was he considered part of the McTavish clan now?

He went down to the house reluctantly, carrying the now-empty thermos. The kitchen was redolent with the scents of bacon frying and a fresh pot of coffee perking on the stove.

McTavish was doing his best to lace rawhide through a broken bridle with one hand. Rose was at the table playing with a piece of toast and some scrambled eggs, and Shannon was dishing up three more plates. She set them on the table without fanfare.

"Sit," she said to Billy and her father. They both sat. Shannon hitched her chair up to the table and spread some raspberry jam on her piece of toast. "This is hard to talk about but it needs to be said," she began, concentrating on spreading the jam. "All of us have ties to this land, strong ties that go way back, but I believe the ties *between us* are more important. Tomorrow our world is about to change, and I understand how painful this change is going to be for the two of you."

She raised her eyes from her toast to look at both of them. "Billy, you said you'd sell me back that house you're working on. I might take you up on that offer, not because I want to live there, but because my father's going to need you no matter where he ends up, and I really don't think he can stay here and watch those towers being built on Wolf Butte.

"So I'm suggesting that we move as a family to a new place and start over. We take ourselves, our mementos, Tess, the horses and we move. Lock, stock and barrel. Before either of you say a word, I'm asking you to consider it for a few days. I have the money to make this happen, and Daddy, so do you. Installing four extra miles of transmission lines just to get around your land is going to cost Patriot Energy a bundle of money. My guess is, if we decide to start over someplace else, we'd have a buyer for this ranch by nightfall, and at a fair price, too.

"We don't have to stay here and suffer. We

could start fresh someplace new. We'll look for a place and choose it together.

"Billy has an idea about starting a horse camp that recruits military veterans to train mustangs for the BLM adoption program. The challenge of working with the horses will help them cope with their PTSD the same way it helped him. It's a great idea, and the two of you could make that work no matter where we live.

"I can be a mother and a daughter and a songwriter and a singer anywhere. And I can help train those mustangs and get the hay in the barn and learn to cook a little better, too, given enough time. I'd even consider getting married again, if the right man were to ask.

"This morning, right after breakfast, Rose and I are going to church. Don't look so shocked. My daughter needs to be exposed to religion, same as I was. When she gets older she can decide for herself which path to follow. When we get back from church, I'm going to ride Khola and nobody's going to stop me. But right now, I'd like to say grace. Rose, put your fork down and fold your hands together, please."

McTavish and Billy sat speechless as Shannon folded her own hands and bowed her head. "Heavenly Father, please grant my own father the patience to *just this once* let me have the last word so we can enjoy a peaceful breakfast together, and Rose and I can get to church on time. We can continue this discussion at the supper table tonight, after we've thought over very carefully everything I just talked about. Thank You, and amen."

SHANNON HAD ATTENDED church regularly and sung in the church choir until her mother died, whereupon she'd announced to her father, "You don't have to drive me to church anymore, Daddy. I'm not going." When she passed through the doors of the tiny white church on this Sunday in late August, she half expected some awful retribution from a god she'd forsaken in her bitter heartbreak, but nothing happened.

The organist kept playing as morning sunlight dappled the worn wood floor and humble pews. She held Rose's hand and they sat toward the back, near the open door. A few members of the congregation nodded to her and smiled, but otherwise all remained focused on the minister.

The majority of Wyoming residents supported open range religion, which included aspects of Native American cultures and the gamut of world beliefs, but Bear Paw's church was Congregationalist. The minister was a pious man who farmed a small holding and fixed cars on the side to put food on the family table. It was the same minister who had officiated at her mother's funeral.

Robert Slocum was fifteen years older now, and those years had left their mark on his weary features and thinning gray hair. The congregation had shrunk considerably since Shannon's childhood. There were maybe fifteen worshippers gathered in the pews, none of them young people with children, and there was no choir dressed in long robes standing by the organist. The minister was talking about the harvest, spinning the theme through his sermon and drawing his flock together through their shared struggles to survive on the windswept plains of Wyoming.

Rose fidgeted constantly, craning to find other young children, sighing loudly when she didn't, swinging her legs back and forth so her heels drummed on the underside of the pew. When someone entered the church and sat behind them, Rose swiveled around on the pew and piped out, "Hello, Mrs. Bannon!" in her bright young voice.

Shannon shushed her daughter even as she recognized Miranda, Mrs. Bannon's daughter, sitting beside her mother. Miranda was the child in college who wanted to be a pediatrician. Shannon smiled at them both and faced front again. Within thirty minutes the service was over and the congregation was exiting the church past the minister, thanking him for the service and heading for home.

Robert Slocum clasped her hands in both of his, smiling warmly. "Welcome back to Bear Paw, Shannon. I hope you're planning to stay awhile."

"Thank you, Reverend, it's good to be home."

As she shepherded Rose to the car, a young voice called her name and she turned to see Miranda hurrying after her. She was a pretty girl with dark shoulder-length hair and a painfully shy smile. "I was hoping I could get your autograph, but if my mother knows I'm asking for it she'll have my hide. I'm Miranda Bannon."

Shannon smiled. "You've grown up."

"I'm in college now," she said, blushing. "I'm a huge fan of yours. I have all your albums."

"Thank you, Miranda. I'm giving a benefit concert at the Grange this coming Saturday for the Hewins," Shannon said, rummaging in her purse. She pulled out a pen and opened her wallet. "I'd love it if you'd come. Tell all your friends. I'll be singing a few new songs I wrote, and there'll be dancing and lots of fun. It starts in the afternoon."

She scribbled in her checkbook then ripped out the check and handed it to Miranda. "You can photocopy this for the signature," she said as the girl's eyes dropped to the piece of paper. "Then deposit that check in your college account and put it toward getting your medical degree."

"Wow." Miranda lifted dazed eyes. "Thank you."

"Miranda, I hope you're not plaguing Shannon like some star-struck tween," Mrs. Bannon called, walking up to join them and smiling at Shannon. "If she is, I apologize."

"We were just getting to know each other again, Mrs. Bannon. Miranda wasn't even in her teens when I left town. All I remember is her pigtails and braces. She's turned into a beautiful young woman and I was just wishing her the best of luck at college."

Mrs. Bannon's expression became somber. "You heard about Patriot Energy rerouting the wind project around your father's land?"

Shannon nodded. "I'm glad it's working out for you."

"I'm sorry, Shannon," Mrs. Bannon said. "Truly, I am."

"Don't be. My mother would understand. Any mother would." Miranda looked between them, frowning with confusion. Shannon tightened her grip on Rose's hand. "Come on, Rose, time to head home. I'm fixing to ride a mustang on a wing and a prayer. I've gotten my prayer, and I'm hoping I won't need the wings."

SHANNON BRUSHED KHOLA head to toe, until his bay coat shone in the bright sunshine. His thick mane and tail streamed in the stiff breeze that blew up the valley. Shannon set the brushes aside and reached for the saddle blanket, smoothing it over his withers and onto his short, strong back.

"Good boy, Khola," she said soothingly into his flickering ears. She wished the wind wasn't blowing so hard. Windy days made even the most placid horses jumpy, and Khola didn't need any help in that department.

She tried to ignore the fact that Billy was hovering in the background, trying not to appear anxious but ready to leap to her assistance. She didn't need his help and wasn't going to ask for it, but it wasn't lost on her that he'd saddled Sparky and had him on standby, just in case.

Her father was banging and clanging on something up in the machinery shed, having refused to bear witness to his daughter's premature death. He'd volunteered to keep an eye on Rose, presumably for the same reason.

"We're just going to have us a nice little ride," Shannon crooned softly as she lowered the saddle onto Khola's back. "A safe, gentle, enjoyable ride in the round pen," she continued, her movements slow and sure as she cinched up the girth, little by little.

"And you're going to be a perfect gentleman for me, so's Billy can stop pacing around and acting as if the world's about to come to an end. He's not the only person around here who knows how to ride a horse. I used to ride a lot. Matter of fact, I was the last McTavish to win that cross-country horse race at the fall fair. 'Course, I was young and wild then, just like you are now, but you're going to be gentle for me today, aren't you, Khola?"

Saddle on, she led him out around the perimeter of the round pen. He jigged a bit, prancing sideways and tossing his head, but he didn't try to buck the saddle off. With his neck arched, and his long, thick mane and tail streaming in the wind, he was stunning.

"I'll hold him for you while you climb aboard," Billy offered, crawling through the round pen rails and walking right up beside her. He took the reins from her hand and brought Khola to a halt, and before she could protest, he bent his head and completely disarmed her with an unexpected kiss. A very tender, sweet kiss.

"I know you can do it, and I like your self-reliant spirit, but everyone needs a little good-luck kiss now and then."

Billy checked the girth, tightened the cinch a whisker more, then cupped his hands for her knee and tossed her lightly into the saddle, all the while holding the reins.

Khola didn't react to her weight on his back. His focus was on Billy. Shannon gathered the reins. "I'm okay," she said. "You can let go now."

"No stunt riding," Billy said, ducking through the rails again. "Just take it slow and easy."

"Yes, sir," Shannon said. "Anything you say."

Billy leaned his forearms on the top rail and grinned.

Shannon walked Khola around the pen, first one way, then the other. He was full of energy and every step was spring-loaded, but he made no effort to toss her.

"How was church?" Billy asked.

"You missed a good sermon."

"You learn anything?"

"We reap what we sow."

Billy plucked a piece of grass and chewed on it. "That right? Guess we should put in a garden next year, start sowing some vegetable seeds."

Shannon reversed Khola again. He was walking smoothly now, flexing his neck up and down and snorting. She rubbed his neck with one hand. "My father won't be able to stay here when the wind company starts bull-dozing Wolf Butte."

"We talked about moving after you left this morning. This land's been in your family for generations, and I love it, too. When I got out of the service and made up my mind to put down roots here, I couldn't wait to be on this soil again," Billy continued. "All I could think about was this valley, these mountains, that big wide-open sky. This land gets in your blood. Your father's right. How do you turn your back on something that's a part of you?"

Shannon reined Khola to a stop, then had him reverse a few steps. She stroked his shoulder. "Good boy." She shifted her weight and moved him forward again. "We have each other, that's the part that counts the most. Rose needs a family. She needs that security, and so do I. We can be a family no matter where we live."

Billy pushed his hat back on his head and chewed on the grass stem. "Sounds like you've done some mighty serious soul-searching."

"I have." Shannon reined Khola in a big re-laxed loop that ended in front of Billy. "It's a big, scary world out there and this has always been my safe place, the place I retreated to in my mind when times got tough. I always thought it was the ranch that held me, the land that drew me back. But it isn't just the land, it's the memories and the people.

"It's my mother. It's Willard at the general store, Al at the Dog and Bull, Mrs. Bannon and her beautiful daughter, Miranda, who wants to go to medical school and be a pediatrician. It's my father, and it's you. The land shapes the people and becomes a part of all of us. I get that. I really do. So if the two of you decide you want to stick it out here, we'll stay. But if you want to move on, we'll make it work."

Shannon dismounted, walked up to the corral fence and climbed the bottom rail to stand face-to-face with Billy. "I guess what I'm trying to say is, my life isn't just about platinum records and sold-out concert halls anymore. I realize there are lots more important things, and the most important one is family. Wherever we end up, I want Rose to have a real family, and I'm hoping you'll be a part of it. I'm willing to wait as long as it takes for you to realize I mean what I'm saying.

"I'm not going to quit you, Billy. But right now I'm going to ask you to give me another good-luck kiss, because I'm about to take Khola for a ride down to the creek so's he can splash in the water, and I'm hoping to stay dry this time."

Billy was just starting to oblige her when Shannon heard footsteps approaching at a run from the direction of the machinery shed. "Momma!" Rose's voice cried out in disbelief. "Are you kissing Billy? Does that mean you're getting married?"

MONDAY MORNING ARRIVED after another sleepless night of wondering what the day would bring. Shannon dressed in the predawn murk, careful not to awaken Rose. She heard the low whinny of a horse and glanced out the bedroom window toward the corrals. Billy was already up, giving hay to the mustangs. Today was the day the BLM would collect them in a big stock trailer, all but Khola. Shannon would pony up the adoption fee for the bay mustang, not because she really wanted to ride him in the fall fair, but because she'd grown too fond of him to say goodbye. But how would Khola take it when his companions were loaded into the trailer and he was left behind? And how would her father take the construction machinery growling onto Wolf Butte? How was this day that was beginning in such sweet stillness going to end?

Then she recalled yesterday, and the brief, tender kiss she and Billy had shared over the corral fence before Rose caught them smooching, and her heart warmed. No matter what the day brought, they'd deal with it. Khola would have Sparky and Old Joe to keep him company. She had Rose and her father… and Billy. Whatever life threw at them, they'd deal with it.

She dressed in worn jeans and flannel, carried her boots down the stairs, said the usual subdued "Mornin'," to her father, who was predictably less cheerful than usual.

She poured herself a mug of coffee and carried it out onto the porch with Tess at her heels, the cool morning air reviving her as much as the caffeine. She heard the first meadowlark give voice to the day long before the yellow streamers of sunlight spilled into the valley. There were no signs of activity on Wolf Butte. All was quiet as the sunrise colored the sky violet and a vibrant golden yellow. She drew a deep breath into her lungs and held it for a few beats while she said a silent prayer for the strength to accept the things she couldn't change.

Then she carried a thermos of coffee up to the corrals and poured some for Billy. Bareheaded and unshaven, he looked as strong and rugged as the land. He took the offered mug through the corral rails and gestured to the mustangs, who were jostling for position amid the piles of hay he'd divvied up amongst them. "They clean up nice, don't they? Remember how scruffy they were when they got here?"

"When's the BLM coming?"

"McTavish said they'd be here before breakfast."

"I'll take Khola for a walk, so he won't see his friends getting trucked away," Shannon said.

Billy shook his head, took a swallow of strong coffee. "I'll ride him out to the back line, maybe check out the cross fencing on the leased lots, that'll keep him occupied. You better stay close to your father. Today's going to be a hard one."

Shannon nodded. This wasn't a day for arguments. "I'll have breakfast ready when you get back."

Her father was standing on the porch when she returned, gazing toward Wolf Butte. "Come inside, Daddy," she pleaded.

He shook his head. "I want to watch the sunrise. I want to remember it this way."

Melancholy followed Shannon and Tess inside the house. Rose was sitting on the kitchen stairs in her pajamas, hair mussed and cheeks flushed. She felt a rush of love and protectiveness when she looked at her daughter. "Go upstairs and wash the sleep off your face, Sunshine," Shannon said, pouring herself a second mug of coffee. "The BLM's coming to pick up those horses this morning, and I don't want them mistaking you for a wild mustang."

IT WAS A morning Billy would never forget. The feel of the strong horse moving beneath him at a rapid walk, the colors of the sunrise staining the landscape in shades of rose and gold and lighting the craggy mountain peaks on fire, the songs of meadowlarks and curlews, the smell of the earth.

He felt more alive than he had in years, full of optimism on a day when his heart should have been on the ground—and would have been, if Shannon hadn't lifted his spirits into the clouds. The promise of her loyalty and the chance to build a future with her, these were beyond his wildest hopes and dreams. Could he believe in that future? Did a half-breed off the rez deserve it?

When Khola started to bunch up under him, wanting to run, Billy let him. The little bay mustang stretched out beneath him in a burst of power and speed. He let the mustang run flat out until they neared the fence line, then gradually reined him in.

When the horse drew close to the rear gate, he took a chance that he could ease the mustang up next to it, and swing it open.

Khola was lathered up and snorting loudly, full of adrenaline, but he let Billy maneuver him near enough to reach the stiff loop of wire encircling the post. He flipped it off, pushed the gate open and rode out onto the leased BLM lands. McTavish didn't run cattle out here anymore but he stubbornly kept the leases, believing the old days of making a profit on grass-fed beef would return and times would get better.

Maybe they would, but it wouldn't be beef cows that improved things. From the way all the Grange members talked, it was going to be wind turbine leases. Billy didn't want to dwell on that. Not this morning. He was going to have this one last ride across a land that had remained virtually unchanged since he'd first laid eyes on it. He wanted to remember it this way, because he didn't want to imagine what it was going to look like sprouting hundreds of thrashing and blinking wind turbines far into the distance.

He rode west, away from the ranch, Wolf Butte and the rising sun, so it was easy for him to spot the plume of smoke rising up in the still dawn. He reined Khola in and studied the golden haze lifting off the valley floor ahead of him.

Not smoke. Dust. Dust being kicked up by large animals. Cattle?

Billy squinted hard. No. Horses. He could barely make out the dark figures on the horses' backs. Hard to tell how many riders were in the group, as they were all bunched up and coming toward him at a trot, perhaps a mile distant and kicking up a lot of dust. Mighty strange sight to see. Nobody ever travelled out here. There were no roads, and people didn't walk or ride anywhere, not anymore.

He walked Khola in a big circle to keep the mustang moving and cool him off. When the riders drew closer, Billy felt a jolt of surprise. Front and center was none other than his grandfather, Henry Crow Dog. Mighty poor day to be paying a social call, too. McTavish wouldn't be feeling too hospitable.

Henry rode right up to Billy and reined his horse in. He nodded solemnly. Billy nodded back and tried to count the riders fanning out behind him. Thirty? Maybe more. Horses and riders alike were tired and caked with dust. They were dressed in ceremonial attire. Most were tribal elders, and their horses, beneath the sweat and dust, had been painted as if they were going into battle.

"You look like some kind of war party," Billy said.

Henry Crow Dog nodded again. "We rode hard to get here. Hardly any rest. Hope we're not too late."

"Too late for what?"

"The tribal council filed a lawsuit against the energy company to stop them from harming our sacred burial ground on Wolf Butte. Our dead warriors are buried there, along with McTavish's wife, Eagle Woman. McTavish told me about the wind project when I was here last. I spoke to the tribal council about it, and we hired an attorney. The papers should be filed in federal court today, but these government things take time, so we came as soon as we could to protect our sacred place."

Billy sat for a few moments, processing this information. He gazed first at the tribal elders on their tired horses, then at Henry Crow Dog. "Grandfather, they're starting road construction today. They're probably already bulldozing the base of the butte."

Henry Crow Dog nodded again. "We will tell them to go back home."

"There's a lot of money at stake here," Billy said. "This is a big deal in Bear Paw, and the law's on the wind developer's side. It's better to wait for the court order. Things could get ugly if you try to stop them. You'll probably be arrested, and you could be hurt."

Henry Crow Dog stared at Billy as if he

hadn't understood what his grandson had just said. Then he laughed, a low chuckle that rumbled out of his chest. He turned and glanced behind him at the tribal elders, and they all laughed with him. When he spoke again, it was to address the horse Billy was riding. "Khola," he said. "You are a warrior's horse. You should be carrying a warrior."

He kicked his weary mount and rode past Billy without another word. The tribal elders followed, stoic and proud.

Billy's face burned as they passed him by. He'd fought a different kind of war as an American soldier, but this fight involved his grandfather, his tribe, his history and his ancestral lands. A history he'd always cursed. A half-breed, he'd never felt he belonged in either the white man's world or with the tribe. Only here, on McTavish's ranch, had he found his true place.

Shannon had said they could move away and still be a family. But could he abandon this land? Who would he be if he did that? Who did he want to be?

The elders filed past him silently, eyes to the front. The dust raised by their passage coated Khola's sweaty shoulders and left a bitter taste in Billy's mouth as he watched them ride away.

CHAPTER SIXTEEN

SHANNON STOOD BESIDE her father up at the corrals as they watched the gooseneck trailer with the mustangs they'd trained depart down the ranch road. "They said we did a fine job, Daddy," Shannon said. "I hope those mustangs all find forever homes at the auction. They're bringing more next month. Twice as many. That's good, right?"

"At this rate it'll be a while before we're millionaires," McTavish said drily, tucking the check they'd given him into his shirt pocket.

"We could open that mustang camp Billy talked about," Shannon suggested. "I bet it would catch on quick and help a lot of veterans."

"Not even shell-shocked combat veterans would want to hang out on a ranch surrounded by wind turbines."

"Then why don't we move someplace else?

People could learn a lot from you, Daddy. You know so much about training horses and dogs. You've worked with so many famous movie stars. The stories you could tell could fill a book."

Her father said nothing, just closed the corral gate.

She drew Rose up against her legs and stroked her daughter's silken hair. "Hungry?" she asked.

Rose nodded enthusiastically. "I could eat a horse!"

Shannon laughed. "Don't let them hear that. C'mon. Billy'll be back soon and I promised to have breakfast ready."

"Too late, Momma, here he comes," Rose said, pointing.

Sure enough, Billy was approaching from the road that went up past the machinery shed. Wearing an expression Shannon couldn't fathom beneath the brim of his hat, he rode Khola right up to the corral, swung out of the saddle and turned to face them.

"My grandfather and all the tribal elders are headed up to Wolf Butte on horseback," he announced without preamble. "They're dressed in full tribal regalia and they've painted their horses. Henry told me the tribe filed a court order to stop construction on the butte, due to it being an historic and cultural site." He looked sharply at McTavish. "Quite a coincidence, them showing up this morning, just one day after we found out about Patriot Energy's plan to start road construction. They rode all night to get here."

McTavish met Billy's gaze with one that would have had Shannon cringing in her boots. She glanced between them. "So, what happens next?"

"Nothing good," Billy said. "I told Henry to wait for the court order to be filed but they're heading over to the butte as we speak to protect what they believe is their sacred ground. There's bound to be trouble."

"This fight's not over till it's over," her father said. "The Shoshone have a good case against Patriot Energy."

"All this will do is slow things down. The project's going to be built, one way or the other."

"Maybe there's another option," Shannon said slowly. "Maybe if Patriot Energy thought this new legal battle with the tribe over Wolf Butte was going to drag things out forever and cost tons of money in legal fees, they might be open to the idea of changing the turbine placement."

Billy's eyes narrowed in thought. "In order to bypass McTavish land and the butte, the only place to run transmission lines would be straight across Bannon's high pastures."

"So, maybe they could put the line of turbines they were planning to erect on Wolf Butte there instead," Shannon suggested. "What do you think?"

"It would save Patriot Energy building another couple miles of transmission lines running to Wolf Butte," Billy concurred, nodding. "They might consider it."

"Why wouldn't they? It's a win-win for everyone. Bannon would get his lease money, Wolf Butte and the historic Shoshone burial and battle grounds will be spared, my mother's ashes would remain undisturbed, and the eagles she loved could continue to fly in free airspace."

"Bannon would never consider that option," her father said stonily. "He wants us to live under those wind turbines and suffer until hell freezes over."

"It's worth a shot," Shannon said. "If we

want to protect Wolf Butte, we have to try. I'll make the pitch to Bannon, but before I go, I'll call the newspapers and television stations. If Henry Crow Dog's riding up there with all the tribal elders, the least we can do is make sure the whole world knows about their fight. This is a big story."

She paused. "I'm sure Henry would appreciate your support," she said to Billy. "Rose has some bright-colored finger paints, if you want to prepare Khola for battle. I'll leave them on the table for you."

"Thanks," Billy said. "I might just do that."

"You'll end up in jail along with the rest of them if you ride up there today," her father warned.

"Maybe, but there are worse things to be jailed for than standing up for a mountain. For my people." Billy looked at Khola and the bay mustang gazed back at him with dark, clear eyes. He rubbed the horse's withers, stroked the damp, sweaty neck, then glanced at Shannon. "Besides, Khola'd look real sharp wearing war paint."

SHANNON'S HEART WAS beating fast as she navigated the dirt roads to the Bannon ranch.

She hoped she could somehow avert what was sure to be a nasty confrontation on Wolf Butte as well as the media event of the year. She wished Rose had stayed with her grandfather, but she'd pitched a fit when Shannon suggested she remain behind. "I wanna see Henry Crow Dog," she'd wailed. "Please, Momma, I wanna go, too!"

Would the bulldozers already be at work, building the thirty-foot-wide road to the summit of Wolf Butte? Would Bannon even listen to what she had to say?

She swung up the ranch road leading to the Wolf Butte trail and pulled to a stop. There were lots of pickups, two big dump trucks with equally big trailers and two huge bulldozers that had already started pushing dirt around. Men in hard hats milled about as two news crews started to set up cameras. No sign of Tom Carroll or Boyd Bannon.

She continued on to the Bannons' house, loose gravel pinging beneath the car as she sped down the dirt road. There were three vehicles there, between the pole barn and the house. "Stay in the car, Rose," she ordered as she parked and got out. "I'll be right back."

At that moment, Boyd Bannon stepped

onto the porch, his expression dark as a thundercloud.

"You're not welcome here, Shannon," he said, hands on his hips. "Tom Carroll just informed me about the lawsuit the Shoshone filed in federal court today. I know your father's behind it." Mrs. Bannon stepped out behind her husband, and Miranda edged out from around her mother. Shannon thought she caught a glimpse of Tom Carroll inside the doorway but couldn't be sure.

"Please, Mr. Bannon, just listen to what I have to say." Shannon's mouth was dry and her palms were sweaty. "It's true that Wolf Butte has historic significance to the Shoshone, and to my father and me it has a deeply personal significance, as well. So what I'm proposing is, instead of wasting a lot of time and money fighting the lawsuit, why not move those turbines from Wolf Butte to your high pastures instead? They'd be a lot closer to the rerouted transmission lines."

"No."

"You'd still get your lease payments and the Shoshone could preserve their ceremonial place and burial grounds."

"That's my land, and I'll do with it what

I want. Now get off my ranch. I won't say it again."

"Please, Mr. Bannon…"

"Do I have to call the sheriff?"

"He's probably already out at the access road," Shannon said. "The tribal elders are up on Wolf Butte, preparing for a standoff. There's a lot of media, too. This is going to be a big story."

"I should've figured your father would pull a last-minute stunt like this."

"It doesn't have to be so ugly. Everyone could win if we just compromised. I know it's your land, but I'm prepared to buy it off you, if you'd consider selling it to me."

"No McTavish will ever own that land," Bannon spat out.

"It's a thousand acres of scrub brush and rock. That's what you always say." Mrs. Bannon spoke up in an unexpectedly tart tone of voice. "You can't hay up there and you can't grow crops or graze animals because they might fall off the cliffs. You always said Wolf Butte was good-for-nothing land the town was taxing you for."

"That was before we could lease it for the wind turbines," Bannon growled at his wife.

"How much, Mr. Bannon?" Shannon said. "How much would you sell a thousand acres of scrub brush and rock for?"

"Every single one of those turbine leases pays me three thousand dollars a year and the lease runs for twenty years. *Twenty years.*"

"Unless they go bankrupt. Then what happens?"

"That *won't* happen."

"How much?"

"It's not for sale."

"What if you lose the lawsuit in federal court?"

"We won't," Bannon stated. "Not a chance of it."

"Your high pastures could hold a lot of wind turbines."

"Tom Carroll's already talking about a project expansion on those pastures, so your talk's empty, Shannon. Either way, I'm getting those turbines on my land, and you can stay off it, starting now."

Shannon clenched her fists tight. Her heart was pounding like a war drum. "Mr. Bannon, I understand why you want those wind turbine leases, but how much money do you need? How much money will it take to make you happy? Half the town's against the turbines. This project has torn our town apart. Is it worth it?"

"It's worth it to put my daughter through medical school. You can't do that raising sugar beets and Herefords in today's market."

"Daddy, Shannon gave me money for college. A lot of money," Miranda said in a small voice.

"Give it back to her!" Bannon bellowed, outraged. "No daughter of mine accepts charity from a punk rock star!"

"Mr. Bannon, I'm not a punk rock star and that's not charity. That's returning the money you gave us for my mother's medical and funeral expenses, along with a little interest. That's an investment in my daughter's future, because if Rose stays here, she's going to need a pediatrician, and with any luck Miranda will set up her practice in this area.

"And, if you sold Wolf Butte to me, you'd get another big chunk of money you might never get otherwise, money that could be used to put her all the way through medical school. If we made it official by making an announcement at the bottom of the access road to Wolf Butte, right now, today, this morning, in front of all the media that's gathering there, you'd be a hero instead of a villain."

"I'm not a villain," Bannon barked.

"Shannon's a country music star, Dad. If you stood against her, you would be the villain!" Miranda said. "I think you should sell Shannon that mountain, and at a fair price, too."

"Momma, *hurry up* or we're going to miss seeing Henry Crow Dog!" Rose's voice piped through the open car window.

"I'll be waiting at the bottom of the access road, Mr. Bannon," Shannon said. "If you decide you want to talk business, or if you want to witness the confrontation between two giant bulldozers and a brave group of tribal elders on horseback, you should come, too."

Shannon's hands were trembling as she turned the key in the ignition. Before she pulled onto the road, she called Billy on her cell phone. "Tell Henry Crow Dog and the elders to start down the butte trail," she said. "The film crews are getting set up and the bulldozers are starting to move onto the access road. Bannon said no to my proposal, but he might change his mind. Either way, I think he'll show up, and he should have a Shoshone welcoming committee."

BILLY TUCKED HIS cell phone into his jacket pocket. The tribal elders stood in a circle around him. Henry was beside the rock cairn, arms folded across his chest. The wind lifted the horses' manes and tails, and fluttered the eagle feathers that adorned several of the elders' headdresses.

"You promised no violence," he said to his grandfather, and Henry nodded stoically. "Shannon says to start down the mountain. The bulldozers are getting started and the news crews are waiting to record the confrontation." Billy hesitated, then added, "I'd be honored to ride with you, if you'd permit it."

"It could be dangerous," Henry said, stone-faced. "You could be hurt or arrested."

Billy met his gaze. "This is my fight, too."

Henry nodded again. "Yes, it is. I'm glad your heart has found itself. We'd be proud to have you ride with us."

The elders moved toward their weary horses. Two of the highest ranking carried lances, but they were for show. None of them were armed. Khola was still tossing his head and full of energy when Billy stepped back into the saddle. Henry started down the mountain, followed by the rest of the tribal elders. Billy allowed a respectful distance to open between them before letting Khola step out.

The distance to the foot of Wolf Butte was less than a mile. They could hear the grind of big machinery as soon as they dropped off the lower plateau, and it grew louder as they descended.

The bulldozers came to a halt when the elders formed a barrier in front of them. The growling engines stopped, and the silence seemed loud. A bald eagle circled above the butte, riding the afternoon currents in search of a meal. The raptor's timely appearance wasn't lost on the small crowd.

Henry moved his horse a few steps in front of all the others. His long white hair streamed back from his face and his expression was solemn as he gazed at the group of contractors, reporters and law enforcement officers. He glanced behind him, caught Billy's eye and motioned him forward with a jerk of his head. Billy moved Khola up beside his grandfather's horse. Finally, Henry spoke.

"You must always be careful with something that is greater than you are," he began in his deep orator's voice. "This land is sacred to us. Wolf Butte is where our bravest warriors fought their finest and fiercest battle against the Crow. Many of our people are buried there, among the ancient rocks. We came here to protect their resting place.

"The white man stole this place from us a long time ago and called it his own, but our hearts and the spirits of our ancestors will always be up on Wolf Butte, up where the eagles fly."

The cameramen and photographers zoomed in, reporters scribbled in their notebooks, and Henry gave them everything they wanted for the evening news.

"What you do here, you do for money, but this land is more valuable than any dollar amount. The land is who we are. The land is all we have. This mountain is a sacred place and should be kept so. Put your big wind machines in your cities if you need them so much. You've already destroyed the land your cities are built on with noise and lights and garbage. Do you have to destroy this mountain, too? If the mountain could speak, it would ask you, why?"

Another pickup truck had pulled in to the staging area. Boyd Bannon with his wife and daughter. It was a good sign that he'd brought them along. They joined the group of people listening to Henry. Bannon looked gruff, but he always did. Tom Carroll hadn't showed up yet, which was surprising. He and his attorney should've been front and center at this confrontation.

When Henry finished speaking, silence reigned for a few moments before Bannon strode forward in his bullish way. He halted directly in front of Henry and Billy and braced his big, work-hardened hands on his hips in a belligerent way.

He gave Billy a hard glare just as the shadow of the eagle's wings flashed across his face. "I'm not here to dispute your spiritual connection to the mountain, but I do want to point out that, at this moment, you're all trespassing on my land," he announced in a raised voice, so all in attendance could easily hear. "We have laws in this country, and in the United States the land belongs to whoever buys it and pays the taxes on it. I own Wolf Butte, and I was within my right to sign the leases with the wind company to put wind turbines up on that mountain.

"But a neighbor came to see me today. She asked me how much money it would take to make me happy and reminded me of the days when neighbors stuck together and helped each other through hard times. She made me think about what this wind project has done to this town and this county, turning neighbor against neighbor, friend against friend. And she's right. That's not the way it should be. If I didn't need the money from those wind leases, I'd never have signed away the rights to my land the way I did.

"So how much money is enough to make me happy? Well, I have four kids that want to go to college, and one of them wants to go to medical school. That takes a lot of cash, and that's why I signed those leases. Not because I wanted to tear the town apart or I wanted to be rich, but because I wanted to educate my kids.

"But good friends are important, too, and good neighbors. I've given it some thought and I'm hoping I can have both. Enough money to put my kids through college, and good friends and neighbors. That's why I've decided to sell Wolf Butte, right here and now."

He reached into his jacket pocket to pull out a sheet of paper, which he unfolded and flagged in the air, turning to scan the faces behind him. "I have a purchase and sales agreement that was just validated by Patriot Energy's lawyer, who's in the process of transferring the lease sites from Wolf Butte to my high pastures. I'd like Shannon McTavish to read and sign this agreement, if the purchase price is agreeable to her, before I smarten up and change my mind about this whole thing."

Shannon lost no time moving forward with Rose on her hip. She swiftly scanned the paper Bannon handed her, then accepted the offered pen and signed the document. They shook hands formally.

Then, in front of the tribal elders, the contractors and the media, and beneath the outstretched wings of the bald eagle that had been circling above Wolf Butte since Henry began his speech, Shannon gave Boyd Bannon an impulsive hug.

And damned if the grumpy old buzzard didn't hug her back.

In that moment, Billy saw his future. The half-breed who hadn't known where he belonged or whether he would ever amount to anything, could, in fact, have all that he wanted. A home. A family. And the woman he loved.

WHEN THEY GOT back to the ranch, her father gave Shannon an awkward, one-armed hug and told her, in a voice rough with emotion, that he'd repay her somehow.

"This land's my legacy, too, Daddy," she said. "And Rose's. Let us be a part of our future. Let me help out around here as much as I can."

Later that evening, after the supper dishes were done and Rose was watching a Western with her grandfather, Shannon walked with Billy down to the banks of the Bear Paw and listened to the river murmuring between its banks. They stood in silence for a long while, looking at the last colors of the sunset fading from Wolf Butte and admiring the twilight aria of a meadowlark.

"I'm glad we're staying put, Billy," Shannon said softly. "I know it's going to be tough for you and my father, living with the wind project, and it'll be tough for my singing career, living so far from Nashville, but for better or for worse, this valley will always be our home."

"And after today, Wolf Butte will always be your mountain."

Shannon shook her head. "It belongs to all of us. Henry was right about that. The land is who we are, and the land is all we have."

"Not all," Billy corrected her, reaching out to take her hand in his. "We have each other."

Shannon smiled and reached for his other hand. "I meant it when I said I wanted you in my life. We can make this work, Billy. I'm sure we can. You can start your mustang camp for war veterans, I can write my songs and sing 'em, too, even if it's just with the Badlands. We can make a family for Rose, and she'll have a good life here. We—"

He stopped her with a kiss, and when he pulled away he said, "Marry me."

She contemplated his offer just long enough to make him suffer. "Kiss me again, cowboy, and I'll think about it."

He took her into his arms, and the kiss they shared was a pledge and a promise that both of them knew would last forever.

EPILOGUE

"MOMMA, WHY ARE you so dressed up?" Rose was standing in the bathroom door watching while Shannon fixed her hair.

"Because I'm singing some of my new songs at the Grange Hall this afternoon, and I want to look nice."

"But you never wear a dress, not like that one."

"You think it's pretty?"

"I do." Rose nodded solemnly. "You're pretty as a picture. Grampy's getting dressed up, too. He's putting on a suit, and he told me to ask you why."

Shannon studied her daughter's reflection in the mirror. "Rose, there's something I want to talk to you about. It's about me and Billy."

Rose's face brightened. "Momma, are you getting married?"

Mother and daughter gazed at each other's

reflection. "Maybe. Would you be okay with that?"

"If you were marrying Billy, I'd be happy. I like Billy, and he likes me. Did he ask you?"

"He did."

"What did you say?"

"I said I would, if you approved."

"Does this mean we're really and truly staying here? Forever and ever?"

Shannon turned to face her daughter. "Would that make you happy?"

Rose nodded vigorously, her face radiating delight. "And if you marry Billy, Henry Crow Dog will be my grandfather!"

"Great-grandfather," Shannon corrected her. "If me and Billy get hitched we might be moving into that pretty little house Billy's building beside the creek. You'd have your own bedroom, and the school bus stops right on the other side of the bridge over the creek."

"Will I be going to school?"

Shannon nodded. "You'll be starting first grade this fall. You'll make lots of new friends there."

Rose frowned. "What about Grampy and Tess? Won't they get lonely if we leave?"

"They'll be right here, right in this house,

where they've always been, and we can come every day to visit. Billy will be working here, same as he is now. You can spend as much time in the house as you like. Tess and Grampy would like that. It's only a stone's throw from Billy's place, just over the hill."

"Will Henry Crow Dog live with us, too?"

"I'm not sure," Shannon said. "You'll have to ask Billy that. Billy was talking about getting one of Willard's pups. Says a house isn't a home until it has a good dog. The pups are little now, just six weeks old, but you could help pick one out. Would you like that?"

"A puppy?" Rose beamed with delight. "Really? Can I have some brothers and sisters, too?"

Shannon laughed. "C'mon, we'd better get a move on. Can't be late today. Billy mentioned there might be a justice of the peace at this fund-raising concert, and he said they can marry people."

"Like you and Billy?"

"Like me and Billy, now that we know it's okay with you. I figured it would be, but I'm glad to hear you say it." Shannon picked up her guitar and took her daughter's hand. Rose paused at the head of the stairs and her fingers tightened around Shannon's, drawing her to a halt. She looked up at her mother.

"Momma, since we're staying, can I have a pony?"

Shannon marveled at how much her life had changed in less than a month. Just a few weeks ago, she'd been wondering if she'd ever feel happy again. She smiled down at her daughter through a blur of tears as her heart overflowed. "We'll have that conversation later, Rose. Right now, I have some new songs to sing and a good man to marry."

* * * * *

Get 4 FREE REWARDS!

We'll send you 2 FREE Books plus 2 FREE Mystery Gifts.

Love Inspired® books feature contemporary inspirational romances with Christian characters facing the challenges of life and love.

FREE Value Over **$20**

YES! Please send me 2 FREE Love Inspired® Romance novels and my 2 FREE mystery gifts (gifts are worth about $10 retail). After receiving them, if I don't wish to receive any more books, I can return the shipping statement marked "cancel." If I don't cancel, I will receive 6 brand-new novels every month and be billed just $5.24 for the regular-print edition or $5.74 each for the larger-print edition in the U.S., or $5.74 each for the regular-print edition or $6.24 for the larger-print edition in Canada. That's a savings of at least 13% off the cover price. It's quite a bargain! Shipping and handling is just 50¢ per book in the U.S. and 75¢ per book in Canada*. I understand that accepting the 2 free books and gifts places me under no obligation to buy anything. I can always return a shipment and cancel at any time. The free books and gifts are mine to keep no matter what I decide.

Choose one: ☐ **Love Inspired® Romance Regular-Print** (105/305 IDN GMY4)   ☐ **Love Inspired® Romance Larger-Print** (122/322 IDN GMY4)

Name (please print)

Address   Apt. #

City   State/Province   Zip/Postal Code

Mail to the **Reader Service:**
IN U.S.A.: P.O. Box 1341, Buffalo, NY 14240-8531
IN CANADA: P.O. Box 603, Fort Erie, Ontario L2A 5X3

Want to try two free books from another series? Call 1-800-873-8635 or visit www.ReaderService.com.

*Terms and prices subject to change without notice. Prices do not include applicable taxes. Sales tax applicable in N.Y. Canadian residents will be charged applicable taxes. Offer not valid in Quebec. This offer is limited to one order per household. Books received may not be as shown. Not valid for current subscribers to Love Inspired Romance books. All orders subject to approval. Credit or debit balances in a customer's account(s) may be offset by any other outstanding balance owed by or to the customer. Please allow 4 to 6 weeks for delivery. Offer available while quantities last.

Your Privacy—The Reader Service is committed to protecting your privacy. Our Privacy Policy is available online at www.ReaderService.com or upon request from the Reader Service. We make a portion of our mailing list available to reputable third parties that offer products we believe may interest you. If you prefer that we not exchange your name with third parties, or if you wish to clarify or modify your communication preferences, please visit us at www.ReaderService.com/consumerschoice or write to us at Reader Service Preference Service, P.O. Box 9062, Buffalo, NY 14240-9062. Include your complete name and address.

LI18

Get 4 FREE REWARDS!

We'll send you 2 FREE Books plus <u>plus</u> 2 FREE Mystery Gifts.

Love Inspired® Suspense books feature Christian characters facing challenges to their faith... and lives.

FREE Value Over $20

YES! Please send me 2 FREE Love Inspired® Suspense novels and my 2 FREE mystery gifts (gifts are worth about $10 retail). After receiving them, if I don't wish to receive any more books, I can return the shipping statement marked "cancel." If I don't cancel, I will receive 4 brand-new novels every month and be billed just $5.24 each for the regular-print edition or $5.74 each for the larger-print edition in the U.S., or $5.74 each for the regular-print edition or $6.24 each for the larger-print edition in Canada. That's a savings of at least 13% off the cover price. It's quite a bargain! Shipping and handling is just 50¢ per book in the U.S. and 75¢ per book in Canada*. I understand that accepting the 2 free books and gifts places me under no obligation to buy anything. I can always return a shipment and cancel at any time. The free books and gifts are mine to keep no matter what I decide.

Choose one: ☐ **Love Inspired® Suspense Regular-Print**
(153/353 IDN GMY5)

☐ **Love Inspired® Suspense Larger-Print**
(107/307 IDN GMY5)

Name (please print)

Address   Apt. #

City   State/Province   Zip/Postal Code

Mail to the **Reader Service:**
IN U.S.A.: P.O. Box 1341, Buffalo, NY 14240-8531
IN CANADA: P.O. Box 603, Fort Erie, Ontario L2A 5X3

Want to try two free books from another series? Call 1-800-873-8635 or visit www.ReaderService.com.

LIS18

HOME on the RANCH

YES! Please send me the **Home on the Ranch Collection** in Larger Print. This collection begins with 3 FREE books and 2 FREE gifts in the first shipment. Along with my 3 free books, I'll also get the next 4 books from the Home on the Ranch Collection, in LARGER PRINT, which I may either return and owe nothing, or keep for the low price of $5.24 U.S./ $5.89 CDN each plus $2.99 for shipping and handling per shipment*. If I decide to continue, about once a month for 8 months I will get 6 or 7 more books, but will only need to pay for 4. That means 2 or 3 books in every shipment will be FREE! If I decide to keep the entire collection, I'll have paid for only 32 books because 19 books are FREE! I understand that accepting the 3 free books and gifts places me under no obligation to buy anything. I can always return a shipment and cancel at any time. My free books and gifts are mine to keep no matter what I decide.

268 HCN 3760 468 HCN 3760

Name	(PLEASE PRINT)

Address	Apt. #

City	State/Prov.	Zip/Postal Code

Signature (if under 18, a parent or guardian must sign)

Mail to the **Reader Service**:

IN U.S.A.: P.O. Box 1341, Buffalo, New York 14240-8531
IN CANADA: P.O. Box 603, Fort Erie, Ontario L2A 5X3

HRCBPA18R

Get 4 FREE REWARDS!

We'll send you 2 FREE Books plus 2 FREE Mystery Gifts.

Harlequin® Special Edition books feature heroines finding the balance between their work life and personal life on the way to finding true love.

FREE
Value Over
$20

YES! Please send me 2 FREE Harlequin® Special Edition novels and my 2 FREE gifts (gifts are worth about $10 retail). After receiving them, if I don't wish to receive any more books, I can return the shipping statement marked "cancel." If I don't cancel, I will receive 6 brand-new novels every month and be billed just $4.99 per book in the U.S. or $5.74 per book in Canada. That's a savings of at least 12% off the cover price! It's quite a bargain! Shipping and handling is just 50¢ per book in the U.S. and 75¢ per book in Canada*. I understand that accepting the 2 free books and gifts places me under no obligation to buy anything. I can always return a shipment and cancel at any time. The free books and gifts are mine to keep no matter what I decide.

235/335 HDN GMY2

Name (please print)

Address

Apt. #

City

State/Province

Zip/Postal Code

Mail to the **Reader Service:**
IN U.S.A.: P.O. Box 1341, Buffalo, NY 14240-8531
IN CANADA: P.O. Box 603, Fort Erie, Ontario L2A 5X3

Want to try two free books from another series? Call 1-800-873-8635 or visit www.ReaderService.com.
